CW01663193

Sparky

My Barn Owl Story

TRACEY ICETON

Cinnamon Press
:: small miracles from distinctive voices ::

Published by Cinnamon Press,
Lytchett House, 13 Freeland Park, Wareham Road,
Poole, Dorset, BH16 6FA
www.cinnamonpress.com

Print Edition ISBN 978-1-78864-199-9

British Library Cataloguing in Publication Data. A CIP record for this book can be obtained from the British Library.

Cover and interior designed and typeset by Adam Craig.
Cover photo of Sparky by John Iceton.

Cinnamon Press is represented by Inpress.

The quote from *Owl* (2009), by Desmond Morris, is reproduced with permission of the Licensor through PLSclear.

SPARKY

My Barn Owl Story

"The owl is a contradiction. It is the best known of birds and the least known of birds."
— Desmond Morris, *Owl*

Author's Note

SPARKY IS A real barn owl, her Article 10* is in my name, I'm responsible for her wellbeing, but I don't own her: we're 'mates'.

Sparky came into my life through an odd set of circumstances; many people played parts, some they're unaware of, and so many things had to fall into alignment that it seems impossible it happened. But it did, leaving me thinking we were fated to meet. Sparky was nearly five years old; I was 44. In captivity barn owls can live to be 20; humans in captivity sometimes live beyond 100. So we should have a long time together which is amazing because she's amazing. That said, owls aren't pets, no bird of prey is. They require specialist care. I'm fortunate to have expert help with Sparky; I only adopted her because I knew this help was available and because I feared for her wellbeing if I didn't. People with no raptor experience shouldn't adopt owls or any other birds of prey.

Hopefully Sparky's story will help readers learn a little about owls and come to regard animals a bit more on their own terms, not ours. In writing the book, I drew on my understanding of barn owls, and Sparky specifically, to portray how she conceivably experiences her lived reality. I wanted to find an alternative, more empathetic, way of writing animals' lived experiences through emphasising that animals live in their own world, be it canine, feline, avian etc., not ours; we're just in it with them. For readers wanting to know more about owls I recommend Desmond Morris' *Owl* (2009), Stephen Moss's *The Owl: A Biography* (2023), Jemima Parry-Jones' *Understanding Owls* (1998), *What an Owl Knows* by Jennifer Ackerman (2023) and *The Secret Life of Owls* by John Lewis-Stempel (2017).

Having a barn owl as a central protagonist was a major writing challenge and readers who know my previous works might be surprised by this book. But, in common with *Green Dawn* et al, it blends fact and fiction. From Sparky's leg ring number, logged with the International Bird Registry (IBR), I learnt her hatch date but, due to data protection, only a few other vague details of her life. I didn't change any known information in my writing and everything from the point we meet is factual but, because of that, I've withheld details which might have been problematic if included. My accounts of myself are as accurate as any autobiographical writing can be. But, knowing nothing else about her until Sparky arrived at the animal centre where I was volunteering in March 2022, everything she experiences before we meet is fiction, based on what her behaviour suggests about her early life and drawing on factual accounts of barn owls in captivity.

Telling Sparky's story raised the question 'how can language convey an animal's wordless experiencing of its life?' Obviously it can't, especially when

---

* A legal document confirming Sparky is lawfully in captivity as she was captive bred from parent birds who were also captive bred.

avoiding writing that portrays Sparky as a feathered human, so I used narrative perspective, structure and, especially, vocabulary that I felt would give the impression of an owl's outlook. My vocab choices were inspired by considering how, if Sparky had language, she'd use it to recount her story. What words/phrases would be relevant to her? I took some liberties, though. For example, owls' night vision means they probably can't discern colours as well as I've suggested and I don't believe Sparky actually knows my name. Such liberties were necessary to keep writing clear and concise for readers' benefit.

Inventing Sparky's life before I met her made me realise something incredibly obvious: all animals in captivity, from the most exotic zoo collections to the cat at your fireside, are utterly at the mercy of their human carers. So if readers take anything from this book, I hope it's this: ensure you can properly care for, and truly care about, any animal you're thinking of adopting. If they could speak, all they'd ask you for is love.

Tracey Iceton
2026

NB: Sparky is not fed any live prey. All her food is humanely killed prior to her receiving it. Descriptions of her 'killing' prey are creative portrayals, based on her behaviour of pouncing down on anything edible, that attempt to convey how she seemingly perceives the meals she gets.

Prologue

14th July 2023

Great Writing International Writing Conference 2023, University College, London

I slip into the classroom mid-session and slide, I hope discretely, into a seat near the door as the chair introduces the second panellist. I've timed this well, his is the paper I want to hear; Noel Sloboda, 'Talking Animals: Poetics of Interspecies Reciprocity'. I listen intently as he outlines how most creative writing about animals imposes human values on them instead of engaging with animals on their terms. Creative writing about animals is a, currently, missed opportunity, he says, to challenge presumptions about animals' lived experiences and foster greater empathy for animals. I leave the session deep in thought.

The lightning fork moment is that night, at home, in bed. The story that's been hovering overhead, readying to pounce on me for months, finally settles gently on my shoulder just as Sparky does. It's her story. Told in a way that doesn't present her as a winged human but that somehow conveys her owlish understandings of life. Can I write such a book, a full length prose work depicting Sparky's lived experiences, known and imagined, avoiding anthropomorphising her, instead being faithful to her barn-owlness? I lie motionless while the idea races around me, hunter and prey. I haven't written anything for over three years, scrapped the last book I was working on, stopped calling myself a writer. Can I still write? Can I write Sparky's story, telling it as she deserves it to be told?

As I stare into the darkness around me, I imagine how Sparky, with her superhero night vision, would see this bedroom. In my head I start writing her description of it.

Now

28th March 2022

HHH

It's a colander, the old fashioned metal kind, punctured with tiny holes, two small U-shaped handles soldered opposite each other on the rim. I pick it up. What's it doing outside the owl room? In the sixth months I've volunteered, a day a week, at this animal centre, I've encountered some odd things. But a colander, like my nan used to have, what that's for I can't imagine. I return it to the concrete with a clatter, open the mesh door and enter the owl room with my buckets and dish scrubber to clean and refill the water tray.

As I set the buckets down something white flickers in my peripheral vision. I turn. Am staring into a pair of onyx eyes, darkly bright against a pure white love-heart face, gemstones in an elegant setting that narrows to a point below the hooked beak. I take in the snowy breast, lightly speckled with black, the feathery white trousers and pale, scaly feet, thin-toed and armed with talons. Dappled tan, grey and white feathers cloak the head, back and wings like a hooded cape as it stands proudly stretched to its full height of 1ft 0. I've been lucky enough to see barn owls up close before, but to have this one standing just feet from me, only air between us, calmly scrutinising me…

It's on the long wooden perch in the corner behind me. It wasn't here before my holiday. I'm used to the animal comings-and-goings at the centre but this watching barn owl is a starkly white novelty. The owl room is where injured wild owls are housed, mostly tawnies but a long-eared owl too. With their muted brown-and-speckled camouflage plumage they hide even in plain view but, being nervously nocturnal, mostly they shelter in the wall-mounted nest boxes, under the twin pairs of pallets leant together to make dark tee-pees in two corners, or perch in the shadows of the tree branch propped against the far wall. Some of the tawnies scurry down a hole in the corner behind the perch this barn owl is on, going to ground, literally, in the drains below, if you catch them out of hiding. None of them ever sits on either of the two long wooden perches in daytime, watching.

But this barn owl is. Do I stare back? The silence amplifies so I break it with my usual greeting.

'Hello, little one. I'm Tracey, one of the volunteers here. Are you alright?' I like introducing myself to new inmates, makes me feel I've started off with them on the right paw, or wing.

Suddenly the owl is airborne, swooping towards me. I stand still, breath held. It lands on my shoulder, so lightweight I feel just the hint of its taloned grip on me. The outer corner of my left eye fills with whiteness. Birds of prey fascinate me. I've done hawk-walks and 'flying experiences' at raptor centres, had falcons and even an eagle, perched on my gauntlet-covered hand and, once, flown a barn owl. Though I'm mindful of how weaponised they are, I'm not nervous around them, unlike some volunteers here. I've already spoken to the centre manager about working with the resident harris hawks and eagle owl, all of which are captive bred, have been trained and flown in the past but now live in aviaries, under-stimulated. As a volunteer I have time for them, it was on my post-holiday agenda. I've got the number of a local falconer who might be willing to help me help the raptors here, was planning on ringing him this week. Now there's a barn owl on my shoulder. Clearly not a wild barn owl. Obviously an imprint owl, hand reared by a human so it'll trust people enough to want to be with them, us: me.

'What are you doing here, little one?' I chatter to it as I slowly walk towards the perch. I can't tell if it's male or female, don't know if this bird has a name so, reluctantly, 'it' and 'little one' will have to do. 'What's your story?' I reach the perch, crouching down so that, on my shoulder, the owl's lower than it would be on the perch.

Little One accepts my suggestion and hops up. I step away. We study each other again. The dark eyes stare at me so intently I know there's a thinking mind behind them, one free of the internal jibber-jabber of human thoughts, a wordless mental processing beyond my comprehension but that's every bit as real and cognisant as my mental monologue. I wish I knew what it's thinking as it eyeballs me. It's clearly thinking something.

OOO

Sparky's on her, now, usual perch in the corner of the fliers' space, where she can watch the narrow gap that humans come and go along. She's waiting, as she has since she was brought here, for a particular human to come. When it comes it'll be her partner in life: her mate. She'll fly to it; it'll feed her. She'll trust it; it'll protect her. They'll bond; be together. It'll be her other half and she'll be its, they'll be a whole, a pair, living a shared life. She's waiting for it to come: her new mate.

Humans have been with her since she hatched, in her world: her life. They're her kin, though not her kind. Some were her mate for a while but none has stayed with her so she knows now they weren't her lifelong other half. She still hasn't found that particular human yet; they haven't found each other. So she keeps watching for it. She needs to find it, needs it to find her, so they can bond, be a pair, get on with living their life.

A human's coming now that Sparky hasn't seen before. Its short red head plumage and blue body plumage is unfamiliar. She absorbs its appearance as it comes along the narrow gap, stopping at the in/out. It bends forwards, straightening up again holding the hard shiny half-shell that some humans put on their heads when they enter the fliers' space. This new human stares at it, puts it down again, not on its head, and enters the fliers' space. It looks right at her, stares, doesn't move. It chatters softly, tilting its head, watching her watching it. Sparky listens for the call, her ss-p-aaarrr-kkee call, that humans give when they want to fly, hunt and feed with her: bond with her. Those humans that have been her mates before gave this call so she listens for it now. Hears in this new human's chattering the sound pattern t-raay-cee.

It's not her call but it's a bit like it; this human could want to be her mate. To find out she'll have to fly to it. If it flaps her away with its featherless wings and screeches at her it definitely doesn't. If it lets her land on its head ledge it might. Sparky leaps into flight.

HHH

Turning back to my duties, I notice the large nest box on the floor in the middle of the room. I creep over and peer inside. It's too dark to see anything but I hear hissing, scuffling, another owl presumably. Maybe this box is something to do with the barn owl on the perch. I'll ask but that doesn't mean I'll find out; info about what's what here is sketchy so the animals' backstories often get garbled, Oriental whispers. With a shrug, I scrub out and refill the water tray before heading to the next room. As I leave the barn owl stands on the perch, head turned nearly completely behind it, watching me go, still thinking whatever it's thinking about me.

OOO

The new human stands still, calm, like her human partners from before, so Sparky lands on a head ledge easily. New human keeps chattering but doesn't give the call that was like her ss-p-aaarrr-kkee call again. It walks her slowly to her perch. She jumps up, turns, head then body, to face new human. They share a look, her dark and its pale eyes. She knows it's sizing her up; she's doing the same. Could they become mates? Then it goes to ss-kk-reee flier's nest box, looking and listening at the hole. Sparky tenses. But ss-kk-reee doesn't come out to try to make new human its mate.

Sparky stays on her perch, watching new human gushing clean fresh water into the pool. Sparky hasn't bathed since she's been in the flier's space; she's afraid of being attacked by a keee-w-ickk flier when her feathers are too water-logged for an aerial escape. Often the water is so murky she wouldn't bathe in it anyway but new human has left invitingly clear water. If only she could be sure she'd be safe she'd bathe. If only she had a mate and they had a space of their own, with no keee-w-ickk or ss-kk-reee fliers. If only new human might be her new mate…

New human leaves; Sparky watches for it returning.

HHH

Another volunteer tells me the barn owl's name is Hoot. I'm also told there's a pair of barn owls in the large nest box plonked on the owl room floor. It's not clear if Hoot and the pair of barn owls arrived together but they're all captive-bred. I also discover the colander's purpose; Hoot's habit of flying to people has spooked those volunteers who're fine entering a room of timid owls in hiding but who don't want a free owl encounter. She (I decided to think 'she' because Hoot sounds somehow feminine) has been known to land on heads, as well as shoulders, so one volunteer brought in the colander to use as PPE. As I go about my duties I remember Hoot balancing, feather-light, on my shoulder, picturing it as a photograph I wish I could've taken, and wonder if Hoot would be as insulted by that colander business as I am on her behalf.

It's late afternoon, time for the carnivore feeding. I collect the appropriate number of day-old chicks from the fridge, counting them into a bucket, and set off on my rounds. The owl room is first.

Hoot's on the same perch. I don't know if she's been there all day or has been in the nest box on the floor and popped out when she heard me.

'Hello, Hoot. We met before but we can be properly introduced now I know your name. I'm Tracey. It's nice to meet you.'

I've just finished speaking when she flies to me, landing on my left shoulder again. Like a parrot. Like she's been trained to do that. But I doubt it's something a falconer would teach a bird of prey; I've never seen them fly to people's shoulders at displays.

'Do you want some tea?'

I grab a chick from the bucket and throw it towards the perch; it lands on the floor nearby. She flies down to it, pouncing feet first like a wild hunter, as if killing the fluffy yellow corpse, before snatching it up and carrying it to the perch, eating while I place defrosted chicks around the room; on the broken tree branch, under the pallet tee-pees, in the corners. I've been watching 'behind the railings' zoo programmes and dangerously think I'm providing stimulation by letting the animals find scattered food. I also leave some piled in the middle of the room too, easily reachable for the disabled owls.

Hoot's still eating so, before I go, I leave a final chick on the end of the perch for her. She looks up, jerking the last of the first chick down her throat before hopping across to grab the second one.

'If anyone asks, tell them Tracey said you could have two,' I say, nodding to her as she clutches the chick in a foot.

I'll ring that falconer this week. And hunt out a book on owl husbandry.

OOO

Sparky's still on her perch, waiting and watching. Soon a human will come with food, maybe that new human who might become her mate. She tunes in her hearing, ears filtering sounds until she picks up the clap-clapping of human feet, her ears seeing them getting closer. It is the new human. Eyes fixed on it, Sparky listens for her call, or the call from before that sounds like hers; there it is.

T-raay-cee.

It's still not her ss-p-aaarrr-kkee call but she wasn't flapped away when she flew to it before and it's a sound-alike call to hers. She leaps into flight, fluttering down onto the head ledge. New human keeps chattering then flies a chick through the air towards her perch. Sparky chases it, snatching it up to the perch to eat.

She's swallowing that chick when new human drops another on the perch end, chattering again, making the t-raay-cee sound. Some of Sparky's before mates had their own calls, like a-ll-eee and d-aann-y-elll.

T-raay-cee. She clutches at the call.

A human that lets her fly to it. A human that feeds her. A human calling to her. A human behaving like it wants to be her mate. But Sparky's been with humans before that behaved like this; some were her mate for a while, then they weren't: none of them stayed with her. Sparky needs to find a partner that'll pair with her lifelong.

Before

4th–5th August 2017

HHH

C'mon, little owlet, time to hatch. I can see you've pipped through your shell and I'm dying to meet you. It's going to be a long hard day of pecking and scraping your way out but you can do it. I'll help if you need me but it's safer for you to do it yourself so keep trying.

OOO

Her space presses tightly around her after so much growing inside it. She taps and scrapes, scratches and pecks at the heavy shell crushing her.

A sudden slip of her beak; the tiny egg tooth breaks through to peck against nothing. She feels cold trickling into the warm wetness surrounding her. She rests but that tiny hole needs scratching and scraping, pecking and tapping at until it's enough to split her too-small space open, freeing her from her eggshell. So she taps and pecks and…

She's exhausted but the tiny hole is a growing crack, creeping around the shell, meeting itself. She wriggles and flops, flaps and kicks at the weight pressing on her. It falls away slowly then suddenly. She's eggless: free. The trickle of cold becomes a stream of chilling wetness but she can't do anything except rest so she lies there, panting breath after breath, getting colder.

A chat-chattering sound drifts down to her. Instinct tells her the sound means safety; she struggles towards it.

HHH

Well done, little owlet, you made it, I knew you could. Come here, lets clean you up, pop you in the incubator. Bless you, you're so ugly, a tiny pink wizened dinosaur, but you'll be a fluffy little bundle in a few weeks and a bonny barn owl by autumn.

OOO

She's being moved, rising up nestled in warmth, the texture enough like her own skin and flesh that it bleeds into her as she settles against it, soaking up the warmth. The chat-chattering sound floats down to her. The warmth and chatter are comforting. She's safe. Whatever's making the chattering call brought her the warmth she needed. She calls back to it with her own quiet chit-chittering. She knows now that there's another here to protect her: the chatterer. If she calls to it, it'll be there for her.

Dry fluffy softness strokes her, rubbing away the chilling sticky wetness coating her skin. Then she's gently floating, landing in more dry soothing warmth, fluffiness under her and air softly blowing over her, ruffling her fine down. She nestles into it and sleeps, holding the reassuring chat-chattering in her ears. Knowing the chatterer's there for her, she's contented.

HHH

There you go, that's better, isn't it? Got all that goo off you. Now warm up, dry out, rest. I'll check on you later, little owlet. Then tomorrow you'll get your first feed.

Now

30th March 2022

HHH

I ring the falconer's mobile, given to me by the animal centre's director who assured me the falconer has happily helped them before with birds of prey. I hate ringing mobiles, poor signal quality and the endless list of things you might be interrupting when you call. I get voicemail, which I hate nearly as much, leave a mumbled message and hope he rings back. Then I flick through the second hand falconry book I got. I haven't found one specifically about owls yet but this'll give me introductory basics for working with the centre's captive-bred raptors; Mildred the harris hawk, Orville the eagle owl, and Sparky.

That's the barn owl's name, the centre director told me, not Hoot. He also told me she was surrendered to the centre by her previous owners who mistook her friendly imprint behaviour of flying to them for aggression; thinking she was attacking them they wanted rid of her, he explains. She's nothing to do with the breeding pair of barn owls nesting in the large box on the owl room floor. I wasn't told where they've come from or why. And I only know what I've been told about Sparky: the teller's Sparky story. Stories are only ever the teller's tale; there isn't such a thing as a true story because the truth is inevitably, sometimes deliberately, impacted by the teller's narration. Only Sparky, if that's her real name, knows her true story but, even if she could tell me, it still wouldn't be the truth; it would be her telling of it. I might as well just make up my own Sparky story…

The falconer rings back. I explain again, hopefully more coherently, about wanting to enrich the lives of birds of prey at the centre, that I've done a bit with raptors before. He's willing to help and we agree a date for him to drop in, suss out the birds and suggest a few things.

I go back to my reading. The book makes it clear I know sod all about training and flying birds of prey. Heat flushes my face. The falconer will have realised that too. The experience days were just flying encounters. I'm a complete novice. But I'm what they've got; Sparky, and the others, will have to make do with me.

OOO

The new human, t-raay-cee, hasn't returned to the fliers' space. Sparky keeps watching for it, though, because it let her fly to its head ledge, fed her, called to her, though not with her proper ss-p-aaarrr-kkee call. If the t-raay-cee human wants to be her mate it'll come again, be with her. It's the human here that's behaved most like it might become her mate so maybe… If she could search for this human, she would, but she can't escape the fliers' space, only humans can use the in/out. She has to wait for t-raay-cee to return to her.

If they do bond, become a pair, they'll leave this space that she's forced to share with the wild fliers, where she's had to learn to survive amongst them. At least ss-kk-reee flier hasn't tried to land on top of her since she fought it off. There's still the night-time chaos though, when the keee-w-ickks, ss-kk-reee fliers and hoo-hoo head-tufts emerge from their roosts, snatching prey from the pile, flying, if they can, around the space, attacking each other. Sparky doesn't fly when they're about unless she needs to escape a keee-w-ickk. She does her flying in daylight; nights belong to the wild fliers so she stays on her perch or the ledge high up the wall, resting watchfully. Whenever she finds her mate, when they've found each other, she'll be safe and contented again. She has to find a human mate; that's the life she knows: needs.

Before

August 2017

OOO

She feels empty inside: hungry. She struggles around, pecking, getting beakfuls of dry, coarse fluff that she can't eat so she makes her chit-chittering as loudly as she can, calling to the chat-chatterer who'll help her when it comes. She calls and listens until she hears its chattering reply to her, knows help is close. Then she chit-chitters continuously, encouraging the chatterer to hurry.

HHH

Alright, yes, you're hungry, I know. Got yummy minced beef for you. Let me get some in the tweezers. There we go. That's it, down the tunnel.

OOO

Something touches her open beak. She snaps her mouth closed on it. A fleshy strand slides down into the emptiness. She needs more, opens her beak again, stretching up, heavy head flopping about on her flimsy neck. But her stretching and straining are rewarded. The touch on her beak again, another fleshy strip slipping down her throat. Morsel by morsel she's fed full. She curls up, feet under her belly, head down, neck muscles relaxing, and sleeps again.

She's been eating, fleshy strands, then bigger meaty chunks, moist and squishy, all passed to her beak by the helpful chatterer. And she's been sleeping, curling up into herself, warmth cocooning her. She only has what she feels and hears to tell her about the world outside the fluttering, twitching body that she's slowly learning to control.

Now there's a new sensation, a flickering, quivering in her head that brings, creeping in, a chink of whitely glowing brightness, a change from red darkness to blue lightness. She finds her eyes, blinking eyelids revealing a thicker slice of light. She blinks more; darker or lighter patches come into focus. Brightness separates out into lines, forming shapes as her eyes open wider. She hears a big shape coming closer, sees it getting bigger, and learns the sound of movement. The moving shape gives the loud chattering she's been listening for. She calls back with her chittering as the chatterer nears her.

Squinting newly-opened eyes, she makes out its head, body, limbs. Blurrily, she studies it, needing to see now so she can recognise the chatterer by look as well as call, matching sound to sight, binding hearing and seeing together into knowing. She compares what she sees it is with what she feels herself to be. The chatterer's eyes face forwards like hers. The chatterer's beak doesn't open like hers though; its an unbeak with a hole beneath instead. The chatterer's body and limbs are similar to hers, legs and feet but no taloned toes; its taloned toes are at the ends of its wings which are at its sides, as hers are. The chatterer's a human, different to her but familiar enough for her to accept it. Now she's seen that it's a human feeding her, keeping her warm and safe she'll bond with it, share her life with humans; make them her kin.

HHH

What lovely dark eyes you have, little owlet, open for the first time today after a fortnight of blindness. Sorry if I'm not the mum you were expecting to see but I want you to have a home where you'll get to fly, not be stuck in an aviary and gawped at, so I need you to imprint on me, not your owl parents. You'll soon get used to me and this way you'll have the best of life: the protection of captivity with the chance to fly free. Ready for some brekkie?

OOO

Now she can see her world opens wide up. She's in a hollow, like half of the shell she cracked out of but bigger. It's filled with pink fluff that she nestles into, cosy and warm: her nest. The nest is inside a large box with sides and a top made of lines in a criss-crossed pattern that stop anything getting in. This is her space.

Beyond her space there's a much bigger space, white sides and top, black-white squares on the ground. This bigger space is filled with lots of lines, straight and curved, that make shapes; flat, square, rounded, pointed, larger, smaller, lighter, darker. Some of the shapes have depth, standing forward or behind other shapes. A tall flat dark oblong patch opposite her space opens and closes; her human chatterer comes in and goes out through this tall dark oblong: the in/out.

Seeing all this she starts mapping this bigger space; it becomes her territory. She keeps mapping until she's tired, falling back into sleep.

She wakes, opening still-developing eyes onto darkness: night. She blinks through the black, seeing into it, seeing all the shapes and lines she could see when light filled her space and the territory beyond. The colours are gone, faded to grey, but her vision is still vivid. She can see around her newly mapped territory as well in darkness as in brightness. Night hides nothing from her. She night-watches.

HHH

Good morning, little owlet. I know, you're wondering where brekkie is but I need to get you ringed first. It's for your own safety; if you're ever lost and found you'll be able to tell people who you are and where you're from so you can get home again. And you're always welcome back here if you're in trouble…

OOO

The sound of her human's chattering wakes her. It's day again, light and colour returned. A few blinks and her eyes are ready; she sees her chatterer coming through the in/out and chitters to it for food, knowing it'll feed her.

But when it reaches into her space it's not bringing meat, held in the shiny thin beak it feeds her with. Instead it stretches out the limbs that are like her wings, the taloned toes at the ends of them coming towards her.

She backs away, calling shrilly, rolling and rocking away from her chattering human because something new, threatening, is happening. A hard, fast thumping in her breast makes her pant. What's happening might harm her. She has to keep herself alive: protect herself.

She can't move any further away so she pecks at her human's reaching toes. They're fleshy but too big for her to pierce with her tiny beak. Then they're surrounding her warmly, the sensation of skin against skin. She's being lifted up. She stops pecking to watch herself being moved through her territory, the shapes in it static around her. She flaps her wings as she's rising, sensing there's a way for her to escape: flight. Not yet, but soon.

She's being lowered now, laid on her back against something that cradles her. She wriggles frantically, trying to get upright, life's hold on her compelling her to struggle. By twisting her neck, lifting her head, she sees her human's toes around her body. There's a fidgeting and a squeezing. Now she can't wriggle so much. She twists her neck side to side, up and down, back to front, pecking randomly at fleshy things, non-fleshy things: nothing.

Something touches her foot, pressing it, bending her toes against each other. She calls out at the strange, new touching, keeps calling as more strange sensations come up her body from her foot; a cold hardness gripping her toes, moving over them so they're crushed together then moving off them, letting them spread out again. Now a cold hardness surrounds her ankle; touching here, there, as she kicks her leg.

The squeezing around her body slackens. She bends forward, pecking at her ankle, beak tip-tapping against a band of hardness that spins around her leg as she strikes it. She grips it in her beak, pulling at it but it stays around her ankle.

HHH

There, that wasn't so bad, was it? Now for some grub.

OOO

She's rising up again, her human holding her gently secure in its toes, moving her forward through air, lowering her. Looking around, she sees the newly familiar map of her territory. She's back in her space. But she's still hungry, calls to her chatterer to feed her. It reaches into her space, this time bringing food, which is dropped beside her, out of beak reach. She shuffles to it on wobbly legs that won't straighten under her, pecks up slippery meaty pieces, gulping them down until she's full. She's not feeling the cold hardness jangling against her ankle now; a soothing drowsiness creeps over her. The new happening, her human chatterer lifting her out of her space, didn't harm her. She's safe, well fed and contented. She knows more trust for her human other half now. She falls asleep.

Now

4th April 2022

HHH

The falconer's coming to the centre today to tell me what I can do for the birds of prey. I fear it's a wasted trip for him. Mildred, the harris hawk, and her mate, have suddenly been rehomed after eight months here. It's good news for them but I was gearing up, literally, to work with them. Harris hawks are the easiest raptors to train, a beginner's bird, so I'm a bit deflated. I even bought a falconry glove designed for their powerful feet. Now I'm not sure what I can do.

The red tailed hawks should, but won't, be nearly as trainable because they've gone feral after so long without human interaction. Hopefully the falconer can suggest things to improve life for the wild kestrels and owls. And I might be able to do something with Orville although he's a grumpy sod. Then there's Sparky; my falconry glove is too hefty for a barn owl but at least I've got a glove. That and the second hand falconry gear I've bought should be enough for a start. The courier lost the flying perch but I have what I need most: the scales. Trained birds of prey have a flying weight, low enough that they're hungry enough to come to someone for food, says the book that's becoming my oracle. I'll need to establish this for any raptors I want to try flying. And I'll need to learn a lot more. I hope this falconer is patient, a good teacher. I go about my usual volunteer duties, on edge for his arrival.

OOO

Sparky hears chattering outside the fliers' space. She's on her perch so twists around, eyes and ears following the sound.

Getting close is t-raay-cee and a human she hasn't seen here before, a human displaying prominent dark face plumage. As they enter the space a keee-w-ickk flier scurries underground like a mouse and ss-kk-reee leaps from the top of its box, circling the space. Sparky's legs tense, ready for take-off, her wings twitching to open into hard-beating flight so she can knock ss-kk-reee out of the air if it comes close. It circles again then disappears inside its box.

Now there's just her and the humans out in the space. They stand chattering, looking at her, so she flies for t-raay-cee's head ledge. As she's wing-beating her way there the face plumage stranger raises a featherless wing with reassuring confidence. Normally when humans want her to perch on their featherless wings they hide their soft wing toes in a covering of thick dark skin then, when Sparky grips with her talons, they don't screech or shake her off. But this face plumage human hasn't done that, it's just raised its featherless wing, behaving like it'll let her land there. So, with a swift wing-tilt, Sparky veers away from t-raay-cee and drops onto face plumage's outstretched perch.

Feeling the fleshiness of its wing toes, Sparky tries to keep her grip light, her talons unpiercing. It's easier than she's used to, standing on this featherless wing, balancing with a loose hold. Face plumage has the most solid perch of any human she's flown to, a natural perch, steady as a stout tree branch. The humans keep chattering. Then face plumage sends her deftly into the air, aiming her at her perch as surely as it held her on its featherless wing.

Sparky lands, turns, sees t-raay-cee and face plumage leaving the fliers' space.

Is t-raay-cee the mate she's been waiting for or this new face plumage human that held her so steady?

Before

September 2017

OOO

Her space has grown smaller around her and doesn't have the nest of pink fluff to nestle into anymore. Instead there's sandy gravel on the ground that she scrapes with her feet. Her territory beyond is smaller too because she's bigger, growing fast, able to stand tall, feet fully under her, legs supporting body, instead of wobbling about on her knees. She stands and walks. Stretching her wings out, she runs across her space, finding her balance.

Her wings are changing too, she feels and sees it happening: a prickling under her thick white down; her skin sore, hot and scratchy; pale points, visible when she twists her head and looks behind her, poke through fluffy down. The points get longer and there are more of them each time she checks. Her skin gets sorer, hotter, scratchier as the pale points lengthen, start unfurling. She pecks at herself here, there. It doesn't ease the soreness, sooth the scratchiness or stop more pale points piercing through her downy plumage. And it's not just on her wings; it's all over her body. She's fledging, feather by feather. The strengthening feathers urge her to run faster, stretching her wings further, beating them harder.

Her call has changed as well, the chittering replaced by a croaky, rasping sound coming from deeper in her chest, a single throaty cawing note, a softly screeching call. The sound and volume of it wells within her so she makes it again, opening her beak wide to let the new call out. From inside her smaller space she screeches raspily for her human to come to her, feed her and be with her because life for her means being with her human other half.

Her human has heard, is entering the territory that's theirs when they're in it together, bringing her food but not just the chunks of flesh she's been eating. Today it's bringing her prey. A tiny white body with a pointed head and pink feet dangles by a pale thin tail. The sight of this furry white body stirs an inherited knowing in her, the legacy of her hunter's ancestry. Mouse: a meal to be caught, killed then eaten. She cranes her neck, caws croakily, eager to crush the mouse's skull in her beak. As her human opens her space, bleeding it with their territory beyond, she jumps up with a wing-beat to catch that mouse.

Her human fills the opening with its featherless wing; stopped, she falls back inside, the mouse following, flying across the space away from her. She tracks its limp flight with her motion-tuned sight, runs to where it lands, beating wings propelling her forward. She pounces on the mouse with both feet, toes strangling it, talons piercing soft flesh. She tightens her hold on it: a killing grip. Her hunter's birthright is a reflex. The mouse doesn't struggle at all but she kills it anyway. It's hers now, a meal earned. She spreads out feathering wings, hiding her catch. Then she crunches down on the skull, thin bone crumbling. She bites at the head until the skull is many fragments that fold in on themselves, making it small enough for her to swallow. Next she tugs sharply, yanking the head off the body, gulping it down. Standing firmly on its belly, she assesses the headless mouse, pecking at it before beaking it up, shutting her eyes and squeezing it down to fill the emptiness of hunger. The mouse settles in her stomach, tail hanging from her beak like a half-eaten worm until it too is swallowed.

She turns now to face her human, calling out her new croaky screech, the one that brought her a whole mouse, rousing hunter-her.

It responds with its familiar chattering. She's started to notice that the chattering has many sounds within it; ooo, eee, arrr, ch, th, ppp, fff and more. She doesn't know what they mean but she can pick them from each other, her ears tuning ever more finely. Now she hears a 'sss' sound. She replies with her raspy hissing call. The sounds are different: similar. Just as her and her human are similar but different. They fit together, though, halves making a whole. She's complete and content as long as her human's there, sharing life with her. She calls again to it as it leaves their territory. Looking back at her, it chatters and head-bobs. It'll return soon.

HHH

You liked that mouse, didn't you? It still amazes me how quickly you grow from helpless hatchling to winged hunter. Only a month old and you're scoffing down whole mice. If it stays warm you'll be able to go out into a proper aviary soon, with room to fly, where you can see a bit more of the world, get ready to join it, little owlet.

OOO

She's grown big enough to leave the space that was her nest; it's too small for her now. But she can't leave until her human is ready for that too, taking her to a new, bigger space that she can share with it whenever it comes to her.

Twisting her neck, she inspects her wings; pale speckled grey-and-tan feathers have unfurled from the long pale points that prickled through her hatchling's down which is mostly gone now. When she unfolds her wings her feathers spread out, the longest few at the ends making a shape like the toes at the end of her human's wing-limb which is featherless. Its whole body is featherless, covered with its own type of plumage but she knows their similarities well enough to accept her human's differences.

Her own newly grown feathers are still soft but stiffening in places, like on her wings. The pecking at scratchy skin has become preening, smoothing and tidying her plumage. Now she has properly feathered wings she needs to look after them. Not all the pale points have unfurled into flying feathers yet so when she beats her wings and jumps she's airborne just for a hop. She can't fly but the urge to is fierce. She'll keep trying until she can. Then she won't have to wait for her human to come to her so they can be together; she'll be able to go to it.

It's come to her now. She starts her croaky call, head bobbing, looking for the dangling mouse it usually brings her.

But it doesn't fly a mouse into her nest space for her to pounce on. Instead her human lifts her out, carrying her across their territory, leaving it.

Something new is happening. She struggles against it in case there's danger in this new happening but her human keeps hold and it's always protected her so she accepts being taken from her territory, away from her nest space, where she's been safe. Maybe she's going to that new bigger space she's being ready for a while since.

They pass into light so bright she blinks against the glaring blaze. Sight returning, she looks overhead into an endless pale blue wilderness smeared with white. The sky: where, when her wing-beating jumps become flight, she'll soar high, swooping down on prey. Her wings twitch and quiver, fluttering against her human's hold. It's her nature, her purpose, her living. She's a flier and a hunter. She knows this about herself now and she's ready to start living that life with her human mate.

She's still gazing into that bright sky as they pass into shade. The sky vanishes. She's set on the ground, free to move, in a new space, dimness above and around her. Standing, she head-turns, inspecting this new space. The sides are solid expect in front of her which is thin lines, like in her nest space. She runs to the lines, searching for the sky that's to be her flying ground, fixing her eyes on it. Behind her, her human calls:

Fff-oooo-dd.

It's a sound she's started to recognise because it comes before the prey is flown down for her to pounce on. Sometimes it's a white mouse, sometimes a yellow chick, sometimes a fleshy bony chunk, furred or feathered but headless, limbless, a bit of something killed for her by her human; she kills it again instinctively anyway.

Fff-oooo-dd.

A white mouse scampers through the air, her human releasing it for her to catch. She quickens her running, wings beating as she goes, adding jumps powered by the wing-beats, shrinking the distance between her and the mouse which lies motionless on the ground, now within strike-range. A strong wing-beat and a stronger pounce land her on the mouse, talons piercing. She looks behind her, grip tight on her prey. Her human steps backwards out of this new space to stand looking in at her, chattering steadily.

HHH

There you go, little owlet, an aviary all of your own with flying space and a sunny autumn day for your first glimpse of sky. Bet you're excited to take off into it but you'll have to wait for your new owner, whoever that'll be, to buy you, train you and trust you to fly back to them. Hopefully you'll be soaring up into it soon.

I'll leave you to settle in and enjoy the view.

OOO

After she's eaten and rested she explores her new space, walking, running and jumping around it, wing-beating as she goes. She hops across ground covered with rocky chunks about the size of a mouse head, feeling their solidness beneath her feet. Reaching a dark corner she pecks at the sides, her beak tapping dully against the wooden surface.

Then she goes to stare out between the lines at the front of her new space, studying the new territory beyond it, mapping the shapes and colours that fill it. Nature and unnature merge together. The natural is all elegantly disordered; twisted trees, lopsided bushes, speckled colours. The unnatural is all clumsily ordered; straight-sided structures, sharp lines and flat solid colours. A patch of grass in the middle of the territory divides and unites the wild and the tame, bringing them together with its natural greenness unnaturally smoothed.

Movement fills the territory too: tiny flying creatures that flit and b-u-zzz close to her space; bigger flying creatures that glide through the sky: fliers like her, like she will be soon.

A yellow-beaked black flier, smaller than she knows herself to be, lands on the grassy patch close enough for her to see its blinking eyes, which are on the sides of its head, not forward facing like hers. The black flier sings a twittering call and pecks at the ground, hops and pecks again, flies away.

W-u-f. W-u-ff-w-uu-f-w-u-f.

She traces the unfamiliar sound to the edge of her territory, near a large red-brown structure. From out of the structure a creature appears, all legs and no wings, tail flapping at its rear: a wolf.

W-u-f. W-u-ff-w-uu-f-w-u-f.

The wolf's call booms as it runs towards her. A human, not hers, chases it, calling to it. She watches as they get closer, her body taut, wings quivering with the reflex to fly. This wolf is invading her territory, threatening her, running to attack her.

The wolf charges right up to her space, stopped by the criss-crossed lines, raising its head. She jumps back, spreads her wings, dips her head and hiss-croaks at it. It lowers its head towards her; she feels warm breath panting over her. Shaking her head at it, she makes herself as menacing as she can, fluffed feathers adding size, bone-deep knowledge teaching her to defend herself when her human mate isn't there.

The wolf raises its head, w-u-f w-u-fs again. She replies with the loudest hissing raspy screech she can managed but it's smothered by the booming w-u-f w-u-f w-u-f.

A shrill note, high and bright, cuts the air. The wolf turns to look. She looks also. The human has caught up, is there now, the shrill call coming from it. The wolf goes to it and they walk away together.

It isn't just her who has a human other half.

Later, when her human reappears, chattering to her, she listens for the fff-oooo-dd sound pattern that she recognises now. Instead, as it enters her space, she hears a new pattern several times: ss-p-aaarrr-kkee.

HHH

Hello, Sparky, how's that for a name? Clive's suggestion because you showed some spark, standing your ground when Doug raced up; he's friendly really, just over-enthusiastic. Sparky, hmm, it suits you. Normally I don't name birds I'm selling but seems you're stuck with me for a while longer. I hoped you'd have an owner to name and train you by now but, as you're fully fledged, I'll make start, don't want you just sitting in there bored. Let me get my glove, get some food.

Right, Sparky, are you going to come to me?

OOO

As her human steps forwards she steps backwards. When it stands still she leans over, tapping its black toeless feet with her beak. They're stiff under her pecking touch. She tilts her head to look up its body to its head, the face round and flat like hers, the eyes staring out and down at her. Then she switches her focus to its featherless wings, watching for prey to appear clutched in the wing toes, about to be flown across the space for her to catch.

But her human doesn't fly any prey. It crouches beside her, covers a set of wing toes in a thicker, darker skin before holding up a yellow fluffy fleshy scrap in the toes now covered by dark thick hide. This is new: different. She doesn't know if it's safe. Cautiously, curiously, she stretches her neck as far as she can, until her beak can reach the piece of food. She snatches it and quickly retreats to eat as another scrap of prey is held out by the dark, thick-skinned wing toes. She gauges the distance between her and the offered food. She'll have to hop closer to get it.

Then she hears the new sound pattern again.

Ss-p-aaarrr-kkee.

The piece of prey wriggles. She steps nearer, eyes fixed on the food as her human calls again with the new sound.

Ss-p-aaarrr-kkee.

She collects the pattern of this unfamiliar call. It's not the fff-oooo-dd pattern she's learned but it's still her mate calling to her, offering her a beakful of wriggling meat. She hops over, grabs, retreats and eats again, eyes on her human, aware of how it and she are a pair. This is their bond growing, strengthening.

It offers her another meaty morsel, too high for her to reach by neck-stretching. She'll have to step onto the dark hide-covered wing toes if she wants that food.

Ss-p-aaarrr-kkee.

She's known this human ever since she hatched. It's protected her, keeping her warm when she was cold, feeding her when she was hungry. It's held on to her but she's never held on to it. She's never gone to it. A decision to make, she hesitates.

The prey piece wriggles temptingly again, it's a chick leg, meaty with a fringe of yellow fluffy down.

Ss-p-aaarrr-kkee fff-oooo-dd.

The new call again, this time with the familiar call, encouraging her to come and eat.

She bends her legs, beats her wings and jumps, landing on the end of her human's featherless wing, feeling the thick skin that now covers its fleshy wing toes as she grips on, her talons unable to pierce the dark hide. As she bends forward to peck up the piece of food she loses sight of it, finding it in touch, feeling it against her beak feathers, snapping it up. With it held securely, she turns and leaps down, eating with her back to her human, wings outspread, hiding her catch. When she's eaten, she turns around, calling for more with her raspy croak. And there is more, but she'll have to hop up for it again.

Ss-p-aaarrr-kkee.

They do this until she's full and tired. As she rests, content, what happened with her mate today seeps through from her ears, eyes and feathers into her bones, muscles and blood, lodging in her mind. If it happens again it won't be new; she'll know what to do.

Now

4th April 2022 (cont.)

HHH

The falconer arrives that afternoon as arranged. I take him straight to the owl room. As we enter a tawny scuttles for the hole in the floor, disappearing into the drains.

'What the…?'

I explain; we have a quick conversation about the problems that hole presents. Christ knows how many owls have buried themselves alive down there.

Meanwhile Sparky's on her perch. One of the other barn owls is also out; it circuits the room, darting back inside its nest box on the floor. It gone, Sparky flies towards us. The falconer puts his left arm up, letting her land on his bare fingers. I'm still worried about her scratching me with talons that make my cats' claws look like cotton buds but he's got her on his ungloved hand, unflinching. He looks her over, checking the leg ring she wears.

'You've got a lovely imprint barn owl here. Female, not very old. She needs to be out of this room though, away from these wild owls. As an imprint she doesn't understand other birds' behaviour. Tawnies are super aggressive, really territorial; a big female tawny could kill a barn owl, especially an imprint that doesn't know how to defend itself. And that male barn owl,' he points to the box it's hiding in, 'if it tries to mate with her she won't like that. She should be in her own aviary, somewhere she can see people, interact with them, not stuck in here with other birds she can't relate to. She needs moving.'

I feel like an idiot; I didn't realise. But moving to where? The centre's crammed with animals. Plus, I'd have to clear it with the centre's director who does things his way. Because he's the only animal expert here no one can challenge him: he's a former zoo keeper with decades of experience; I'm a volunteer with an NVQ level 2 in animal care. A suggestion from me that something's not right won't be appreciated.

Sparky bobs her head like she's agreeing with the falconer and flicks her dark eyes onto me, as if asking for my help. I know then I'll do whatever I can for her.

'O.K., I'll sort something out.'

Once we've left Sparky, finished touring the birds of prey at the centre, we natter about the paths our lives have followed, how we've ended up having this conversation. Life's labyrinth: how you get where you were always heading without knowing the destination. At least people have the illusion of free will, choice: control. Animals in captivity don't even have that. They end up wherever, have to put up with whatever. They can't go where they want, do what they need, can't even choose death to escape cruelty. Wild animals have their freedom but that's all. Everything else they have to struggle for; if they fail they suffer: die.

Captive animals can have a longer, more comfortable, life but only if people give them that.

I don't know what life Sparky's had from people before coming here but what she's got now isn't good enough. She's got me, though. It's like Sparky and I were always on converging paths. Neither of us made this happen, we couldn't have because it was unimaginable. But here we are. Maybe I can be the person who gives Sparky the better life she deserves…

I flick aside philosophy; there are practicalities to focus on. I have the falconer's number, some basic advice to get me started. He's got books I can borrow, a leash and swivel I can use for Sparky. He'll have seen through me, realised I'm cabbage green, but he's willing to help, lives fairly close, says I can phone him any time, drop in to get the books and gear. It sounds easy; it won't be. But picturing Sparky, remembering our first meeting, her on my shoulder, I know I have to do all I can: whatever needs doing.

Before

September–October 2017

OOO

Her human is here again, coming in, sharing her space, as it does ever day, calling to her with the now familiar ss-p-aaarrr-kkee sound pattern. As soon as she hears it she hops, runs and jumps over to her mate because they're a bonded pair and that call is her mate's greeting. She is ss-p-aaarrr-kkee because that's the call her other half gives when it comes to her, wants her to come to it. Hearing that sound, absorbing it, she's become it, knowing that sound brings them together, makes them whole, completing her: she is Sparky now.

Her human holds out its featherless wing, the toes covered with the thick dark skin that her talons can't pierce. Sparky watches these wing toes, waiting for a piece of prey to appear between them. There it is.

Ss-p-aaarrr-kkee.

She maps the distance to the food, hunter's eyes and ears catching the prey-like wriggles and rustles, hunter's mind reckoning pounce height. She crouches low, springs up, beating her wings, snatching for a foothold before slipping, falling off. She needs to wing-beat harder. She knows there's lift for her that way. She just needs to find it.

The prey piece wiggles again as her mate calls her.

Ss-p-aaarrr-kkee.

She leaps higher, flaps faster, feeling her own weight suspended in air. Then her feet are grabbing at a landing, her toes curling around her mate's wing toes, them holding on to each other. She's made it. Head bending, she beaks up her reward.

As she eats she's lowered to the ground, the featherless wing tilting so she steps off backwards, watching for more meat, ready to calculate her next wing-beating jump to it. Sparky opens her fully feathered wings wide, displaying intricate white, black and grey diamonds dappled against a softly warm tan background, her feathered cloak deftly woven by nature. Fringing this cloak are her primaries, long and strong, made for flight, more purely white with faint smears of tan and grey. Head turned, this is the detail she sees: her sparkling speckled plumage. But she's focused on her human now, waiting for the sight of a ready meal.

There it is.

Ss-p-aaarrr-kkee.

She jumps, wing-beats, foot-grabs. Makes it, perching on the featherless wing. She's learning to fly.

They do this again and again. Each jump-flight there's food for her, fleshy morsels, pink and bare or yellow and fluffy.

Her mate stands tall now, chattering and rubbing its legs. Then it reaches into a hole hanging at its side where it finds the food it offers her. This time her human pulls out an innately familiar form: a mouse. Not just food to eat but prey to hunt; the sight of it buzzes primal urges through Sparky.

She focuses unfalteringly on the white-furred meal. It's further, higher, from her, than any prey she's caught from her human before. If she waits it'll crouch down so she can hop easily up to her mate and its food offering. But she doesn't need to wait. She's ready. She springs up, keeps wing-beating, muscles straining and flexing, the effort drawing her closer to the waiting prey, further from the ground. She's airborne: flying.

Sparky jolts down, wobbling, on the wing toes, struggling for balance. Her mate gives a shrill sharp call that startles her, stumbling her already clumsy landing. She misses her footing, slips, tumbles back into flight. With frantic flapping she holds herself up, lowers herself groundward. The mouse falls too. As they pass silently in mid-air, Sparky glimpses its whiteness, eyes tracking its dive, landing herself a short hop from it. She runs into a pounce, striking fiercely with both feet, talons piercing. But now she gasps for breath, the exertion of first flight, an almost vertical take-off, exhausting her.

As her breathing slows into a steadier rhythm she feels the quivering of muscles fatigued by flight and folds her wings behind her, treading her feet on top of the mouse, talons buried securely in the white flank, until she's able to eat.

The quivering fades, replaced with a thrumming of energy, bright and strong: powerful. The feeling of flying, having flown: being able to fly. It hums through her whole body with a light floatiness, bubbling up then gently calming, leaving her contented, her mate chattering away behind her as she eats her catch.

HHH

Sorry I startled you, Sparky, but you caught me out there, flying up like that. It's all right for the books to say you'll fly at ten weeks but you haven't read the books, have you? You'll fly when you're ready, and that's today. Well done for finding your wings, though. We can move on with the training, now. Soon have you flying across the aviary to me, eh, Sparky? I'll dig out a flying perch later so you can practice take-offs and landings.

OOO

Her human returns as the day becomes night.

It's carrying a strange thin tree, brings it into her space, planting it in a dark corner. Sparky hops over to her human, sidestepping around the clumping toeless feet until her mate bends down, offering a wing limb for her to step to, a scrap of meat there for her if she does. And she does, because she wants to and knows her mate wants her to, so they are together, holding on to each other. As she gulps down the food her human walks her to the planted tree.

She studies it, this odd spindly trunk topped by a single stunted horizontal branch. Not a real tree; an unnatural tree. But on that branch she'd be perching safely off the ground. Her mate brought her it, has lifted her up to it, so must want her to perch there. Not an odd tree: a perch. With a head bob, Sparky maps the distance in wing-beats then springs herself towards the odd tree perch.

She's in the air, moving up, propelling herself forwards, focusing on the branch as she nears it. Another few wing-beats and she'll be there. She holds her feet out in front, readying to grab it.

There's a jarring stop.

Swaying, she tightens her talons around the solid branch beneath her feet. Wings flapping, she fights for balance until the motion of flight stills and she's where she wanted to be, on her new perch, facing her human, not having to tilt her head back to see its wide pale eyes facing forwards above its unbeak and face hole.

She rotates her head, taking in her space from this new vantage: the sides and top that she's much closer to now; the rock-lumpy ground that she's much further from, the view ahead out across the grass and away into the darkening sky. She's closer to that sky up here on this new perch.

She twists her neck again, facing her human who's head-bobbing at her and chattering, sometimes making the ss-p-aaarrr-kkee sound: her sound. Hearing her mate calling to her, she replies with her gently croaking rasp. They call to each other, drawing closer together. An urge grows in her to be nearer to it but her mate isn't holding out its featherless wing for her. She studies it. Up this high she notices short, straight ledges either side of its head, somewhere she could land, perch. It would take only a few wing-beats and she'd be with her other half.

She pushes off, flapping at the same time, spanning the short gap between them and landing, more steadily, on a ledge beside her human's head. It calls out as she settles there, chattering rapidly as she faces where she was. Looking back from her human's head ledge, Sparky sees they're walking towards her new perch. When they reach it, her mate drops down so Sparky's lower than the perch; the head ledge she's on jerks up and down so she jumps across to her new perch with a single wing-beat, landing more smoothly, finding her feet on this stable branch perch.

She turns to see her human stepping out into the territory beyond. The night's much darker now; her eyes soak up the little light left, seeing the shapes hidden by dusk. Her other half is a shadow at the front of her space. It chatters to her briefly then goes. But it'll return in the morning; tonight Sparky can perch up high, watching for its coming.

HHH

Now I know you're excited about flying, Sparky, but it's bad manners for birds of prey to sit on people's shoulders, even cute little bright sparks like you. You're not a parrot so we'll have no more of that, please, Sparky. Goodnight, see you tomorrow.

OOO

Alone, Sparky walks the length of her new perch, sideways steps then forwards-backwards. It's several steps long. She paces it a few times then settles in the middle, entering the night outside with her ears and eyes. From up here she has a wider view of her territory.

There's waiting to be done now, until her human returns. She flits between watching the activity of night fliers in her territory and practicing her own flight, jumping and flapping herself up to and down from her odd-tree perch, learning to control her newly hatched aerial movement so she'll be able to fly to her human even if it's far away from her.

The next morning Sparky's on her new perch when her mate appears. She bobs her head, leaning forward, calling it with her croaky greeting. It chatters a reply then goes across the space as far from her as it can. There it raises its featherless wing, a piece of fluffy yellow prey between the hide-covered wing toes, and calls her to it.

Ss-p-aaarrr-kkee.

Instead of flying up to it, she has to fly across to it, further than she's flown before. She hesitates, mapping the distance of this horizontal flight, waiting for the moment of it to come to her.

Her human calls again, a meaty morsel wriggling temptingly in its grip.

Now.

Sparky plunges into flight, body straight, face forward, ears and eyes fixed on her target. And she's there, swinging her feet out in front, grabbing her landing on the wing toes, finding the yellow fleshy food, swallowing it.

Her mate turns with her still on its featherless wing, so she's facing her new perch. She finds herself pushed into the air, flaps to hold herself there and fly herself back to her perch. She makes it easily, it's only a few wing-beats, and turns to her other half, ready for more flying to it: with it. So when the featherless wing rises again, fresh prey offered for her, the ss-p-aaarrr-kkee call pulling her, she doesn't hesitate. She's made this flight before so she knows she can do it again. She knows she's a fully fledged flier now. The exhilaration of flight fills her. She flies, pounce-lands and eats, is turned around, sent back into the air, finding her wings, propelling herself to her perch with newborn confidence.

They do this together, her and her human, until her wings are heavy and her hunger gone. Her mate sees she's tired, they're a pair, know what each other needs, so it leaves her to roost. She settles down into herself, satisfied, resting to be ready for when they fly together again.

HHH

Top marks, Sparky, you're picking this up fast, a bright spark right enough, one of the best I've trained. Your owner, when you get one, will have a fantastic little barn owl. I'll make sure you go to someone who deserves you, who'll look after you, give you your best life. I'd keep you myself but that wouldn't be fair; with so many other birds to care for I couldn't give you all the attention you should have. I've always thought it's not possible to have too many birds, 'til now: 'til you. It's a funny old game, I'm in, Sparky. Sometimes I wonder why I do it. For the love of birds, I know, and the chance to pass on my passion. I just want everyone else to love all of you as much as I do. Maybe that's too much…

Now

11th April 2022

HHH

The centre director agrees to me moving Sparky into her own aviary, where no other owls can stress her and where I can man her, the falconry term for handling a raptor prior to beginning its training.

I ask two volunteers to help me set up Sparky's new accommodation.

It's much smaller than the owl room, only about 4ft wide, 6ft deep and 8ft high. There's hardly any flying room in it but once she's flying to me she'll get her exercise outside the aviary so that'll be O.K. Plus, birds of prey, like all predators (humans included), are naturally sedentary, only active when necessary—one thing I already knew. So as long as I fly her regularly the smaller aviary will do. Ideally she'd have one large enough to fly in if she wanted, between sessions with me, but this is the only available space. It's mid-terrace, one of three aviaries, inside the wildlife room, which houses injured kestrels and corvids. Sparky'll have neighbours but they won't be flying around her space although she'll see them in theirs. Set against the whitewashed wall, the aviaries are simple wooden-framed, chicken-wire walled constructions made by the volunteer odd-job man, using materials donated or scavenged: make-do constructions.

I muck the aviary out, put fresh wood chips down, find a water tray for her. I'll have to take one of the two screen perches, as I've learned they're called, from the owl room for her. They're a wooden frame 5ft long, 4ft tall, standing on legs which split into two feet for stability, making them 3ft wide at the bottom. They're like the mobile white boards that got shoved from classroom to classroom in my former teaching life. But instead of a wipe-clean surface set into the frame there's mesh, stretched taut so if a bird tethered to the top of the frame jumps off it can climb back up, using the mesh. Sparky won't be tethered though; she'll be 'free lofted'. I'm learning a new language as well as everything else…

Bate: when a bird tethered to a perch/glove tries to jump off
Cast: to throw a bird off the fist to get it airborne
Creance: the long line birds are tethered to during their initial flight training
Fist: common term for the gloved hand a bird of prey perches on
Jesses: leather ankle straps used to tether a bird
Leash: length of cord used for tethering a bird
Swivel: metal fastener with two rings that turn freely about each other, used to join jesses to leash

… but book learning, words, I'm good with; it's practical skills that challenge me. Training Sparky will be up there with guitar playing and motorbike riding; I do both, still sometimes fudging strings and clunking gears after years of practice.

But I don't stop trying, and I won't now, for Sparky's sake.

The screen perch is too large for the aviary but it's all I've got for her. With difficulty, the two volunteers and I wrestle it out of the owl room, down the corridor, into Sparky's new quarters. It'll only fit in corner-to-corner, leaving me just enough space to stand in. I'll manage, I have to.

Now I just need to get Sparky out of the owl room, down the corridor, into the wildlife room then into her aviary. Just!? I've never carried a bird of prey on my fist without professional supervision; it's been three years since I did it with supervision, at a bird of prey centre. If I cock up she'll be flying around the corridor, panicked, difficult to catch, stressing us both. And if someone opens the outer door she could escape. I've read that's fatal to captive-bred imprint owls because they've never learnt to hunt; although they have the instinct they lack the skills. Even wild owls, raised in that lifestyle, usually only survive it for five years; it's said half die in their first winter. I cannot mess this up.

I get a large net, telling myself I could trap her in it if she does fly off my fist. Chances are I couldn't but I need the safety blanket of that lie. Then I step into the owl room.

Sparky's on the remaining screen perch, the one she's claimed as her own, nearest the door, where she can people-watch. We took the other, from the opposite corner, because she was sat on hers, supervising as we wrangle the cumbersome item, flying overhead as we, cursing, clumsily manoeuvred it through the doorway.

Now she fixes me with dark eyes. She knows something's happening, if only because something else just happened: the removal of her perch's twin. But I believe she knows because she senses it too, the way nature equips all creatures to anticipate changes that might affect them. She flies to my shoulder. Does that mean she trusts me, in this moment of potential danger?

I have my brand new falconry glove on, the leather stiff, the fingers inflexible. Awkwardly I reach up with it, trying to grab her jesses to lift her onto my hand. I can't see what I'm doing, am reluctant to feel around for the jesses with my other, bare, hand, in case she claws or pecks me. After some faffing I'm lucky and, somehow, Sparky's sitting on my glove, the two of us appearing like we know what we're doing. She might. I definitely don't.

I haven't had chance to collect the swivel and leash from the falconer so I can't tie her securely to my glove. I thread her jesses between my fingers, hold the ends with my free hand and hope my grip is strong enough that she can't fly out of it. But I have to let go to open and close the owl room door. The perilous moment passes without incident. We're in the corridor.

I talk to her as we walk to the wildlife room and her newly furnished aviary. More peril as I again have to let go of my hold on her jesses to open that door. But we're through it safely. Now if she does slip away she can't escape into the wide, grey yonder outside to starve or become an RTA statistic. Just a few more steps.

We're in her aviary. It took less than a minute but probably knocked a week off my lift-expectancy. Worth it, though. I slacken my hold on her jesses, point her at the perch, which is only arm's length from me. She hops to it, turns, looks at me, around her new home, back to me.

'There you go, Sparky, this is better, isn't it? No other owls bothering you. A private suite. Hopefully the neighbours won't disturb you.' There's a magpie in the left-hand aviary, two chickens in the right-hand one. But barnless barn owls can't be choosers.

I leave her on the perch, settling in.

OOO

It's been a few days since t-raay-cee came. Last time it brought the face plumage human but today it brings other humans, a pair Sparky hasn't seen in the fliers' space before. She darts to t-raay-cee, landing on a head ledge only to be walked back to her perch. T-raay-cee and the other humans chatter together, facing the perch across the space from hers. Sparky takes off again, flying to them but as she gets close enough to plan landing on a head ledge they join themselves to that perch with their featherless wings and drag it along. Sparky wing-pivots into a turn, circling back to her perch. From there she watches t-raay-cee and the other humans haul the perch across the space and through the in/out.

She waits, muscles tense, wings primed, to learn what this new happening means. Hoo-hoo head tufts is on the crooked branch against the space's far side, eyes closed, but Sparky knows it's also waiting, watching with its ears, for what happens next. The keee-w-ickk that can fly is on top of a nest box high up the side; it didn't have chance to scramble down the hole when the humans came so now it's trapped out in the space, also waiting for what will happen to happen so it can scarper into hiding. Both hoo-hoo and keee-w-ickk wait motionlessly. Sparky's waiting is restless sidesteps and wing-flaps on her perch.

T-raay-cee returns alone. Sparky flies to its head ledge. As soon as she's landed its wing toes peck around her feet. There's a tugging; Sparky feels herself drawn up and forwards so she steps onto the end of t-raay-cee's featherless wing. The familiarity of perching on a human like this settles inside her. Nothing urges her to fly away. This doesn't panic her because she's done it with her before human mates and they protected her, kept her safe. T-raay-cee is behaving like they did so maybe it's going to be her new mate. If it becomes her new mate it too will protect her; she has to give it chance show her if it wants them to bond.

T-raay-cee crosses the fliers' space, stepping into the narrow gap, walking along it, chattering. Head turning, Sparky watches them leaving the fliers' space behind. Facing forwards again she spots slivers of sky high up the sides of the narrow gap and remembers the euphoria of flying free under and up into it with her before mates. Maybe t-raay-cee's going to…

No. T-raay-cee takes her into a new space, dimmer and smaller. Sparky's eyes absorb the dark light, catching a flicker of flapping motion, a white and black flier over here. Her ears search the space, locating the scratching of feet scraping the ground over there. Alert, tuning in to the flashes of movement, the snatches of sound she finds nothing warning her to flap off t-raay-cee's featherless wing.

They pass into an even smaller space and t-raay-cee points Sparky towards a perch, her perch, from the fliers' space; it's here for her. Reassured, she jumps to it, turning to this human who's behaving like her mate, letting her perch on it, flying prey to her and, now, finding them a new space away from the wild fliers.

It's chattering to her; she hears her call in amongst the sound patterns. Then t-raay-cee leaves. But if it's to be her new mate, it'll return, fly with her, they'll become a pair, whole together. T-raay-cee could be a suitable mate.

Sparky explores her new space. It's smaller than most of her before spaces, just a few wing beats to cross it. If she sidesteps from this end of her perch to that she's moved through most of the space. The space's sides and front are made of criss-crossed lines that let her see out but the rear is a solid white surface. There's a long straight branch high up the rear that she flies to; it's wide enough to perch on, just. She lands there, surveying her surroundings.

The white-and-black flier is to that side of her. It's smaller than she knows she is, with a pointed head but an unhooked beak. She watches it flapping around on its side of the criss-crossed lines; it can't get to her, isn't a threat. On the other side there's a pair of fliers like none she's ever seen, with tiny heads on long thin necks and big, rounded bodies. They wing-flap but stay grounded. They can't get to her through the criss-crossed lines but even if they could she'd easily escape them.

Ahead of her, in the territory beyond her new space, there's a large water pool and small human perch with legs, like those she's seen humans resting on before. A tangle of branches is planted in a dark corner, a perching place for fliers. She ear-scans, detects the flittering noise of feet shuffling and scratching. Now her eyes hunt through this branch-tangle for the flier, quickly spotting the stuttering flutter of wings. It's smaller than her but with a pointy head and hooked beak, mottled brown plumage. Flight reflexes open her wings. But it's outside her space. She's safe here, in the space t-raay-cee has chosen for her to roost in; no other fliers can attack her.

Sparky draws her gaze back into her own secure space, notices a gleaming shimmer on the ground beside her perch: a water pool of her own. She drops down to it, gripping the edge with her toes, curling them round, recovering her balance as she bends over the water, letting her beak prick it. With no fliers to attack she can bathe later. Hopping off it, she lifts herself into vertical flight, landing on the perch. Her perch in her own safe space that t-raay-cee found for them; it must want them to be together, mustn't it?

Before

October 2017

OOO

It's day again, soon her human will come to her space, their space, so they can do their flying and hunting together. Sparky waits, ready to go to its featherless wing when it calls her, perching there to eat whatever prey it has trapped in its wing toes for her before flying back to her tall perch so she can return to it again for more food. This is how they fly and hunt together, in the space that's Sparky's when she's alone but theirs when her mate joins her.

But today, when her human comes it brings another human, both of them entering her space. Her mate's never let a strange human invade their space before. It's always protected Sparky, keeping others away.

Sparky stays on her perch, muscles taut, anxious about this stranger in their space, trespassing between them. Will it attack? She studies the stranger for threatening behaviour but it just stands quietly beside her mate.

It's shorter and thinner than her human, with lighter, paler body plumage and longer, fairer head plumage. It chatters to her mate who replies. Her mate then raise its featherless wing.

Ss-p-aaarrr-kkee.

Her human is calling her to fly to it but having a stranger there that might attack them makes Sparky stay on her perch, guarding against potential danger. They can't do their flying and hunting until she's certain they're safe.

Ss-p-aaarrr-kkee.

Her human calls again but she doesn't risk going to it, for both their sakes. It steps away from the stranger, closer to her.

Ss-p-aaarrr-kkee.

She snatches a glance at her mate, noticing the piece of wriggling prey it's brought her, just like it always does. To keep their bond strong she needs them to do what they always do: their flying, hunting and feeding. But the new human might be a danger to them. She flashes her eyes between her mate and the stranger, wings paralyzed by the uncertainty of what happens if she flies, what happens if she doesn't. The piece of offered prey keeps wriggling; the stranger keeps still. Her human keeps calling her, its featherless wing ready for her landing. Slowly Sparky's muscles relax.

She flies over, snatching the food with her beak, gulping it, head raised, ears and eyes on the stranger then darting to her perch, turning instantly to keep watch over her mate and the stranger that's invaded their space. Her mate steps closer to the stranger and they chatter together again then leave.

Sparky goes to the lines at the front, where she can look out at her territory.

Her human is walking away from her with the stranger. She calls to it, her raspy croak more urgent than usual. It stops, comes back to her, crouching down and chattering through the criss-crossed lines to her, before rejoining the stranger.

HHH

Don't worry, Sparky, I'll be back in a jiff, just going to get Michelle a cuppa and grab your anklets and jesses, find a leash for you, do the formalities. You're heading to your new home today. I'm going to miss you but it's time for you to leave the nest, go out into the world and be 'owl'. That's all I want for you; I'd rather let you go to somewhere you'll be loved and cared for than cash in for you to spend your days alone in an aviary. I've covered costs, you've got a good family home and Michelle gets to share her passion for birds with her teenage son. A result all round.

OOO

Her mate soon reappears: alone. Sparky flies to its head ledge but it walks her back to the perch, nudging her to step up to it. As soon as she's on it, before she can turn, she's grabbed. Struggling against the hold, battling to beat wings pinned to her sides, hissing as menacingly as she can, Sparky fights the attack. Twisting her head around, trying to peck her foe, she sees it's her human that's holding her.

A memory in bones and flesh, a felt memory, floats to the surface: her human held her like this before she could fly. But instinct won't let her stop struggling; being pinned down is what happens to prey before the kill. She jabs at the wing toes wrapped around her body but can't reach them.

Then the world falls away from her. She's on her back, lower in her space, looking up at her human's face from underneath, something warm and firm pressed against her wings, the grip on her still tight. Writhing her whole body, feet snatching at empty air, she can't right herself. All she can do it hiss and kick. Her mate touches her feet, pecking at her ankles. It's unfamiliar behaviour; Sparky doesn't know what it means. She hisses again, the sound becoming an insistent screech. Her human chatters back to her as it holds her, touching her legs. Sparky feels something wrapped around each of them.

Suddenly the hold on her bursts. She claws herself upright, flaps to her perch.

When she lands she picks up a foot, side-stepping for balance, but her foot won't move as far up or along as she wants. She tugs at it but each jerk only brings it up so far, not as high as she wants. She studies her feet. There's something dark looped around each ankle. She pecks, feels a skin thicker than she can tear through. She pulls at each dark loop in turn. They stay around her ankles, cuffs of skin that isn't hers. She stretches up to study them from the most distance her body allows. Dark strips of skin hang from these ankle cuffs, coiling around, over, under her talons and the perch. She bends forward, jabbing, snipping and scuffling with her beak, trying to uncoil them, grabbing a hanging strip in her beak. She tugs but the dark skin strip slips free. Now though, when she lifts her foot she can move it as high and far along as she wants.

Her mate's outside her space, peering in at her, chattering, her ss-p-aaarrr-kkee call and other sounds. She flies to the front lines again, watching as it leaves, hopping along to keep it in view. But the skin strips dangling from her ankles tangle around her toes and she has to stop hopping to peck and shake her feet free. Her human is out of sight when she next looks for it.

HHH

Sorry, Sparky, but, you'll soon get used to wearing jesses. At least now you're kitted out for the rest of your training: flying outside where you can stretch your wings, enjoy life.

Don't worry, Michelle's had birds of prey before so you'll be safe with her, Sparky. We've had a good long chat about you and she knows to ring me if she needs any help. Her son is dying to meet you; you'll be his Hedwig. We need kids like him to love birds of prey if you're to have a future, wild or captive, so you'll not only be a friend to a young lad who needs one but, hopefully, you'll set him off on a lifelong obsession with raptors that'll be good for all your kind.

OOO

Her human and the stranger return, the stranger staying near the in/out. It carries an oblong object, a box, that it sets on the ground. Sparky scrutinises the stranger, keen senses searching for innately recognised signs that this new human is readying to attack. Her mate won't let it attack, though, coming to stand between Sparky and the stranger. Sparky switches her focus to her mate, waiting for them to do their flying and hunting together. As long as her human other half is with her, she should be safe: they're safe together.

Her mate raises its featherless wing, offering her food.

Ss-p-aaarrr-kkee.

She flies over, feet gripping the wing toes, talons piecing the chick head it's brought her. Head swallowed, she turns to launch back to her perch so she can fly to her human again. But when she leaps up she's jolted down. She jumps, wings flapping, straining to get airborne but every spring only gets her a brief moment of static flight before she's jerked back to the wing perch. She looks; the skin strips dangling from her ankles are twisted between her human's wing toes, holding her down.

Sparky tries again to get away. Her human won't let her go, it's joined her to it, a new bond between them but a not pairing: a tethering. Panic swells inside her as a rapid heartbeat, a burning in her chest, a quivering in her muscles: the reflex to fly, to flee. This human that's protected her, been her lifelong partner, is now endangering her, stopping her from being free to fly: to escape. She lunges, leaps, flaps, stays tethered down: captured.

Her human crouches, Sparky still fighting to fly off its featherless wing even as it leans towards the box the stranger brought and pushes her inside, shaking her off its wing toes.

She croaks a hiss, turning quickly to face forwards as she's trapped in the box by a criss-crossed in/out that close behind her. Her mate is outside, peering in at her, chattering softly, its face hole stretched into an upward curving line. It head-bobs, finishing its chattering with her ss-p-aaarrr-kkee call, then stands so all she can see are its grey legs.

HHH

It's alright, don't worry. I know it doesn't seem like it, but this is a good thing; you're going to your new home, Sparky. Your life's starting today. And it's going to be a wonderful life, I'm sure. It'll be new and scary at first but you'll settle in quickly and you'll love it, especially once you get flying outside properly, Sparky.

OOO

The box jerks up into a stilted kind of flight, swinging awkwardly low through the air. Sparky slips towards the rear, feet sliding out from under her, banging her against a hard surface. Scrambling for a foot hold, she struggles upright only to slither sidewise as the furry covering beneath her toes rucks up, sliding with her. The box's jolting flight levels out, letting her stand, steadier this time. Twisting her head around, she plucks at a feather, bent by her crash against the box's rear. Then she hears her call, further away than usual but still resounding in her sharp ears, and faces forwards again.

Through the criss-crossed in/out she see the box is moving through her territory, heading towards and passing by the features she mentally mapped from inside her space. Her human walks ahead, chattering to the stranger who's reply comes from closer to Sparky, above her. It's carrying the box, like it did when it entered her space. Only now she's inside the box. It's carrying her.

The pattering, panting panic swells in her again, urging her to fly away. The flustering heat of near danger, of harm and death, floods her chest. She flaps, feeling primary feathers bending against the box's sides. There's no way she can save herself. But her human has always protected her. She calls to it, a croaky cry. Still walking ahead, it turns and stoops to look at her, chattering softly, its face hole making an upturned line again. Then it looks away.

She traces its gaze; they're getting close to an oddly shaped structure, boxy and standing on round feet. It's lower sides are black and shiny but the upper sides are mostly made of colourless reflections, like those on water. They get closer to it until it's so close, this odd structure, that it fills her eyes. The box jolts to a clumsy landing beside the odd structure's round feet.

Her human grabs at the structure's side, pulling the side away from the structure like an outstretched wing, making an in/out. Sparky's lifted towards this in/out, her human's chattering soft and warm before it disappears from her hearing as she's past through the in/out, the structure swallowing her.

HHH

There, there, Sparky, don't panic. You'll be safe with Michelle. I know this is a big change for you, lots of new experiences: adventures. You won't be in the car too long so try to keep calm. Have a fantastic life, Sparky. Good bye, take care of yourself and your new family.

OOO

The box has settled on a flat surface inside the odd structure's space. Sparky stares and listens, eyes and ears collecting details of the structure's dark interior which is illuminated by light pouring in from the shiny surfaces high up the sides. Sparky pads round inside the box, trying to see more of her surroundings through tiny gaps in the box's sides. Dark shapes loom around the box. The only sounds come from outside the structure. Then the new human appears, blocking Sparky's view by leaning over the box. There's a klunk-klikk sound. The stranger retreats. A loud sharp bang reverberates around the structure's space and inside Sparky's head then fades to silence.

This is all new, different: threatening. She calls to her other half but there's no ss-p-aaarrr-kkee call in reply, no reassuring chatter. She wing-flaps again but has to fold them away because of the box's too-close sides. She lowers her head, shaking it, pecking at the furry thick ground inside the box. Then she pecks at the hard smooth sides, hissing at the realisation there's no escape. A human trapped her; only a human can free her. Her human, her mate, it's always kept her safe, taken care of her; it'll free her. It'll let her out so they can be together because they're a pair, a whole, their bond is their life. Craning up to her full height, neck-stretching and head-tilting, Sparky searches for her mate, spotting it in among distorted glimpses of her territory that she finds high up the odd structure's sides where light comes in through the shiny surfaces, letting her see out through them. Her other half raises a featherless wing, flapping at her. Sparky calls to it again but another juddering bang smothers her raspy cawing.

The juddering bang vibrates the space; Sparky recoils, losing sight of her mate. The stranger has entered the structure, in front of her. It twists around, looking at her, chattering. In amongst its chatter, she hears her ss-p-aaarrr-kkee call, sounding softer, brighter than how her mate makes it. But definitely this stranger called to her with her own call.

Sparky shuffles to the rear of the box, huddling into the fragile shelter of the dimness there. The stranger stays facing her for a moment, as if expecting something from her. Then it turns away.

The loudest noise she's ever heard rips through the air, a thunder of sound. It trembles through Sparky's whole body, setting off a frenzied pattering in her chest and an urgent quivering in her legs and wings. She leaps and flaps, leaps and flaps. The noise settles to a deep, rumbling, roaring growling so powerful it moves the odd structure, like a howling wind moves trees. Sparky feels the movement outside her body, outside the box she's in. Head-tilting, neck stretched towards the structure's shiny see-through surfaces, she snatches at views of the outside world racing past; tall trees, rolling hills, cloud smears and many structures of different sizes, shapes and colours. She's still; the world is moving. The growling structure she's inside is moving the world around her: it's a moving growler, a growling mover.

The world passes by her for a long time. She stays huddled at the rear of the box, feet sometimes slipping away from her, fighting herself upright again. When the world stops moving her human will be there to take care of her. It's always been there, with her, will be waiting for her when the moving and growling stops.

Now

11th April 2022 (cont.)

HHH

After settling Sparky in her new aviary I go about my volunteering duties, finishing with the carnivore feed. I make my rounds with the bucket of chicks, sticking to my routine because I don't want to miss any of the animals depending on me. But I'm glad Sparky's room is second on my mental 'to feed' list.

She's at the end of her perch, head facing the door as I enter the wildlife room, eyes staying on me as I go into her aviary. The falconer advised giving her as much food as she'll eat for a few weeks, to put her at her fat weight. Then I can start training her and, by seeing what she doesn't do at that weight, get an idea of how much she'll need to lose to do anything for me: with me.

He also advised 'deyolking' her meals. The day-old chicks, Sparky's staple diet, are a waste product from the egg industry, cockerel hatchlings with no value, gassed and sold for pennies as reptile and raptor feed. All newly hatched chicks have absorbed the egg's yolk into their bodies, it's their first meal. Because the chicks Sparky's fed were killed before they digested that yolk it's still in their bellies. But it's not good, not natural, for raptors to eat more than the occasional yolk so I should remove them, he said. I didn't dare ask him how the hell I do that.

Luckily there's a YouTube video of a woman pinching a chick's bottom between fingers and thumbs, pulling its belly apart like a crisp packet. The yolk pops out whole, the gooey yellow liquid contained in a hygienic membrane. She draws it out, detaching the yolk-filled balloon from the chick's intestines, and she's ready to feed that chick to her barn owl. When I try the membrane pops; I have egg all over me. Telling myself it's just yolk doesn't help; the floppy lifeless chick in my gungy fingers is not a cracked egg: it's a dead animal. This is not for the squeamish. But it's what Sparky needs me to do so, pragmatic but grimacing, I'll do it.

I place three deyolked chicks on the perch near her. She jumps on one straight away, flying with it to the far end as I slip out. I watch her pull the head off, swallow it and unpick the innards, the intestines slurped down like spaghetti. I won't know if she'll eat the other two and I can only leave instructions that she's fed three a day and cross fingers other volunteers do that 'til I'm back in next week. For now I've done what was urgent: got her into her own safe space.

On the drive home I picture Sparky in her new aviary, away from the wild owls that might have mobbed, even injured, her. I volunteered at the centre to do what little I could to help the animals there. Today I helped Sparky. I can do more for her but she's one of hundreds, thousands, of animals in need. I zoom up my mental picture of Sparky in her new aviary, superimposing it over countless real and imagined images of captive animals in their manmade suffering.

OOO

T-raay-cee is back, coming into their new space, bringing her food, like her before mates used to. But instead of calling her to its featherless wing for her to take the offered meal, it leaves several chicks on her perch, demonstrating its ability to find and catch prey for her: more bonding behaviour. It steps out then, making her feel safe enough to hop along the perch and snatch a chick. It's a behaviour Sparky remembers, from humans that became her mate before. None of those humans has stayed with her, though; they're all gone now. She learnt to trust them, paired with them, but they left her anyway, leaving her only half of herself. Maybe t-raay-cee will be her lifelong mate but she'll only know that when they've had a lifetime together. For now, all she knows is that it's acting like it wants to be her partner, finding this safe roosting space and bringing her food. She hops to where it left the chicks for her, taking another and eating. If it keeps behaving like this she'll start trusting it, as she did her before humans.

Before

October 2017 (cont.)

OOO

The growling movement stops. The strange human climbs out of its place in front of Sparky. Through the tiny gaps in the box's sides, she sees it leaning over her, over the box, before she feels the box rising up and bobbing through the air with a swinging motion. Sparky shuffles to the front, her steps clumsied by the swinging. But she makes it those few steps forwards and, tilting her head, sees the wide open sky above, darkening from pale to deeper blue.

The sky is the same. But, looking around now, she sees nothing else is. She's been brought to a new territory, much smaller than her old territory; a little grassy patch bounded by stunted bushes and spindly trees, surrounded by high wooden sides. In the middle of the grassy patch is a tall perch. Her wings itch to fly to it and she flaps wildly for a few beats, stopping as she feels flight feathers brushing against the box's sides.

They head towards the furthest corner of the territory where a small structure, tree-bark brown, stands alone. As they get close to it, Sparky sees the front is made of criss-crossed lines. Looking through them she spots things similar, but not the same, as were in her space before; a tall perch and a shallow water pool. There's also a shorter perching place that's a tangle of branches. It's like her before space that she shared with her mate. But it's not. It's a new space and her mate isn't here. She's alone.

The box is taken into this new space, lowered, the in/out opened. Sparky backs away from the opening.

Ss-p-aaarrr-kkee.

The stranger is making her call but differently to how her mate sounded it: an imitation.

Ss-p-aaarrr-kkee.

The stranger crouches, holding out a featherless wing, offering her a mouse. Sparky stays huddled against the rear of the box, its hardness reassuring against her back; nothing can attack her from behind. She only has to watch for danger coming from ahead, from the stranger.

For a while neither of them moves. The stranger gives her ss-p-aaarrr-kkee call a few more times, buried amongst other chatterings, and pokes the mouse towards her but Sparky doesn't go out to it, or even call back to it.

HHH

Here you go, Sparky, welcome to your new home. I've done my best with your aviary, hope you like it. Oh, god, you look terrified. Please don't be scared. You're safe here. Look, Sparky, I've got you a mouse for tea. Aren't you coming out? No, O.K., I'll just leave it there, let you explore. Please come out and eat, Sparky, you need to eat. I'll be back to check on you later, Sparky.

OOO

The stranger stands; Sparky tracks its footsteps as they crunch away across rocky ground. Then she waits, listening and watching, until enough time has passed without sound or sight of anything threatening, that she's able to risk reaching for that prey.

She creeps forwards, her walking awkward now because she keeps tangling her feet up with the skin strips wrapped around her ankles. But she makes it, grabs the mouse, scanning the space for somewhere to take it: the tall perch. Leaping and wing-beating she dives to it, lands and, catch hidden under outspread wings, eats quickly, urgently getting food into her while she can.

Meal devoured, she inspects this new space. There's nothing here that she recognises as danger. She has this new space to herself. As well as the tall perch and the branches perch a ledge runs around the sides and rear. She flies to it. Her head feathers ruffle against the solid top surface but there's enough room for her to perch on the ledge. She side-steps along it so far, then back the other way, finding a crevice here, a gap there; places she could stash food in case prey is scarce in this new territory.

The whole space is small but big enough to fly a few wing-beats across so she does: over, back, here, there, up, down, tracing a web of routes around it; perching now on the tall perch, now on the ledge, hopping onto the branches perch, walking to the shallow pool, looking through the clear water to the pool's solid bottom. Sparky touches her beak to the surface, pricking the trembling reflection, making it ripple apart. She can bathe in it but only when she's explored this new space thoroughly, mapping it and the territory beyond, ensuring she's safe.

She goes now to the front, looking out between the criss-crossed lines, at the patch of grass and the perch that she'd fly to if she could. She flies now, leaping into vertical flight that powers her towards the top of the criss-crossed lines. Twisting her wings, she flaps herself onto them, grabbing with her feet as she bangs into them, feeling the lines' sharpness pressing against her breast and cutting across her toes as she clutches her upright landing place, feet stretched in front, wings half opened for balance. She stares out: a perch under the sky. She never flew under the sky in her before territory. Maybe here she'll fly outside in this, her new territory, if she stays here, in this new space that will also become hers if she stays, the space the strange new human brought her to. It brought her food too. If it keeps bringing her meals, flies with her, takes care of her it will also be hers; a new human partner to share life with. She'll have to wait for it to do those things though, before she'll know if it is her new mate.

Her wings and feet tire holding her on this vertical perch so Sparky hops down and into the water pool; it's big enough for her to splash around in, shallow enough for her to climb out of. Bathed, she shakes wet feathers, flies soggily to the ledge, hunches her head down onto her shoulders and sleeps.

A chattering fills her ears. Opening her eyes a sliver, Sparky sees the stranger standing outside her space, staring in at her. She lowers her resting leg, standing on both feet in case it enters her space and she needs to take off; she doesn't trust it yet. But it stays on its side, chattering, the darkness of night closing around it. Then it leaves.

HHH

Sorry to wake you, Sparky, but I just wanted to make sure you're O.K. Have you eaten that mouse? And is the aviary O.K. for you? I guess if you're sleeping I must've done a decent job. Now get yourself a good night's rest ready for tomorrow. Daniel's dying to meet you; it's a big day for both of you. He's so looking forward to it. Once he's back from his dad's after school we can see about flying you. You'll just have to be patient with me, it's been a while, too long, since I had birds in my life and you're not a harris hawk so fingers and feathers crossed, eh, Sparky? Hopefully between us we'll work it out. Yes, we will. It'll all be fine, something Daniel and I can enjoy doing together and a lovely life for you. O.K., I'll see you in the morning. Night-night.

Now

16th May 2022

OOO

Sparky's spent many days and night in the new safe space that t-raay-cee brought her to. Even though there isn't as much flying room she's more comfortable in it, life's easier. Humans come, putting chicks on the end of the perch or flying them towards her; she eats when she wants without keee-w-ickk fliers or ss-kk-reee to mob her. She hasn't felt hunger since t-raay-cee brought her into this space that's now hers. She's been able to bathe too, with no fliers to attack while her wings wetly ground her.

Sometimes t-raay-cee comes to her, holding out its featherless wing, calling her to fly to it, offering her prey. But this human doesn't come often enough for them to bond so Sparky doesn't always fly to it. She doesn't know if it's trying, wanting, to bond with her. It needs to show her, behaving like her mate, sharing life with her. She waits for t-raay-cee to show her.

Each morning she stands on her perch, ears tuned to the sounds drifting along the narrow gap outside her space and its territory, her eyes focused on the in/out, watching to see if the human she hears coming is t-raay-cee. It's the human since she came here to behave most like it could be her other half so she waits, the hollowness of a life alone, unshared, growing inside her, an ache throbbing slowly towards pain.

HHH

Today's the first day of Sparky's training. I've had to wait, Sparky's had to wait, until now, getting everything as ready as possible.

In the past month I've been back to the falconer, collecting a leash and swivel for her plus two more books on falconry then buying, second hand, the only book on keeping and training owls that's available. Reading it I discover why, amongst countless falconry titles, there's only one slim volume about owl husbandry, most of which is devoted to breeding with a solitary chapter on training: owls aren't falconry birds. People breed them to sell to raptor collections in zoos, for conservation or education purposes; some go to private individuals doing owl experience events, photo/video shoots or flying displays. Consequently there's no market for books about owl training because the typical owl keeper is already an expert raptor handler, not a novice. Not me.

Worse, owls, especially small ones like barn owls, aren't beginners' birds; they're too easily killed when dieting them to their flying weight. I'm doing this wrong before I've even started! But this past month of waiting Sparky's been in limbo. I can't leave her there any longer. She's had too much uncertainty in the short time she's been here and who knows how much during her life before? She needs routine, stability. I'm good at routine so that would be easy if it was just me and her. But it's not.

The volunteering MO at the centre makes getting Sparky consistency impossible. There are so many volunteers, coming in ad-hoc, with a rapid turnover of faces. A few have a lifetime of hands-on animal care, a horse rider, a cat lover, a dog breeder, former farmhands and current smallholders; others are willing but inexperienced; some have special needs and are there more for their own good than to help the animals. Communication between volunteers or with the centre director isn't that effective. There are only two other staff members so volunteers work with minimal supervision. Consequently, people establish their own, sometimes odd, ways of doing things. Besides the director, I'm the only one with raptor experience. Just making everyone call her Sparky was a fight; 'Isn't she called Hoot?' 'I was told her name's Barny.' 'Sparky doesn't suit her.' I had to make a sign for her door because I need her to recognise the name I'll call her with, the name I've been told is hers.

And, despite the instructions I left about what and when to feed her, other volunteers have done whatever they pleased. One week I came in specifically to try getting Sparky to feed from my gloved hand to find she'd already been fed by someone who decided the carnivores should get breakfast, not dinner. So a wasted opportunity for me and more confusion for Sparky.

I've now arranged to come in Monday to Friday, making sure she has a proper routine that I control. I'll do my usual volunteering duties on Mondays, allowing for time with Sparky, then pop in for an hour each day the rest of the week, to feed and fly her. There's a reliable young volunteer in on weekends; I trust her to feed Sparky correctly on Saturdays and starve her on Sundays so she'll be keen for me on Mondays. Wednesdays are the carnivores' usual starve day, a practice meant to mimic a predator's wild eating habits because they wouldn't hunt successfully every day. But by Sparky having her starve day on Sunday I'll be able to manage her weight and training better Monday-Friday. Thank goodness for that reliable young volunteer; she cares about animals, hopes to work with them, will do her best for Sparky.

I've also made two more signs, using my limited DTP skills and a borrowed laminator, to pin on the outside of the corridor doors, warning people when there's a 'barn owl flying session' in progress so they don't come blundering in, frightening Sparky, giving her an escape route.

Now, with all this sorted I arrive today eagerly nervous to take the first real steps with Sparky only to find there's nothing to feed her, or any of the carnivores; the delivery of day-old chicks hasn't arrived, wasn't ordered in time. It might turn up later. If it doesn't come before I need to leave I won't be able to do anything with her. I'm frustrated, annoyed, consider ringing the falconer to see if he has any chicks spare so I can do as planned. But I don't want to ask for more help than he's already willingly given me. It's not his problem the centre's supply ordering is disorganised and he didn't need to help me at all so I'm reluctant to push my luck;

one day we, Sparky and I, might really need a favour. I can still weigh her, see what she's like with me. Maybe the chicks will turn up. I'm also going to try changing her jesses. One's snapped, the leather grown old and brittle. A set came with my basic falconry kit which will do for now. If I can get them on her.

I finish the morning feeding and watering jobs then go in with Sparky. She's on the perch, facing the door as I enter. Was she watching for me? I want to think so but we haven't built up any kind of bond. Yet. Carrying the little digital scale complete with perch, also part of my starter kit, I go in.

OOO

Today t-raay-cee appears, carrying a short perch, a set of its wing toes covered by thick dark skin; this means it wants her to perch on its featherless wing. It calls to her.

Ss-p-aaarrr-kkee.

She's hungry, no human brought her food yesterday and now here's the human that might be her new mate, calling her to fly to it. Eagerness swells in Sparky. That's enough for her; she goes to t-raay-cee, landing on the short perch which is easier than dropping onto its head ledge.

T-raay-cee stands the short perch on her perch, Sparky balancing on it, its wobbliness beneath her feet faintly familiar. She looks up at t-raay-cee, it's face hole is the upward curving line, making the rest of the face warm and bright. Then t-raay-cee tugs gently on the skin strips dangling from her ankles. This is familiar too. She's done this before, knows what's next. Sparky steps off the perch, onto t-raay-cee. They'll fly together now.

But they don't. They stay in the space, there's more tugging then harder jerking so Sparky's repeatedly unbalance. She wants the jerking to stop so she jumps, wing-flapping, into the air, finds herself yanked down again. She can't fly away but the panic rising in her, a wave of energy that urges her to escape, won't let her stop trying. She keeps leaping and flapping as a growing heaviness from her ankles sends a quaking feeling into her body, tightening muscles, stretching nerves.

All through this t-raay-cee chatters, sometimes soft and low, with Sparky's call nestling in the chatter. Other times the chatter is still low but harsher, with no ss-p-aaarrr-kkee call. Its wing toes peck persistently around Sparky's ankles and it won't let her go. Then suddenly it offers her up to her perch. She hops across. T-raay-cee leaves. They didn't fly together. Sparky doesn't understand this behaviour.

T-raay-cee soon reappears, stepping her back onto its featherless wing.

Held there again Sparky tenses, readying to jump, wing-beat, fight herself free of the tugging around her legs which heavies her ankles. She leaps, hop, flaps: fights. Manages to pull herself from t-raay-cee, heading for her perch but her furious wing-beats only keep her in a stationary horizontal flight; the perch stays a flap away. Her chest trembles, a throbbing spreads through her. She closes her wings: falls.

Her space is topsy-turvy, the ground above her. She swings in this upside down space briefly, chest heaving. Then, toes scrabbling, feet running in mid-air, her talons grip something solid. Tightening her hold, Sparky pulls herself up, climbing back into her right-way-up space, standing again on the end of t-raay-cee's wing.

There's more tugging on the skin strips around her ankles that Sparky fights against. She stops when t-raay-cee takes a shiny pointed stick from amongst its body plumage, opening and closing it like a beak. It's held to Sparky's skin strips, there's a feeling of release then more tugging. Sparky tries again to escape into the air but all her flapping only lifts her into a hover. She fights to fly until she has to stop, is again hanging upside down.

After another scramble up to perch on t-raay-cee's wing and a final tugging her next wing-beats do get her airborne. She swoops up to the ledge high at the rear of her space, head-turns so she can stare over her folded wings, down at t-raay-cee who's chattering softy as it leaves her again.

They didn't fly together. It didn't even offer her food. It did call her to it. But it held on to her, captured her. Its behaviour is a tangle of bonding and threatening. Sparky is bewildered by this human; it doesn't know what it wants with her and neither does she.

HHH

As I leave that afternoon I'm worried, upset, that I've damaged what little bond I had with Sparky. I've had to stress her out and couldn't even reassure her with food. I realise I should've left changing the jesses for another day, when there was food, to make it a more positive experience for her. I hope she's a forgiving bird, or, at least, a forgetful one. A terrible start to Sparky's training after I'd prepared so hard. The best laid plans of novice owlers…

That night I start a training log for my sessions with Sparky because it's the only useful thing I can think to do after the day's disaster. I'm a writer; words are my fallback. By recording what I do, what she does, I'll hopefully learn to understand her and make myself understandable to her.

16/5/22
No chicks so couldn't fly her/call her to fist. She was keen to come to me though (starved 15/5?). Landed on scale perch and managed to get weight: 12.6oz. Also managed to change jesses but had a struggle and had to get scissors to cut one off. Result was stress to Sparky—she kept bating off fist (don't blame her) but showed she can right herself when hanging upside down. After weigh and jesse change she was sat on beam at back of aviary so think she was spooked. Hopefully she will calm down over night and still come to me tomorrow…

Before

October 2017 (cont.)

OOO

Sparky opens her eyes, remembering she's in the new space the strange human brought her to. She spent the night roosting on the ledge high up at the rear where she knew danger couldn't creep up on her while she slept. She stretches out her wings, flaps the few wing-beats needed to take her to the tall perch, side-stepping along it end to end. This new space is enough like her before space for her to accept it. Now she has to wait to learn if the strange new human is enough like her before mate for her to accept it too.

While she waits she studies the territory beyond her space, focusing on the perch that's planted in the grassy patch, somewhere for her to fly to and from like she did with her mate except they only flew inside her space; does that outside perch means outside flights, in the sky? A small brown flier with red breast plumage lands on the perch. She rasps her hissing caw. It glances at her then flits away.

She flies to the criss-crossed lines, hanging on them, head rotating, eyes and ears absorbing her new territory, mapping it. Furthest away from her is a large square structure with a pointed top. Set into it is a white in/out and several squares shimmering with reflections of the pale grey sky.

As she's mapping this structure the strange human steps through the in/out. Beside it is another human, shorter and, her long range sight tells her, younger: a juvenile. They're coming out of the structure so must have spent the night inside it; it's their space, where they eat and roost. Now they're coming towards her space, the juvenile bounding forward, loud, shrill calls streaming from it as it rapidly covers the ground between it and Sparky. She retreats to the ledge, as far from it as her space lets her be.

When the juvenile reaches Sparky's space it stops abruptly, pressing against the criss-crossed lines, its unbeak poking between them, its wing toes clutching at them. It chatters incessantly, a deluge of sounds, filling Sparky's ears until her skull thrums with noise and she has to stop listening.

Tilting her head, she scrutinises this juvenile's face: creamy coloured skin; pale blue eyes; unbeak rounded, not hooked like her real beak, but speckled like her breast; curled brown head plumage. The whole of it looks freshly fledged.

Suddenly it calls to her like they're mates.

Ss-p-aaarrr-kkee.

It wants her to go to it but she doesn't.

Ss-p-aaarrr-kkee.

It's not her mate. Her mate left her, broke their bond; she does need to find

another to share her life with though. Maybe this juvenile human... Curious, knowing it can't hurt her because it's outside, Sparky swoops to the lines and, feet raised, grabs hold of her vertical landing. The juvenile springs backward as she lands where its face was, but it keeps chattering.

HHH

Oh, wow, Sparky, you are so cool! Awesome. Amazing. You flew to me as soon as I called you. We're going to be best friends forever, Sparky. Even better friends than Harry and Hedwig. Promise.

OOO

D-aaannn-y-elll. D-aaannn-y-elll. D-aaannn-y-elll.

The stranger runs now towards them, calling that sound so clearly Sparky's sharp ears learn the pattern of it instantly.

When the stranger reaches the juvenile it drags the juvenile away from the front of her space with its featherless wings, like it's protecting the juvenile from danger: parent and chick. They screech at each other. The screeching settles to chattering. Sparky hears the d-aann-y-elll call a few more times, sees juvenile bobbing its head, then lowering it but not head-shaking like she does when something unsettles her. Humans use their bodies differently to her because they are different but she's learning to understand the language of their bodies and behaviour.

The humans stop chattering and enter Sparky's space. She flies to the tall perch, where she can watch for danger from them. In the last day and night she's survived several new happenings, lost the familiarity which made her comfortable. Her body shakes now, nerves pulsing, wings throbbing, flight shuddering through her feathers, ready to flap her away if she needs to escape.

But they don't threaten; they offer food. The parent human does it first, raising its featherless wing, a piece of prey trapped at the end, calling Sparky to come catch the food.

Ss-p-aaarrr-kkee.

She's hungry. But she'll have to go to a human she isn't bonded with, can't trust yet. It could hurt her.

Ss-p-aaarrr-kkee.

The chick leg wriggles around in the stranger's grip. She waits, watching, thinking: deciding.

Ss-p-aaarrr-kkee.

The only way to know if she's safe flying to these new humans is to do it. They've brought her food; if she wants them to be her mates she should respond by going to them for it. She balances the risk against the reward for a moment then flaps over, diving in, talons clutching the prey. Standing on this foot, bringing that foot to her beak, pecking blindly, she gets the chick leg into her mouth, swallows and looks at the parent human, across to the juvenile, back to the parent. It points Sparky at the tall perch, like her before mate used to in her before space. So she does as she did before; returning to the tall perch, facing the humans when she's landed, watching for them to offer more prey. It's the familiar flying, hunting and feeding, similar but different.

The parent human calls her, feeding her a few more times, the feeling of safety growing inside Sparky each time she flies to and from it unharmed, her hesitation shrivelling to nothing. Then the juvenile steps forward, parent human chattering to it, the d-aann-y-elll call among the rapidly flowing sounds. Juvenile head-bobs, raises its featherless wing, a wriggling prey piece trapped in the toes.

Ss-p-aaarrr-kkee. Ss-p-aaarrr-kkee. Ss-p-aaarrr-kkee.

She's drawn to it by her call, it's food offering and by what she's learnt of herself, humans and life since she hatched. Its wing dips as she lands, wobbling her but she find the morsel, eats, lifts her head and looks into its pale blue eyes. Juvenile looks back, into hers. Neither of them blinks.

The parent calls to them both. D-aaannn-y-elll. Ss-p-aaarrr-kkee.

Sparky knows her call. Juvenile knows its. Now they know each others'. Their bonding begins.

Now

May 2022 (cont.)

OOO

After enduring so much unpredictable change there's the beginnings of stability for Sparky. T-raay-cee comes most days, into her space, offering food, calling her to it. Sparky still sometimes feels the tremoring urge to fly away from it though. Mostly that's when there are sharp noises outside her space, startling her. Or if strange humans come, not doing what t-raay-cee does. These disturbances unsettle her, the randomness of strangers and noises making Sparky wary of going to t-raay-cee's featherless wing, even when there's wriggling prey for her to catch and her call urging her. She hasn't been with this human long enough to trust it, to bond with it, yet.

When nothing disturbing happens Sparky hops up to t-raay-cee readily, taking the offered meal, returning to her perch to eat, going again to stand on t-raay-cee's wing toes, her talons gripping the thick hide covering them. Often she feels safe enough that they can do several short hop-flights together, like she has with her before mates, and reassuring contentment glows faintly in her, gradually brightening.

But just when she's relaxing with t-raay-cee, feeling a lightness in her muscles and a steady beating in her chest, something startling often happens, another harsh noise sounding or a threatening human appearing. The contented glow dims again; anxious, Sparky flees to the ledge high up in her space where she's out of reach, can face any coming danger.

If t-raay-cee arrives when she's been panicked up to the ledge, Sparky can't fly to it, her wings won't let her, no matter how many times it calls her or what food it's brought her, no matter how much she needs to find her human other half and pair with it. But t-raay-cee keeps trying, reaching up for her, tugging the skin strips to make her step to it. If she can, Sparky flies before it gets to her, darting about her space, bouncing against the sides, gripping onto the criss-crossed lines for a moment's breath, wings held out, fluttering with traces of flight, before springing back into the air. It's a chase. It always ends with t-raay-cee catching her but each time it does, it feeds her and doesn't harm her. It wants to bond with her even more than Sparky wants to bond with it. As much as she needs a human mate, she still must overcome her uncertainly about this human, beat down her inherent fears and trust her own knowing of life shared with humans.

Is this the beginning of their life together, them learning to be a pair? Sparky waits, flitting between agitated and calmed, for their bond to brighten, strengthen, as it has with humans before, into them flying free under the sky, with nothing but their bond tethering them together.

HHH

I muddle through the first few training sessions with Sparky in the confines of her 'it'll have to do' aviary.

17/5
Was a bit spooked by other volunteer feeding crows so had to lift her onto scale with some bating. Weight registered (12.75oz) but she flew off scale then wouldn't come for food. Left alone for a few minutes. Wouldn't come to glove for chick leg but did come to perch for it. Then fed wing to beak. Did come to glove for chick body but wanted to fly off straight away. Need to get her to come back and forth to glove for small bits of food.

18/5
Nervous and wouldn't come to scale so had to get her and put her on, after a bit of chasing her around aviary. She bated off glove but got her weighed and put her on perch then she came for chick leg and wing as treat. Got her to fly to glove for leg and head. Then got her to fly to glove for chick body and let her take it to perch to eat as reward.

19/5
Had to lift her by jesses to scale. She flew to beam at back of aviary after weigh-in so gave her chick wing to beak while she was there. She then came from perch to glove for wing, 2 legs and head but she didn't want to stay on glove and returned to perch to eat. Then returned to beam. It took a while for her to then come to glove for chick body but she did eventually.

20/5
Bit of a cock up—screw missing from scale made perch loose and scale tipped over when I was trying to get her on it so had to repeat process. Not ideal. Gave her leg as reward. Came quite readily for food five times but was initially trying to grab food from ungloved hand. So had to hold food on glove with left thumb and keep hold once she landed to stop her taking off with it. Once jesses secured she flapped to get away each time and won on 2 or 3 occasions. But I did manage to hold her on fist for a few minutes and put food to her beak. She is reluctant to eat on fist… I think she doesn't like being held on glove.

23/5
Was keen (11.9oz, down from 12.2 on Fri) this morning after starve day on Sunday. Got her on scale easily enough with jesses then gave her wing while on scale as reward. Then flew to me six times for food. She got more reluctant as session went on. Flew twice to my shoulder to try to get food while not sitting on glove but I didn't let her have it. Made her go back to perch and come to glove. Twice she came to glove sleeve rather than fist for same reason—trying to get food and get away from fist to eat it.

24/5
She came readily three times but still wanted to fly off so held her on glove. Once she flew to shoulder and twice to glove sleeve so lifted her onto fist and gave her 4 more bits of food over two fist visits so encourage her to swallow on glove and see glove as somewhere she can eat safely. Think she will fly readily between 12–12.2oz once she trusts me.

I don't really know what I'm doing, am making it up, and messing it up, as I go along. Worse, I think Sparky doesn't know what I'm doing either. If only I knew what she's used to. What I do know is that she's smart, trying to get food off me without playing my game.

OOO

Each day Sparky waits for t-raay-cee coming. It isn't like her before humans, all of which left traces in her, bodily memories like painless scars. They were part of her; being with them made her whole. They're gone but Sparky feels them still, faintly, in her muscles and nerves, bones and blood. T-raay-cee isn't like a-ll-eee who let her fly around their large shared territory; nor matt-ee who sent her flying far and high; not even like d-aann-y-elll but maybe a bit like d-aann-y-elll before it grew, stopped being her mate. Sparky senses a twitching in t-raay-cee, like prey alert to a hunter nearby. But, with enough days spent together, they can settle into bonding. If they have many days together they could become each other's missing half, paired up at last, lifelong.

So she waits for t-raay-cee each day.

Before

October 2017 (cont.)

OOO

Days and nights pass. Sparky settles into her new space, her new life with her new mate, d-aann-y-elll, and its parent, m-uuu-m; they're bonded now, living life together. M-uuu-m and d-aann-y-elll come into her space every day, she flies to them, catching the food offerings they bring. In the beginning she mostly flew to m-uuu-m but now she mostly flies to d-aann-y-elll, its her real mate, m-uuu-m is just there too. Sparky's world now is all she needs; a roosting space, a bathing pool, prey, the safety of everyday routine and humans to complete her. But her wings itch to fly further, higher, like other fliers she sees swooping and soaring, sometimes landing on the perch planted in the middle of her territory that she's yet to fly from.

Today when m-uuu-m comes into Sparky's space, d-aann-y-elll stays outside. M-uuu-m comes straight to Sparky; she doesn't know what'll happen next because this hasn't happened before so she flies to the ledge. M-uuu-m comes up to her again. On her ledge, wings pressed against the solid surfaces behind and beside her, head feathers brushing the top, Sparky can't escape. She hiss-caws, muscles rigid, ready to struggle.

Chattering softly, m-uuu-m reaches out. A tug on her ankles makes Sparky step to its featherless wing. She searches for food, finds none. This is different. She leaps up, trying to escape, is jerked down. There's more tugging on her ankles; she strains her feet against the tugging but can't lift them. M-uuu-m, still chattering gently, is studying her feet; Sparky looks too, sees its wing toes pecking at the skin strips dangling from her ankles, joining them to a shiny ring thing and wormy line. The tugging stops. The line tethers Sparky to m-uuu-m. She remembers her before human doing this, then it abandoned her. Panic mobs her now. Sparky flaps frantically as m-uuu-m, chattering more urgently, crosses the space, heading for the outside, taking Sparky with it. The last time a human took her out of her space she never returned there, never saw that human again even though it had been her mate since she hatched. Sparky fights to fly from m-uuu-m's featherless wing, back into her space that she shares with d-aann-y-elll, her mate, where they fly together. But she can't. She's outside now. She looks at the sky stretching endlessly away overhead in all directions. The opportunity dawns in her. Now her wings flap to fly her into that aerial wilderness.

They go towards the perch on the grass. D-aann-y-elll stands near it. When m-uuu-m gets them there it and d-aann-y-elll chatter, there's more tugging on Sparky's ankles then she's held up to the perch so she steps onto it. This is different but similar; her humans are here and she's on a perch like when they're in her space. Her panic floats away; she waits calmly to be called to fly to them as usual.

D-aann-y-elll stays near the perch, chattering to her while m-uuu-m walks away. Sparky faces d-aann-y-elll but it doesn't call her.

Ss-p-aaarrr-kkee.

She head-swivels. M-uuu-m is calling her, from near the grey path between the grass and the big structure that's her humans' roosting space. M-uuu-m raises its wing, a chick leg trapped in the toes.

This is further than Sparky's ever flown. She doesn't know if she can fly that far; she doesn't know she can't. A coolness ruffles her feathers, gentle wind blowing towards her. She's never flown with a wind blowing her before. She's never flown out under the sky before. But it's in her to.

Ss-p-aaarrr-kkee. Ss-p-aaarrr-kkee.

She springs off the perch, wings beating hard, cool breeze lifting her, carrying her skyward as her wings power her forwards, air whooshing against her face, into her unblinking eyes, rippling her plumage. M-uuu-m gets bigger; Sparky gets closer. Then she's there and, feet out, tries to drop down. The breeze holds her in mid-air. She tilts her wings downwards, lowering herself. A foot finds a hold, talons tighten; the other foot scratches around, clutching at nothing until it too finds a hold. And she's on m-uuu-m's wing, beak full of food.

M-uuu-m turns, facing Sparky at the perch she's just flown from. Now she's come so far it looks nearer. M-uuu-m pushes Sparky into the air: into flight.

She reaches the perch. It's the most wing-beats she's ever done. Beak open, she pants in rapid breaths, freedom and fatigue flowing over her. Checking behind, she sees where she's been; where she knows she can go.

Beside her d-aann-y-elll is beating its wings together with a clap-clapping sound, and chattering her call and other sound patterns. Its face hole stretches into an upwards curving line.

HHH

That was awesome, Sparky, you're so clever. I knew you'd do it. Mum said you might not but I knew you would. You're the best!

OOO

There's a buzzing energy inside Sparky. She's flown the furthest she's ever flown, knows she can fly further, higher. She takes off, pointing herself at the sky, climbing into it.

But a sudden jolt snaps her out of flight. She falls and flaps, fighting to keep herself airborne. There's a long moment of wing-beating then she rights herself, is flying, not falling, landing in the grass, cool and feathery beneath her feet.

She's away from the perch and d-aann-y-elll, closer to m-uuu-m. She lowers and shakes her head, pecking at her ankles, her darkly glowing eyes tracing the line attached to her ankles by the skin strips, tracing it sharply all the way to a short branch planted into the ground between the perch and m-uuu-m. The line attaches to the branch at that end and her legs at this end; that line pulled her out of her skyward soar. She pecks it again.

M-uuu-m's beside her, holding out its hide-covered wing toes for Sparky to perch on, pulling gently at the line so Sparky finds it easier to step up than not. M-uuu-m takes her to the perch. When it's walked as far away as before it turns, calls her, offering more food.

She's being called to fly, hunt and feed: a variation of the familiar routine. So she does, grabbing the morsel as she lands. When she's eaten and m-uuu-m has turned so she's facing the perch again, Sparky returns to it without waiting to be nudged into the air.

They do this a few more times. Then m-uuu-m and d-aann-y-elll swap places and d-aann-y-elll calls her. Sparky sets off before it offers her food. She doesn't need prey to draw her to d-aann-y-elll; it's her mate, this is what they do; fly, hunt and feed together. She lands on its head ledge, feeling it bob down as her feet grip its body plumage for balance.

M-uuu-m calls to d-aann-y-elll, chattering more harshly than usual then it puts a piece of meat on the perch.

Ss-p-aaarrr-kkee.

She doesn't go though. She stays with d-aann-y-elll. M-uuu-m keeps calling but she still doesn't go. Finally d-aann-y-elll walks towards the perch. When they're close to it Sparky jumps off, flapping down onto the perch, grabbing the food scrap and turning, still swallowing, to be ready for d-aann-y-elll to call her again.

This time her mate offers her food at the same moment it calls. She flies straight to its featherless wing, eats and returns to the perch just so she can fly again to her other half.

They do several flights. She doesn't try flying up into the sky because she wants to fly to d-aann-y-elll and doesn't want to be dragged groundward. She wants fly as high and far as she can to show her mate their bond is strengthening by returning to it from further and further away.

The flying stops. There's a quivering, achy feeling in her chest, wings and legs as well as the usual full feeling in her gut. So when d-aann-y-elll tugs on her ankles then walks them back to their space, m-uuu-m following, Sparky rests.

Inside her space m-uuu-m leans in close, pecking at her ankles, untethering her from d-aann-y-elll but, her body still quivering, Sparky stays on the featherless wing. D-aann-y-elll takes her to the ledge. She steps to it. Both humans leave her space but d-aann-y-elll stays just outside, chattering to her. She settles into herself; the quivering feeling fades, contented warmth spreads through her, her mate's chatter quietening.

HHH

You did so great today, Sparky. Sorry you have to be tied to a line but Mum says you'll fly away otherwise. I know you won't 'cos we're best friends and you won't leave me. Mum doesn't get it, but she'll see, we'll show her you won't fly away.

Then you can fly free and that'll be even more than amazing.

OOO

It's night now. Sparky perches on her ledge, a leg tucked up, downy feathers warming the scaly skin on her ankle and foot. When that leg's warmed and rested, she swaps, tucking up the other. She's tired, her whole body aching from flying harder than she ever has. But she's contented; she wasn't taken away from her space, she'll see d-aann-y-elll, and m-uuu-m, tomorrow. She knows there'll be more flying with them, then roosting in her space. She doesn't know if it'll be flying in her space or out under the sky or if she'll ever be able to fly as far as she wants. But there'll be d-aann-y-elll and m-uuu-m and her, bonded together: a whole.

She hears footsteps, her humans are coming. Rousing herself, Sparky goes to the lines, grabbing hold of them, wings outspread, suspended there, a white shadow in blackness. M-uuu-m appears, chattering softly, coming closer to Sparky. Her call and d-aann-y-elll's are swept along in the flowing chatter. It stays a moment then returns to its space across the grass.

HHH

Thank you for today, Sparky, for making Daniel smile at last. Since the divorce it's been difficult for him, for us. I've been so worried about him, he was becoming too withdrawn, shutting himself away from me but now he's got you he's coming out of that. We've got something we can share, enjoy, love together: you. We're not just mother and son, we're becoming friends so thank you, Sparky, thank you for bringing us back together, making us a happy family.

Now

May 2022 (cont.)

OOO

T-raay-cee and Sparky establish a routine. There's more hunter's confidence about t-raay-cee, matching Sparky's own; she's learning to trust it, knows their bond is developing, fragile but there, cobweb thin; cobweb strong. Soon they'll fly together.

But today, when t-raay-cee comes into her space and she flies to it at her call there's a change to their routine. It tethers them together with the shiny ring thing and the wormy line before they leave her space. Sparky remembers that, with her before humans, this led to them flying outside. As they cross through the territory beyond her space and head into the narrow gap she exercises her wings.

They walk in the gap for a while, t-raay-cee offering her food as they go. Sparky eats but her focus is on mapping the narrow gap, extending her territory to include it, her eyes noting the shapes and colours displayed, ears collecting the sounds that drift about. It's a long enough space to strengthen their bond by flying it.

But after walking together, t-raay-cee returns Sparky to her space. There's no flying. Sparky doesn't know why; her before humans didn't walk about with her like this. They flew with her. Maybe it doesn't realise that flying together is what they need to form a lifelong bond.

HHH

The falconry books say it's a mistake to wait too long before progressing your bird's training. So now she's coming to me fairly readily in the aviary I decide to take the next step. Or, literally, steps, by tethering Sparky to my glove and walking along the corridor, her perching on my fist, feeding her titbits as we saunter. She's calm, head-turning curiously to take in her new surroundings, thankfully doesn't test my iffy falconer's knot. She seems to be enjoying going on a wander with me. At last I feel we're getting somewhere, going somewhere, together, even if it's just a stroll in the corridor.

OOO

The walking is repeated the next day, and the next and the next. Sparky thoroughly maps the narrow gap, extending her territory into it. She relaxes, perching on t-raay-cee's featherless wing, eating the offered prey while surveying her new patch of territory. The walking routine reassures her she's safe out there with t-raay-cee. But they still haven't flown together.

Sparky stares at the slivers of sky visible high up the sides of the narrow gap. It's out there in all its vastness. Every feather tingles for more than the few flaps needed to cross her small space. In this new territory she could fly many wing-beats, more even than in the spaces at a-ll-eee's. But not as many as when she flew, a long while ago, with matt-ee, in the wild sky. These before mates did fly with her though. T-raay-cee hasn't and it must if they're going to pair up; Sparky needs a mate to fly with. She's ready for that; t-raay-cee isn't.

HHH

I don't know how many walks to take her on before flying her in the corridor and put off the leap from having her securely fastened to my falconry glove to letting her have the freedom of flight, even if it is indoors. I want to get there with her but fear what happens when I do. I wish I could explain that to Sparky but I just keep hoping she's patient, understands my reluctance to let her go.

Before

November 2017

OOO

Sparky waits for d-aann-y-elll and m-uuu-m to come, as they have every day since she arrived at her new space and they bonded, giving her the comfortable routine of flying, hunting and feeding with them.

Today though, it's just d-aann-y-elll who comes, calling her to it, chattering to her while it pecks around her ankles, joining them together with the shiny ring thing and wormy line, which takes longer than when m-uuu-m does it. Finally they go out to the perch on the grass. They're going to fly, d-aann-y-elll and her, alone, as a pair. She leaps from its featherless wing as they near the perch, eager to fly with her mate as they should, just them.

At the perch it pecks again at her ankles, untethering them, like m-uuu-m does before it attaches the long line that tethers her to the short branch planted in the ground, the line that pulls Sparky out of the sky if she flies too high. D-aann-y-elll doesn't tether her to this long line though. She feels the lightness of its absence, sees only the skin strips dangling from her ankles as her mate steps her to the perch. There isn't anything to stall her flight. Now she can show her mate how strong their bond is by returning to it from far away.

D-aann-y-elll walks to the furthest edge of the grassy patch.

Ss-p-aaarrr-kkee.

She leaps into the air, the freedom of no tethering line exhilarating, and flies, a strong breeze lifting her, filling the nothingness under her wings. Flying higher than ever she heads for d-aann-y-elll; it wants her to go to it and she wants to be with it. Sparky wing-beats the air back, reaches her mate and drops onto the featherless wing, swallowing the offered food as it turns to send her to the perch.

With a nudge, she jumps again, this time feeling wind behind her, pushing her onwards, speeding her towards the perch, sending her over it even as she's trying to land. Twisting her wings, she manages to turn tightly, scrabbling for the perch, clutching clumsily, jolting down with a lurch. She faces d-aann-y-elll; it's already offering her more food.

Ss-p-aaarrr-kkee.

She soars easily but, before she reaches her mate, the wind strengthens. A sharp gust pushes her backwards, sideways, pressing her down and away. She flaps frantically, tries to gain height, struggles determinedly towards d-aann-y-elll. She reaches it, chest burning and wings throbbing with the exertion of battling the wind. She's panting too much to eat, needs to recover. But d-aann-y-elll is already facing her at the perch, raising her into the wind which buffets her from behind. Sparky's still swallowing as she's thrown into flight by another sharp gust.

And now she's fighting to slow herself, wrestling the wind for control of her wings, the gust flapping them for her, flinging her forward too fast. She's swept over the perch, hurtling towards the trees and bushes marking the end of her territory, scanning them frantically for a landing as she tries to press herself backwards into the tailwind, to stop it hurrying her onwards. In the next wing-beat she'll be out of her territory. Out of her territory is into danger. Desperately she struggles against wind-blown flight to rejoin her mate; away from her mate is towards a half life, unpaired: alone.

The gust suddenly drops. Sparky drops with it, down into a low bush at the edge of her territory. Her wings splay out as she scrambles for a foothold on flimsy branches that bend beneath her. Toes curling, she finds a shaky perch, bobbing around on it, and turns, searching for d-aann-y-elll to help her out of this low, awkward place; to reunited them.

Her mate stands motionless across the grass from her, eyes wide, face hole gaping. She gropes for a more stable perch, slips deeper into the bush, feeling spikes prodding and poking her, feathers bending and snapping. She tries to take off but jumping pushes her further into the bush, pinning her to it, wings now raised above her head as though frozen mid-beat.

Behind d-aann-y-elll, m-uuu-m emerges from their roosting space, charging closer, covering its wing toes in the thick hide as it runs, chattering loudly to d-aann-y-elll who retreats from it. But m-uuu-m swoops down on d-aann-y-elll, stealing food off it then running on, towards Sparky, slowing when it's within a few strides, chattering more softly. Sparky hears her call, tries to flap her trapped wings, leap up to m-uuu-m but can't.

M-uuu-m reaches her, crouches and holds out a featherless wing, offering the food. Sparky stretches her neck, pecking around for the feel of flesh in her beak. But before she finds it, she realises her wings are hers again. A single step and she's up on m-uuu-m's wing perch. M-uuu-m walks them to Sparky's space.

Inside it, m-uuu-m calls loudly.

D-aann-y-elll. D-aann-y-elll.

It shuffles slowly to them. There's more harsh chattering from m-uuu-m. Sparky sees d-aann-y-elll offer it food, a whole mouse, trying to appease it, but when m-uuu-m takes the mouse it passes the offering straight to her. Sparky accepts, crunching the skull in her beak then flying to the rear ledge to eat away from m-uuu-m and d-aann-y-elll's harsh cawing; the noise stabs her ears.

As she eats they leave, the squawking chatter fading as they walk to their own space, d-aann-y-elll following m-uuu-m, its head dipped below its shoulders. M-uuu-m is head-shaking and wing-flapping furiously. Sparky's never seen humans behaving like this with each other before but her natural knowing of animal behaviour tells her they're squabbling, m-uuu-m furiously, d-aann-y-elll defensively. If they stop being a pair Sparky won't be able to share her life with both of them. D-aann-y-elll is her real mate so she'll go with it: they're bonded together lifelong.

As daylight weakens m-uuu-m and d-aann-y-elll come to Sparky's space but only m-uuu-m enters. It gives Sparky a chick, chattering to her as she flies to it, then walking her to the front where d-aann-y-elll stands on its side of the criss-crossed lines.

HHH

Hello, Sparky, sorry about today. I hope you weren't too upset by it all. I'll make sure it doesn't happen again. Here's some extra nosh for you, a peace offering.

Now, Daniel has something to say to you, Sparky.

OOO

Sparky pulls the head off the chick, gulping it down, before she looks at d-aann-y-elll. Its face is paler than usual, its unbeak is red-sore and its eyes wetly glistening. Hanging its head, snatching a glance at her then a glance at m-uuu-m, it chatters to her.

HHH

Sorry, Sparky. I shouldn't have done that, it was wrong, I know that now. You could've been hurt and I don't want to hurt you, honest. I just wanted you to fly free, I thought… Mum's going to fly you for a bit but I'll still be here, watching. We'll fly together again soon, Sparky, and I promise I won't ever do anything that might get you hurt. I'm sorry, Sparky. I hope we're still friends.

Now

30th May–1st June 2022

HHH

After a weekend of deliberating I make my mind up: it's time to try flying Sparky, short distances in the barn corridor. I need to do it now, before I spend too long imagining all the potential disasters and before she gets bored walking up and down on my fist. We should be safe enough flying indoors, even without any expert supervision, and I need to trust her if I want her to trust me.

OOO

The next time t-raay-cee comes it doesn't tether them together, they just go out into the narrow gap. Sparky is keen but calm on its featherless wing; are they going to fly together?

T-raay-cee takes Sparky to a perch. When she's stepped onto it t-raay-cee walks away from her, facing her, watching her. They are going to fly together. Energy charges through Sparky. She chases after t-raay-cee, landing on a head ledge because there's no featherless wing raised. T-raay-cee returns her to the perch and retreats a few steps again. Lodged inside her, Sparky locates a memory of before that matches now. She waits for her call.

Ss-p-aaarrr-kkee.

All those moments in her space, when t-raay-cee called her and Sparky hop-flew to it; all those occasions before with other humans who called her to fly to them, they hatch now. It's what Sparky and her new mate have been heading towards; enough trust to be apart so they can return to each other: so they can fly together.

Sparky springs airwards, gliding to the other half of herself, wings drawing her on. It's been such a while since she's flown with a human like this that it rushes over her in a flood of energy that sweeps her through the air without thought for what happens when she reaches t-raay-cee. She has to land on the head ledge, is stepped onto the featherless wing and returned to the perch. That flood of energy ebbs; she flies again, this time to the featherless wing, landing decisively and being offered food. She tingles from wing-tip to wing-tip, vibrant with the power of flight.

T-raay-cee nudges her into the air. Sparky holds herself in a hovering flight before dropping back onto a head ledge. Now she's flown to this human, when it called her to it, their bond is affirmed. They need more flying though. She's pushed into the air again. But in the rush of responding to her call and flying to her new mate, she's lost sight of the perch she took off from. Her focus was on where she was going, not where she'd been, so she can't find her way back. Now she's airborne she needs to land somewhere. Scanning rapidly, she spots a box high up the side.

Perching there, Sparky realises the view is wrong; this isn't where she took off from. Up here she's looking down into the narrow gap, at t-raay-cee reaching up for her, tugging at her skin strips until Sparky steps back to its wing toes. Together, Sparky perching and t-raay-cee walking, they head along the narrow gap, the perch coming into view. Sparky hops to it, watching and listening for another raising of the featherless wing, another call.

Ss-p-aaarrr-kkee.

She flies again. Lands again. Eats again. Is carried to the perch again.

After a few flights to t-raay-cee, Sparky locates the perch she's taking off from, picking it out amidst the cluttered background objects and colours in the narrow gap. She marks the perch's location on her map so when t-raay-cee next pushes her into the air Sparky is able to return straight to it. As soon as she lands she faces about, readying to fly to her new mate again.

Ss-p-aaarrr-kkee.

They do another few flights. It's not many wing-beats more than she needs to cross her space but it's more like the flying she's known before with mates, the flying, hunting, feeding they live for, together completing each other.

In her space, as night falls, Sparky roosts, perching on this leg, that leg tucked up, wings folded, eyes closed. For a while she's had a fluttering feeling inside that couldn't be stilled. This fluttering had been irritating her so long she'd stopped noticing it, but tonight she's aware of it because it's gone, has been calmed by flying to her mate. She rests, readying herself for when t-raay-cee comes and they fly together again.

HHH

30/5
Took her into corridor and got her on perch. She flew once to shoulder so put her back on perch and called again. She came but wouldn't fly back (why?) when cast—landed on shoulder again then on fuse box. Had to put her on perch for first 3 flights but next 2 she flew back to perch after cast and returned for food. Will increase distance slightly tomorrow.

Although my training log doesn't record it, I'm elated at having Sparky fly to me. I doubt she's as pleased as me, though. A few metres in a corridor is hardly fulfilling her owlness.

OOO

After flying with t-raay-cee, even just those few short flights in the narrow gap, Sparky knows they're bonding more earnestly; maybe they'll even pair up for life.

So when t-raay-cee comes again the next day she's anticipating them flying. T-raay-cee takes them straight into the narrow gap and they start. Sparky gets lost initially, trying to find the low perch she's to go to so she can return to t-raay-cee, but after she locates it, remarking it in her territory map, she's able to just fly; to t-raay-cee, to the perch, to t-raay-cee. Then a loud bang crashes into her ears. Startled, Sparky flees to the perch, warily watching, eyes trained on the furthest end of the territory, where the bang emanated. A pair of humans enters: invaders. It's the wizened, shrivelled human that trapped her in the fliers' space and another she doesn't recognise. They walk along the space, chattering. Sparky doesn't trust shrivelled human; it's disturbed her with strange behaviour before, leaving her anxious that it was a threat to her. Sparky stays focused on the trespassing humans, keenly watching for signs they're going to attack. Though it's calling her, she can't fly to t-raay-cee with the trespassers there; her wings are tense, legs stiff and chest tight. The invading humans disappear through an in/out at the side of the narrow gap without attacking. Sparky's fluttering panic settles.

Ss-p-aaarrr-kkee.

She flies now. They do a few more flights before t-raay-cee takes them to her space, leaving her with food to stash. When it comes again they'll fly more, further, as long as no strange humans invade their territory…

HHH

Buoyed by my initial success flying Sparky in the corridor; even though she only came a short distance to me and it took a bit of learning on her part to return to the perch then to me when I called her, judged against the fact that I've never flown a bird of prey without an expert beside me I think I did O.K. I suspect Sparky did better. I don't know what training she's had before, whether she's ever flown indoors, other than in a small aviary, if she's always been flown tied to a creance line or was used to flying outside, free, and how long it's been since she flew with someone like this. She must've had some training, some previous experience flying with people, from how quickly she picked it up. She certainly seemed keen to stretch her wings with me so I'm as confident as I dare be that, carrying on like this, gradually getting her to fly further, eventually the whole length of the corridor, about 50 metres, we'll be O.K. After that first session, seeing her fly, having her fly to me, I know I have to give her this opportunity, even if it's a ghostly imitation of the flying she should be doing outside: free.

Unfortunately, it's not as important to anyone else at the centre, including those that should care enough to at least heed the signs I put up when I'm flying her to stop us being interrupted. I can't believe the centre director just breezed in like that. I'm furious but daren't say anything to him: he's the almighty here, presiding over his motley animal kingdom. I make do with fuming to John when I get home that night, using a word that I reserve for especially infuriating events or people, or both. It was both today, so I use the word twice and hope I won't have cause to use it again tomorrow…

1/6
Came after some hesitation from perch to glove then straight into corridor. Flew readily first 2 or 3 times. Then interrupted, again, by director's son and girlfriend visiting animals. Sparky could hear them in the room so was hesitant again. Once they had gone she flew 4 or 5 more times with a little more hesitation but wasn't put off by another volunteer watching.

Before

November 2017 (cont.)

OOO

Several days come and go; m-uuu-m takes Sparky to the perch on the grass, flies with her. D-aann-y-elll watches from the edge; it doesn't fly with her. It's her mate; she doesn't understand why it's not flying with her. But m-uuu-m is, it has food for her and she's hungry so she goes to it, watching d-aann-y-elll whenever she returns to the perch to see if it'll call her instead. It doesn't. Maybe it doesn't want to be her mate anymore.

Then a day comes when d-aann-y-elll takes her out to the grassy patch. They're going to fly together again; they're still a pair. But it takes her to a low perch, not the tall perch she flies from. As soon as d-aann-y-elll turns away, she jumps into flight; she can land on a head ledge, start their flying, hunting, feeding, reminding it they're partners, a whole, sharing life. But she's jolted to the ground a short way from the low perch. She's tethered to it, can't fly to d-aann-y-elll, doesn't know what this new happening means.

M-uuu-m appears now, wing toes covered in smooth bright yellow plumage and carrying a deep water pool and a long stick with taloned toes at the end. As m-uuu-m passes Sparky she sees white foamy water swirling around inside the deep water pool which it takes to her space, where d-aann-y-elll waits. There's lots of chattering and flapping of featherless wings. D-aann-y-elll crosses the ground close to Sparky again. She jumps towards it, calling it with her raspy caw, but her mate doesn't come to her. When it reappears, it's dragging a long coiled line that uncoils when dragged to Sparky's space. D-aann-y-elll points the tip of the line into her space and water rains out of the tip in a fast arcing stream.

Sparky stares, curious, at this new happening.

While d-aann-y-elll rains water inside her space m-uuu-m claws the ground with the taloned stick then dips its yellow wing toes into the foamy water, bringing them out clutching something small, flat and with many dark stiff twigs growing out of it. M-uuu-m rubs small flat twiggy object over the sides of Sparky's space for a bit then passes the it to d-aann-y-elll who continues the rubbing. Then there's more water raining and ground clawing.

Sparky loses interest. The sky's blue today, with feathery clouds. She stretches her wings and springs off the low perch but the line stops her flying into that blue expanse. She pecks the line, shakes her head, pecks again, hops back to the perch, leaps off again because the urge to fly doesn't let her stop trying even though she's found she can't. She flap-jumps, is grounded, pecks the line, hops to perch, flap-jumps again. After a while her wings and legs ache like when she's been flying. She rests, hunter's instincts warning her to save energy for when there's the chance to fly and hunt with her mate. She does a final hop up to the low perch, giving a gentle screech, and observes her humans.

Finally they finish inside her space. D-aann-y-elll runs to her, crouching down as she jumps as high as the line lets her, trying to meet her mate in mid-air. It chatters to her; she croakily replies, stepping onto the featherless wing as soon as it's held out to her. They'll fly together now, after too many days of not. She feels d-aann-y-elll's eagerness to soar welling up, melding with her own. There's some tugging on her ankles then d-aann-y-elll faces the tall perch, starts walking towards it. Sparky doesn't wait to be walked there. She leaps into the breeze, swooping to it. Only the pull of the line that tethers her to the short branch planted in the ground, quells the thrill of her flight. They fly; to-and-from, to-and-from, over and over, m-uuu-m watching. Some flights there isn't food for her because she's returned to d-aann-y-elll before it's had chance to offer her some; just being able to fly with her mate is enough to satisfy her. Together as a pair, they have all they need. They have each other.

HHH

Today was brilliant, Sparky, well, once we got your aviary cleaned. That was a bit gross but it didn't take too long. Just as well, Mum says we'll do it every week from now on. That's O.K. I want to look after you properly. And it was worth it: we got to fly again since I'm not grounded anymore. You knew straight away it was flying time, came right to me, even without food. Guess you love flying. Who wouldn't? It must be so cool. Definitely the superpower I'd pick. We'll fly together all the time now. Promise. Friends forever.

Now

June 2022

OOO

Sparky's bond with t-raay-cee is still flimsy, she flies with it, but not out under the sky with the wind taking her, free to soar as she did before with matt-ee. Flying in the narrow gap, though, is more flying than she's done in a long while and it happens most days, with t-raay-cee giving her ss-p-aaarrr-kkee call, Sparky flying to it because that's why they're together: it's their life. If it was just them, a pair, bonded by their flying, hunting and feeding, their life would be easy. But it isn't just them.

When they go into the narrow gap there's often other, strange humans lurking, like predators waiting to pounce. So Sparky has to watch them watching her and t-raay-cee to make sure they're safe. Then she can't focus properly on their flying. She doesn't know why these humans keep stalking them, as if readying to mob her and t-raay-cee. It should just be them, hunting together, like it was with her before mates, especially matt-ee who never let other humans threaten their flying together.

HHH

Sparky starts attracting an audience, just my family and other volunteers. I know it's too soon to put on a show but people are fascinated by owls, eager to be shoulder-to-wing to one; their humanlike faces, their wildness and their magical myths. In meeting Sparky I've been gifted a rare, enviable, opportunity and feel obliged to share it, especially with other volunteers who, if I impress them, might tell the centre's director there's a reason to keep Sparky here. Selfishly, now we've found each other, I don't want to lose Sparky. If I train her so she and I can do mini displays to fund-raise for the centre she'll maybe be enough of an asset that he won't rehome her like he did the harris hawks I was planning to fly. So, while I know it's not the best thing for Sparky right now to become a sideshow, I blunder on anyway.

2/6
Easy weigh-in but took a while to get her to come from perch to glove. Think she could hear John and Mum talking in corridor so was a bit unsure. But once she came took her straight into corridor and flew her. She came quite readily most of the time, straight away on occasions but she was more hesitant the other flights. She flew back perfectly each time though and I extended the distance to about 7m so all good!

3/6
She was on back beam this morning so called her to glove, came with some hesitation. Then weighed her, 12.2oz, and took her straight into corridor. I put the perch further away so she was curious and looking around quite a bit. But once she started flying she was quite responsive and even flew to me once before I offered food. On one cast she flew round and landed on my shoulder, think extra distance had confused her but after that she was very reliable back and forth.

6/6
She was a bit hesitant at first, partly as John's parents came to watch. But once she got going she was fine, even flew once without food. On one trip she hopped up to my shoulder with the food so I put her on glove and cast her back to perch but all other flights were spot on. Didn't do quite such a distance as Friday, will extend more tomorrow.

7/6
Was keen and waiting on perch this morning. Two volunteers watched. She was more hesitant at first but did fly well and was reasonably responsive. They watched about 4–5 flights then left and I did a few more, extending the distance to 12m. She was quicker to respond for the final few flights when it was just me and her.

But my plan to keep Sparky by making her an asset here backfires. The animal centre is a charity. It's main income is from the paying public who, for a few quid, can wander round to view the non-exotic animals; poultry, small furries and farm animals. But they also organise a range of fund-raisers, mostly behind-the-scenes open days and animal encounters on and off-site. Today the centre director informs me that the volunteer who does the off-site animal encounters has a coffee morning booked for the coming weekend and will take Sparky with her, along with a few other furry or feathered residents, to help charm cash from the crowd. I'm to show this volunteer how to fly Sparky today, he tells me, like Sparky's a wind-up toy and I only need to hand over the key. I'm stunned; all I do is mutter, 'O.K.'

Sparky isn't performance-ready so how the hell can someone who's never handled a barn owl, let alone flown one, do this without it ending in disaster? How can he think this is right, safe, for Sparky? I picture her flying around inside a village hall, panicked, injured by cack-handed attempts to recapture her or, worse, escaping through a carelessly opened window.

But if I refuse I might have my Sparky privileges revoked. I'm only a volunteer; I have no rights to her, or even to come here. The director can easily banish me. Then what happens to Sparky? Spending so much time here for the last few weeks, I'm starting to spot things that concern me, that I can't dismiss as the accepted difficulties of under-funding and resourcing that animal charities face. Things like Sparky in the owl room, in danger from those wild tawnies, housed there by the centre director who now wants to put her at risk again…

Sparky would need an Article 10, a legal document required to use certain raptors, including barn owls, for 'commercial purposes'. It applies even if the money raised is for charity. If I can mention this legality while I'm flying Sparky to the volunteer maybe she'll decide against breaking the law for a few extra donations, she's one of the charity's trustees so surely wouldn't want legal problems. I set off for Sparky's aviary, anxiety churning my stomach, mentally drafting a script.

OOO

It's not just a strange human watching today. It's a strange human calling her to fly to it. T-raay-cee is there too, and calls her initially but then the stranger takes her mate's place. It doesn't give her call like t-raay-cee does. It isn't standing the way t-raay-cee does. She doesn't know this human at all, doesn't feel safe flying to it; doesn't want to fly to it because it's not her mate. If she flies to it that would be a breach in her bond with t-raay-cee which is still fledging.

Sparky doesn't fly to it, even when the stranger calls and calls her. As soon as t-raay-cee calls her, she flies to it, several times, showing this interloper who her real mate is.

HHH

Thankfully Sparky solves the problem herself, flying only to me so my speech about the A10 is unnecessary; Sparky is excused fund-raising duties. For now.

Before

December 2017–January 2019

OOO

Except when it's raining or very windy, d-aann-y-elll comes to Sparky and they hunt together on the grassy patch, m-uuu-m watching. There's always the line to ground her if she goes too far into the sky or leaves their territory so she doesn't fly anywhere except in their territory, to her mate. Maybe there'll be a day when she isn't tethered by the line, like before with d-aaann-y-ell, so she checks often for the chance to fly further away so she can fly further back to her mate, proving their bond is strong.

If it's raining or very windy d-aaann-y-ell comes into her space and she flies short hop-flights to its featherless wing instead so they still get to hunt together. This is their shared life. She has everything she needs; a pool for bathing, a safe roosting space, plenty to eat, energy for flying and her human other half. She's content.

Sometimes m-uuu-m comes into her space without d-aann-y-elll and balances Sparky on the short perch which bobs up and down a bit. Sparky doesn't know why m-uuu-m does this because d-aann-y-elll always does it too, but she knows she can trust m-uuu-m so she lets it balance her on the low bobbing perch then she flies to its head ledge and it walks her to the perch in her space, which she jumps to, then m-uuu-m leaves. Other days she's taken out of her space and sat on a stable low perch on the grassy patch while d-aann-y-elll and m-uuu-m rain water in her space, rub the sides and claw at the ground. Then she flies with d-aann-y-elll.

The seasons pass from frosty dark winter to fresh bright spring and fiery dazzling summer. Her feathers fall out, new ones unfurling like the flower petals that are blooming around her territory. Sparky preens, plucking out old feathers, straightening new ones, bathing more often helping her moult until she has fresh new plumage combed smoothly into flying order. But these changes are nature's gentle rolling pattern; they don't ruffle her. Her life here, with d-aann-y-elll and m-uuu-m is settled, she knows it so well she's completely at ease in it.

Even when strange humans come, which they do especially during the heavy, long summer days, to stand watching her and d-aann-y-elll hunting and feeding, she's confident enough to fly with her mate as they always do. The strangers' squawking chattering doesn't alarm her and she isn't upset if they come near, staring at her, because she's perching on d-aann-y-elll's wing. If she goes near them when they're within range they scatter. Only a few times has any other human stood still long enough for her to land on a head ledge before flying to d-aann-y-elll when it called her. And if they come to her space, peering in at her, she always flies to the front, hanging on the criss-crossed lines, talons hooked, toes gripping, wings unfolded, peering out at them. If they poke their wing toes through at her, she pecks them. Then there's squealing and they go away, d-aann-y-elll chattering furiously at them.

There was a day when a strange human invaded her space. Sparky was on her tall perch. It stepped through the in/out. She flew to the ledge, getting as far away as possible from the trespasser, her muscles taut, wings beating ready. But d-aann-y-elll called out and the stranger retreated even as d-aann-y-elll ran to it, attacking it, protecting her. The stranger called back, the noise bouncing around inside Sparky's head. Then the stranger leapt up and swung a featherless wing at d-aann-y-elll's head but d-aann-y-elll crouch quickly, swung its featherless wing at the stranger's body, striking it, making it bend forward and growl, before it walked away, its featherless wings wrapped around its body.

That stranger didn't come again; d-aann-y-elll had fought it off, defending Sparky's space, protecting her as mates do. Since that day no others have invaded the space she shares with d-aann-y-elll. Sparky knows d-aann-y-elll would fight them off again if they did so she feels safe; her mate will always protect her, defend their territory.

Summer mellows into an autumn of crisp days and damp days. Sparky notices d-aann-y-elll's call starts sounding more like her own; croaky, rasping, sometimes squeaking like the mice that run through her territory at night. She learns this new croaky rasping sound of her ss-p-aaarrr-kkee call. She also sees d-aann-y-elll is growing. Its legs and wings stretch. Its body fills out. She recognises this natural change. It's life's order; hatching, growing, living, dying. Like the seasons and her own moulting, there's nothing in this change to unsettle her.

Then suddenly there is an unsettling change; d-aann-y-elll stops coming to hunt with her: disappears. Only m-uuu-m comes, chattering softly. The days are short and cold now, the nights long and colder. M-uuu-m brings her food but after sunset, and they don't fly together even though Sparky can fly as well in darkness as in daylight with her night vision and feather-drop hearing. Without flying her life is reduced to an existence, easy and secure but like a grey winter's sky. More days pass; d-aann-y-elll doesn't reappear. It could've left her for another mate. It could've died. Sparky watches and waits, darting from perch to ledge to criss-crossed lines to perch, always alert for the sound or sight of her mate returning. Although m-uuu-m is still there, bringing her food and chattering, Sparky is distressed by her mate's absence. She needs it to return because they complete each other.

HHH

I know, you're missing him, Sparky. But it's his dad's turn to have him this Christmas. Don't worry, he'll be back soon and you'll fly every day again.

OOO

The sun rises pinkly in a white-blue sky; Sparky's wings twitch instinctively to soar up into it. The ground shimmers with flecks of brilliance, as though covered with tiny stars scattered by the night. Sparky shudders deeper into her plumage, numbing air circling her. As the sun drifts higher it casts a golden glow into her space. The surface of her water pool gleams with sudden light. Sparky flies down to investigate. Faint warmth washes over her when she lands in the sunbeam. As she hops up to the edge of her water pool, the gleaming light shrinks to a narrow shining sliver across the pool which looks as it always does, the dark green bottom visible through the pool's clear water. There's a scrap of uneaten meat in the pool. Sparky pecks at the food. But the surface doesn't ripple at her touch like water should; it's solid. She steps onto the solid surface, feet slipping apart, talons unable to grip the smooth hardness beneath her toes. It's frozen: ice. This fascinating new phenomenon, something she can see through but not get through, holds her attention, lodging itself in her knowing of the world. The piece of meat stays trapped behind the ice.

A crunching footfall shifts her focus. She leaps to the criss-crossed lines. Is it d-aann-y-elll? M-uuu-m walks with small, cautious steps, across the sparkly white ground to her. Sparky retreats to her perch; there'll be fresh food now. But still her mate is missing. Maybe it too is trapped somewhere by ice, unable to get through, return to her?

Now

June 2022 (cont.)

HHH

I need time with Sparky, just the two of us, to establish a routine, learn each other's ways.

9/6
No dramas and no audience today. She was waiting on perch—her weight is quite stable now at 12oz. In corridor she was hesitant first 2–3 flights then did 3–4 more quite readily but as I kept extending the distance she was hesitant again for last few, coming eventually 15+m. I messed up casting her back twice so she ended up hovering and circling until she found her way to the perch. She is doing really well, better than me!

But that's just one day. We need several, many, like this, all in a row.

OOO

They're flying together when a strange human invades their territory again, coming raucously into the narrow gap, its behaviour boldly threatening. Sparky feels the swell of panic and instinct launches her into flight. But she can't escape the stranger in the narrow gap. A rapid pattering in her chest urges her to keep flying, wing-beating frantically, staying airborne: harder to catch. She flies in circles, gets nowhere. When her wings heavy and her chest throbs, the nowhere flight draining her, she has to drop onto the perch.

Then t-raay-cee comes close, offering prey, chattering softly. The fluttering panic inside her fades but Sparky's wary of the stranger now; it keeps stomping along the gap like it's claimed their territory for itself. And t-raay-cee doesn't do anything to chase it off. Her mate must be feeling the same tremoring panic as her. Muscles trembling from her failed escape, Sparky rests on the perch briefly, eyes locked on where the stranger comes and goes from. It doesn't reappear so she takes the chance to do a short flight, and another short flight, to t-raay-cee, because that's what they should be doing together.

The stranger charges down on them now, disappearing through an in/out at the side of the gap. Sparky follows it with her ears, listening to the unnerving noise of it clattering and banging out of sight, her ears trying to see what it's doing. She daren't fly any more, no matter how much her mate calls her to it; she needs to keep her focus on this stranger; it could attack them.

HHH

Despite my 'barn owl flying session in progress' signs a workman crashes into the corridor, spooking Sparky. I know he's got a job to do but she only needs quarter of an hour, not a lot to ask, surely? He comes and goes a couple of times. On his third intrusion I ask him if he can give me a little time to fly this barn owl, please? But he's busy, 'got to get on.'

'Yes, but every time you open the door, you're risking her escaping and that's death to a captive barn owl.'

'Oh, I know all about birds of prey,' he tells me cockily, 'my mate keeps them.'

Then why don't you sod off and let me fly her in peace, you berk, I think. But I can't say that. He's the centre director's pal, doing this govvy job as a favour and I'm permanently on guard against anything that might ruin things for Sparky and me. I ask about when he takes breaks; I'll have to plan flying sessions around his sodding lunch hour.

The longer I spend here the unhappier I am about how things are for the animals, all of them; I'm no longer sure they're better off for having been rescued by the centre. Is this actually a rescue centre with its paying visitors, breeding programme and practice of trading and selling animals? Sparky is becoming the emblem for concerns I don't know how to tackle. All I can do for now is trust that what needs to happen will happen and take up my role in it when that moment comes. Until then I'll carry on doing what I can for Sparky.

13/6
Did ten good flights up to 10m. Some hesitation after first 3 or 4 and came once before I got food out to offer her. That time she landed on my shoulder so I put my glove down and she returned to perch herself then we got back on track with rest of the flights.

14/6
V. similar to yesterday. Up to 15m distance again now and she is definitely more relaxed and enjoying it. We're getting there now.

OOO

Today they go out into the gap, just her and t-raay-cee. It's been just them the last couple of times they've flown so they could get on with being together, doing what a pair of mates should. And they'll do more of it again today.

But as they walk into the gap Sparky sees it's bare and dark, filled only with harsh, honking noises. The perch is there but everything else is gone; it doesn't match her map. This isn't their territory. Sparky can't see what's making the honking but such a loud, deep, painful sound must mean danger. She launches into the air, swooping down the narrow gap that's not her territory, right to the end where an in/out bars her escape. She turns, a wing tip dipped, another raised, pulling her into a tight arc. She has to fly back towards the noise. There's nowhere else to go.

She lands on the perch. T-raay-cee calls her.

Ss-p-aaarrr-kkee. Ss-p-aaarrr-kkee. Ss-p-aaarrr-kkee.

Sparky knows her mate wants her to fly with it. But she can't make herself take off. It comes close, offering her food, giving her chance to go to it with only a few wing-beats.

Ss-p-aaarrr-kkee. Ss-p-aaarrr-kkee. Ss-p-aaarrr-kkee.

She calculates the risk is low enough because it's so close, and makes the flight, snatching the food t-raay-cee's got for her then darting to the perch. Standing there, the painful honking throbbing her ears, her chest constricted, her focus on this strange foreign territory, not t-raay-cee and their flying, hunter-her scans the surroundings with eyes and ears, searching for threats and opportunities. That's how she locates it; a white scurry, down there, scampering around for a hide-e-hole. She stretches up tall, eyes fixed on the mouse, waiting for it to move or stay still, gauging a pounce on it, predator soul awoken. But t-raay-cee bends over the prey, watching it, then stands in front of it, blocking it from Sparky's view. She steps along the perch, craning her neck to see the mouse, hunter's curiosity overriding survivor's caution now. The mouse stays hidden; she keeps watching. After a while of this t-raay-cee tugs Sparky onto its featherless wing and they return to her space.

That night Sparky's restless, darting about in her space. Now she has her other half, she's nearly her whole self again. If only there was always just them, no strange humans, no startling noises, no foreign territories; she could always fly to t-raay-cee then because she'd know they were safe. If they had that they could be a proper pair together, lifelong mates.

HHH

15/6
After two great days another disaster. Took her into the other half of corridor as workman was in ours again but guinea fowl spooked her. Then she spotted a mouse (think it had been poisoned as it didn't run away when I moved the bucket it scampered behind). That distraction plus noise and new setting meant she wouldn't fly so I had to give up!

But I can't, won't give up on her. We were always heading for this moment, life intended for us to meet. We'll stay together until we're sent our separate ways. But that isn't now.

Before

January–July 2019

OOO

D-aann-y-elll returns to her at last, grown taller and older than when it left her. But nothing else changes. They're still a pair, bonded for life. Sparky's distress disappears, she's contented again. They hunt together every day, outside when it's flying weather, in her space when it's not. This is Sparky's best life. It continues steadily, surviving another winter, blooming into another spring.

Then d-aann-y-elll vanishes again. But it returned to her before so it will now, just as summer always returns, no matter how bitter the winter. Sparky waits for her mate's return.

After several days it appears, at night, running towards her space, pressing against the criss-crossed lines and chattering to her.

HHH

Sorry for being away all over the Easter hols, Sparky, but Dad was getting married again so there was no way of getting out of that. It wasn't all bad though, yeah, weddings are lame but Daisy made up for it. She's a stunner, just like you. Can't wait for you to meet her, Sparky. She's going to visit when school breaks up.

OOO

A new human appears with d-aann-y-elll. Sparky studies it, noticing the red-brown head plumage hanging to the head ledges, the black body plumage but blue legs. Its feet are as white as her own breast feathers. D-aann-y-elll brings it into her space. Alarmed, reflexes fly Sparky to her perch; d-aann-y-elll doesn't let strangers invade their space. She side-steps to the end of the perch, edging away from them, looking behind at the ledge she could fly to if she needs more distance.

D-aann-y-elll raises its featherless wing.

Ss-p-aaarrr-kkee.

She hesitates. It's her mate, with food for her, doing what they always do together. But that stranger is beside it and there's no way for Sparky to know what it'll do if she flies near it.

Ss-p-aaarrr-kkee. Ss-p-aaarrr-kkee.

D-aann-y-elll steps in front of the new human, so it won't be easily able to attack her if she flies over.

She goes, landing flutteringly. D-aann-y-elll chatters to the new human, turning so Sparky faces it. Sparky hears her own call and another, that sounds like daay-zee, repeated in her mate's chattering. The new human flaps a wing at Sparky, saying her call then saying the daay-zee call: its call. It might be trying to bond with her and d-aann-y-elll. As they go to the perch on the grass Sparky observes its behaviour closely for signs of what it wants.

D-aann-y-elll and Sparky do their flying, hunting, feeding; daay-zee watches from nearby but it doesn't do anything threatening so Sparky relaxes. Her mate's here, it's protected her before from humans and she trusts it. So when daay-zee gets closer, until it's beside d-aann-y-elll, there's no reason for Sparky not to keep flying to her partner.

They've done several flights, Sparky's starting to feel full from eating all the prey d-aann-y-elll has caught for her. When she starts feeling full they stop flying. But today they don't; they fly on, d-aann-y-elll stepping to the edge of the grassy patch so Sparky has to fly as far as the tethering line lets her. Every time she lands on d-aann-y-elll's wing it faces her at daay-zee, chattering to it. Every times she lands on the perch, turning to d-aann-y-elll, she sees it and daay-zee preening each other with their wing toes and face holes.

This flight, as she lands and turns on the perch, she notices daay-zee covering its wing toes with that thick dark skin her talons don't pierce. D-aann-y-elll stands behind daay-zee, like they're tethered together. It raises its and daay-zee's featherless wings in unison, calling to her, a mouse wriggling in the wing toes.

If she wants that mouse she'll have to fly to this stranger, that her human is acting like its bonded with. But d-aann-y-elll is her other half, they're already a pair. She needs to go to it, show it she's still its mate, reminding it of their lifelong bond: theirs is the only pairing.

She lands with a wobble as daay-zee's featherless wing bobs beneath her. It lets out a slight squeal but stands still enough for her to find the mouse and start eating, watching her mate in between eye-closing gulps. D-aann-y-elll comes around from behind daay-zee, standing facing Sparky. She finishes the mouse, tail slipping down last.

She's already eaten a lot today. The mouse fills her up. Now she needs to empty herself. So she does, hunching forward, squatting down and squirting out.

Daay-zee screeches. Sparky's thrown off its wing perch, flying out of the fall, up and away from the screeching, heading skyward, going until the line's pull halts her. She flaps hard, holding herself in mid-air for a wing-aching moment before having to sink down.

She's beyond the grassy patch, on hard, grey ground, her feet splayed uncomfortably on the flat surface; she can't curl her toes, grip with her talons: perch. It's not where she'd choose to stand. She searches for d-aann-y-elll.

It's away over there, with daay-zee. They're chattering and flapping their featherless wings, pointing, looking at daay-zee's leg and foot. The blue plumage has a streak of whitey-yellow down it and a brown dropping has splattered onto the white foot. Still squawking, daay-zee darts away.

D-aann-y-elll calls after it but it doesn't return. Sparky calls to d-aann-y-elll, her raspy croaking call. Her mate turns to her now. Its face is puckered around the eyes and face hole; she senses darkness in it. Her mate makes a short, sharp noise, ff-u-kk, then comes to her, tugs on the skin strips, dragging her up to it, taking her to her space, chattering harshly as it does. She's thrown inside, scrambling into a falling flight, landing on the ground. When she turns, d-aann-y-elll is chasing after daay-zee.

HHH

Bloody hell, Sparky, thanks a lot. After I told Daisy how great you are you go and do that! You've ruined everything. You better hope she forgives you or else.

Stupid bloody owl.

Now

June 2022 (cont.)

HHH

I tell a friend I'm teaching a barn owl to fly. He asks why can't it fly. I realise how little people know about captive birds of prey, despite the fascination with them, and how much I've learnt, got still to learn, for Sparky's sake.

Falconry books say birds of prey, unlike dogs, have no loyalty to, or love for, their human companions. They fly to you because you've got food and you've kept them hungry enough to risk landing on your fist, taking their eyes off you to eat. They tolerate you because they've been trained to. But imprinted birds are different. The layman's understanding is that, having been reared by a person, they think they're human so readily bond with people. But, reflecting on Sparky and me, that's an oversimplification. She's aware of herself, all living beings are, and that wordless sense of 'I, Sparky' must mean she knows I'm not the same as her. I'm external to her, different from her, but shared experiences, like flying together, bond us. It's a unique relationship, crossing the species barrier. Her human-rearing means she's familiar with people but not fearless of them; I've still had to win her trust.

Falconry books don't say what animals birds of prey are like but I find a useful, to me obvious, comparison between owls and cats. Both obligate carnivores, skilled nocturnal hunters with excellent night vision and hearing; naturally solitary and quick to become mistrustful of humans if their bond with people is broken; both fight by rolling onto their backs and striking with their claws. Forward facing eyes give them humanlike appearances so they're both embedded in myth, linked to the sinister and magic. For good reason the owl and the pussy cat go to sea together. Cats are flightless owls; owls are winged felines. Viewed this way Sparky is a familiar, I just need an owl's eye view of the world and we'll be O.K. together.

I try to be hopeful, not my usual outlook; Sparky is flying to me more reliably, coming further, hesitating less. Are we finally becoming friends?

OOO

Sparky needs stability, routine, to be confident flying with her new human; she does what little she can herself to make each different day the same. She waits for t-raay-cee on the high ledge at the rear of her space. When it enters her space, Sparky goes to the perch. There she waits for the featherless wing to be raised, which it is as soon as she's landed. She hops to it so she and her mate are together, united: whole.

That's all Sparky can do to make life for herself and her mate reassuringly routine. T-raay-cee does what it can too; it also wants them to have a stable life. So it always starts by balancing Sparky on the short, slightly wobbly, perch it brings with it, offering her wriggling prey. Then they go together into their narrow territory where it takes Sparky to the flying perch before walking away facing her, watching her as she watches it, both anticipating the moment when it's walked far enough.

Ss-p-aaarrr-kkee.

Then they fly and hunt together. If nothing disturbs them, Sparky flies unhesitatingly to t-raay-cee, wanting them to be together. Their bond solidifies. Sparky knows they're each other's mate: a pair.

Before

July–September, 2019

OOO

Life starts changing for Sparky.

Some days she and d-aann-y-elll hunt together on the grassy patch like they should. Some days, even when it's flying weather, d-aann-y-elll just comes to her space, sending a chick or mouse towards her but not calling her to fly to its featherless wing. Sparky follows the prey with her bright eyes, sharp ears and silent wings, pouncing on it, taking her catch to the ledge. When she looks up after eating d-aann-y-elll is crossing the ground to its own space on the legs that are still growing. There are more days when her mate does this; fewer days when they do their flying, hunting, feeding together like a pair should.

Then there are some days d-aann-y-elll doesn't come at all. M-uuu-m comes instead, into her space, letting her fly to it for food, always, last of all, a mouse. On a few occasions, when she hasn't been hunting outside with d-aann-y-elll for a long while, m-uuu-m takes her and they fly together. Sparky does it, but half-heartedly; it's not flying with her true mate.

Whenever d-aann-y-elll appears from its space, her ears and eyes lock onto it and she flies to hang on the criss-crossed lines, watching and listening for it to come to her; seeing and hearing it go away from her.

Spring becomes early summer, then midsummer, then early autumn. Fluffy light down, sprinkled like snow, and stiff white and tan leaves drop from her, littering her space because d-aann-y-elll doesn't come to claw them away. Discarded feathers cover droppings and pellets to be covered with more droppings and pellets then more feathers. As she waits for d-aann-y-elll to come, new feathers grow. She preens and bathes, when there's water in the pool, preens again, coaxing fresh plumage into a smooth cloak, keeping herself in flying order for when her mate returns and they fly together. It's always returned to her before. But when it does come, after clawing away her old feathers and raining water that dissolves droppings and pellets, it doesn't take her outside to hunt. She races across her space to it, landing on a head ledge as it's leaving. It walks her to the perch, nudging her onto it, walks away. She chases it down again. It chatters stiffly, sharply, pushing her off its head ledge and slipping outside as she tumbles into a clumsy flight-fall, bumping to the ground, righting herself just to see it leaving her.

HHH

Stop it, get off, Sparky. I've got better things to do than mess about with you. If

Mum's so worried about you, she can bloody look after you. Not like she's got a social life. It's her fault for getting you, anyway. What kind of dumb parent gets their kid an owl? She should've known I'd get sick of you. Now she's nagging me all the time about you. Why don't you do us both a favour and fly off?

OOO

Days pass, each shorter and cooler than the previous. D-aann-y-elll comes to her at last. Sparky stays on the ledge in her space, listening for it to call her so she knows it wants her to fly to it. Too many times this summer it's flapped her away when she's flown to it; it doesn't always want her to be with it now, even though they're still each others' whole-half.

Ss-p-aaarrr-kkee.

She launches towards it, energy surging through her as it takes her outside. Seeing the perch, she sprints to it, getting there so she can fly to d-aann-y-elll as soon as it calls her, while it's here with her, being her mate. But as she flies she feels a lightness, a dragging weight gone. Landing on the perch she raises a foot, inspecting; the skin strips that dangle from her ankles are there, as always, but not the shiny ring thing that joins her to the line which tethers her to the ground. She's untethered. A memory, faint as a shadow on a cloudy day, fades through her.

Ss-p-aaarrr-kkee.

D-aann-y-elll's raised its wing. The memory drifts away. She flies to her mate, a feeling of floaty freeness buoying her through the air to her other half and the prey it's trapped for her. When it points her at the perch again she launches herself, not waiting for the nudge d-aann-y-elll gives her; she doesn't need that extra lift now she has this lightness to her flight, this freedom.

Ss-p-aaarrr-kkee.

She takes off, springing skywards with her usual force, beating her wings as hard as she's learned she needs to, finding herself propelled further than ever, looking down at her territory from higher than she's reached before, swooping towards d-aann-y-elll in a wide arc, flying over her territorial boundaries on the way, thrilled by the liberty of nothing to stall her flight: nothing to ground her. She can go as far as she wants from her mate for the satisfaction of returning to it. She lands on d-aann-y-elll's wing, eats and takes off again.

This flight she arcs around that way, towards and over her space, looking down on it, beyond it, into the neighbouring territory. It too has a grassy patch but no perch. Dipping a wing, she pitches her flight back towards her own territory, where d-aann-y-elll is, going to her perch, waiting there for her call, revelling in this wild free hunting, saving them just as their bond was beginning to splinter like a dead tree.

They fly several flights, Sparky going higher, wider, circling their territory, patrolling it, feeling freeness and lightness filling her but never straying further from d-aann-y-elll than she can fly back to it.

Ss-p-aaarrr-kkee.

D-aann-y-elll has a white mouse for her. After the mouse she'll be taken to her space so she makes this hunting flight as high and far as possible without leaving her territory, flying past d-aann-y-elll, towards its space, there turning, swooping, gliding behind d-aann-y-elll, coming to it from above the opposite edge of her territory, diving down to catch the mouse.

Clutching the prey, she gasps at air, cooling the burning in her chest, too breathless to eat. She can eat in her space. But d-aann-y-elll just chatters to her then pushes her towards the perch. Sparky wing-beats into a stuttering flight, still clutching the mouse in her foot as she gains height, swooping to the perch, landing awkwardly, dropping the mouse. She flaps down to recover it, leaping up to the perch with it, looking for d-aann-y-elll as she does.

It's running away from her, heading for its space. She chases after it. But it vanishes through the in/out before she catches up, her wings heavy, slowed by all their high, far flying together. She drops to the hard grey ground, staring up at the huge structure where d-aann-y-elll and m-uuu-m roost, scanning the white in/out and the shiny reflective squares for a way inside. She hovers upwards, tries to perch on the in/out but it's slippery and smooth, her talons slide off, she fly-falls to the ground. There is a narrow ledge, though, below each shiny reflective square, so she flaps up to the nearest.

The ledge is so narrow her beak bumps the shiny reflective square. But this close she realises it's not shiny or reflective. She can see through it as clearly as air, as water, like it's not there. Except it is; she taps it, hearing the sharp spiky tip-tip-tipping of her beak against it. A memory, of a frosty winter dawn, seeing through and standing on frozen water in her pool, drifts to her.

Leaning back so her beak isn't tip-tipping against it, she looks through the expanse of ice rising up in front of her like a cliff face. Sees d-aann-y-elll behind it. She calls an urgent screech. Her mate turns, gapes at her, its eyes unblinking, face hole open. Then it flaps its featherless wings at her and chatters, the sounds muted, as though buried. Even with ears straining, she can't pick patterns from the chatter clearly, can't hear if her human's giving her call. The ice dulls noise like clouds dull light. She hisses her raspy croaking call anyway; it's all she can do. Her mate comes close to its side of the ice. But the solid ice stops it reaching her. It raises its featherless wings, the toes curled into themselves, strikes the expanse of ice with them. The noise is a thunderous banging that shudders the ice and judders into Sparky, alarming her into a brief hovering flight.

When she flutters back to the ledge her mate's vanished from view.

Sparky doesn't know what to do now. She could wait here for d-aann-y-elll to reappear. She could fly to the perch on the grass or to her space. She waits on the narrow ledge until her legs tremble, then on the ground until her splayed feet ache. D-aann-y-elll doesn't reappear.

She flies to the perch on the grassy patch, keeps watching for d-aann-y-elll. The sun drifts towards the horizon. She alternates watching for d-aann-y-elll and glancing around her territory. Her space is near but the in/out is closed. Normally by now she'd be inside on the ledge, resting. She eats the mouse, forgotten when d-aann-y-elll left her. Then she flies to her space, hanging on the closed in/out, looking at where she should be. But her legs start to quiver after a while of tight gripping. She returns to the perch, eyes and ears trained on her humans' roosting space, the shiny squares that she now knows are ice; solid but see-through, her mate unreachable behind them. She could fly across again…

The wind gets stronger, buffeting her, ruffling her plumage uncomfortably. A gust strikes her, sidestepping her along the perch, nearly off the end of it. She shuffles back to the middle. Rain mists down, the wind swirling it around her, wrapping her in it. She's coldly wet, like when she first hatched. With sodden feathers she can't fly to shelter, has to stay on the perch. She huddles into herself.

The rain thickens, the day darkening to night well before sunset. Her ears catch a distant click. She faces the sound, sees d-aann-y-elll reappearing, at last. When it reaches her, it raises its featherless wing. She steps shakily up as it chatters to her, the sharp piercing chatter she hears from it more and more. It takes her to her space, sending her flying through the in/out. But her rain-heavy plumage drags her downward. Wing-beating urgently, she tumbles to the ground, scrambles upright, turns. D-aann-y-elll is already leaving her again. She shakes water from her feathers, tries to launch herself to the ledge. Flops to the ground. Trudges to the low branches perch, climbing into it, sheltering among its twisted limbs.

HHH

Stupid owl, you didn't fly away. Don't you realise you're not wanted anymore? Why couldn't you just piss off while Mum was at work? Serves you right if you freeze to death. Whatever happens to you now it's your own fault. You had the chance to go and didn't. Bloody stupid owl.

Now

16th June 2022

HHH

As I'm daring to hope we have a future flying together I'm told Sparky's leaving the animal centre, the director hunting me down while I'm in her aviary, weighing her as part of our pre-flight routine.

I'm outwardly calm as I listen to him, inwardly fighting the storm threatening to overwhelm me. He's lying; I don't want him realising I know that. Handily he doesn't know much about me, including how well I remember the stories people tell me. My nan always said good liars need good memories; he's forgetful so, consequently, a terrible liar. What he's telling me now doesn't match what he's told me previously—that Sparky ended up here because her owners, ignorant about imprint behaviour, thought she was attacking them. I play along, nodding, saying, 'Oh, O.K., I didn't realise,' letting him shovel his hole neck-deep. When he leaves I need a moment to gather myself before calling Sparky to me.

Calmer, I get her on my fist, fingers fumbling as I hold her jesses, adrenalin shaking through me. Out in the corridor we fly together, me hoping she can't sense the nightmare thoughts mobbing me. Before leaving I photograph her leg ring number.

OOO

Today Sparky comes down from the ledge onto the perch then up to t-raay-cee's featherless wing. Everything's normal. Now they'll go out into the narrow gap and…

Shrivelled human appears outside Sparky's space. Sparky recognises its wizened, lifeless appearance and crackly chattering because it's tethered in her memory with being in the fliers' space, when she was threatened by keee-w-ickk and ss-kk-reee fliers. She doesn't trust shrivelled human so flap-jumps away to the high ledge, flying almost vertically to escape.

From there she watches over t-raay-cee and shrivelled human. They each stand on their own sides of the criss-crossed lines at the front of her space. T-raay-cee is on Sparky's side, where it stays, chattering to shrivelled human who chatters back for a short moment then leaves.

Sparky waits until she's heard its footsteps retreating along the narrow gap. Then she flies to t-raay-cee's featherless wing. They'll go out and fly now, as long as she sees and hears it's safe.

Outside, Sparky perches for a while, looking and listening, eyes searching the furthest limits of her territory, ears searching beyond it, for signs shrivelled human is returning. Only when she can't detect and sight or sound of it is she reassured enough for them to fly.

They get several steady flights together then a noise from outside catches her scanning ears, hyper-alert for threats after shrivelled human's appearance. Sparky has to stay on her perch, even though t-raay-cee is calling her to it, until she's heard the sound leave. Then she can relax enough to fly again, knowing the danger has past.

Before

September 2019

OOO

Sparky keeps watch for d-aann-y-elll. Mostly it appears but doesn't come to her. She hangs on the lines at the front, calling out to the other half of herself; she can't let go of it, even though it's abandoning her day by day.

M-uuu-m starts coming to her space every night. Sparky flies to its featherless wing; she trusts m-uuu-m but it's not d-aann-y-elll, not her mate. M-uuu-m balances her on the low wobbly perch, lets her fly to its featherless wing, fills her water pool, clears droppings and feathers from the ground of her space, feeds her, even flies with her outside some nights. Always it chatters to her. Sparky listens, head tilted, collecting m-uuu-m's chatter, especially when she hears her own call in amongst the other sounds. This becomes her new life, her and m-uuu-m: without d-aann-y-elll.

HHH

So sorry about Daniel, Sparky. I've tried talking to him but he won't listen. I don't know what to do with him. I never thought he'd be like this. It's all my fault. You don't deserve this. You deserve to be with someone who wants you: loves you. I promise I'll find you that someone.

OOO

Sparky only sees d-aann-y-elll on the far side of their territory now. It's grown a lot, is taller than m-uuu-m. It doesn't fit in her space anymore.

M-uuu-m still fits, it comes to her and they do what they've been doing since d-aann-y-elll stopped coming, a new but similar routine of flying, hunting, feeding. Sparky feels the strengthening of her bond with m-uuu-m; she's known it for so long that she accepts it readily. Gradually the loss of her mate heals; m-uuu-m becomes her mate.

The nights lengthen; it's dark when m-uuu-m comes so they fly inside her space. Tonight, after they've flown, when Sparky's caught the mouse and swooped to her ledge to eat, instead of leaving, m-uuu-m stays, chattering and watching her. Sparky opens her wings to hide her meal, eating it head first. As the tail wriggles down her throat she hears her call, turns to m-uuu-m. Raindrops trickle from its eyes. Sparky follows a drop as it falls from m-uuu-m's face, vanishing into the ground. A snff-snff noise comes from its unbeak. Sparky studies m-uuu-m closely; the pale blue eyes have a swollen soreness and more rain drips from them.

Then m-uuu-m holds its featherless wing out, another mouse clutched in the wing toes. She's not hungry but hunter-her knows to take food when she can; she'll stash it for later. Sparky flaps over to m-uuu-m, feet grabbing the extra meal as m-uuu-m points her at the ledge, letting her take the offering there. From her favoured spot on the ledge, Sparky notices m-uuu-m is outside now, walking towards its own space. It doesn't look back at Sparky like it always does when it leaves her space. It just shuffles, slowly, across the ground, head low, body trembling.

HHH

Sparky, bright little Sparky, your last meal here so you deserve a feast. There you go. So much for promising I wouldn't cry.

Don't worry, you're going to a great home. Matthew's a lovely lad, he'll look after you properly. He's worked in a bird of prey centre for six years so he's a proper falconer, knows what he's doing, not like me. Now he's setting up on his own, already has a tawny owl, a harris hawk and a peregrine falcon but I know you'll be the star of the show. You'll finally get to fly properly. You'll be better off with Matthew, Sparky.

OOO

The day dawns grey and heavy. Sparky kept the extra mouse on her ledge last night, is just swallowing it when she hears humans approaching. She flies to the lines. Is it d-aann-y-elll?

It's m-uuu-m. And a new strange human, taller than even d-aann-y-elll, with golden curly head plumage and dark green-brown body plumage. The stranger carries a box.

They enter her space. Sparky goes to her ledge, putting what distance she can between her and this stranger. Body rigid, nerves twitching, she studies the stranger for threatening behaviour. It's so tall it seems to fill her space, has to stand with its body folded like she folds her wings if there isn't space to open them.

The stranger puts the box down. M-uuu-m comes to Sparky, holding up the featherless wing for her to step to. But something different is happening. This isn't the routine she knows and trusts so she doesn't step to it. M-uuu-m reaches out, tugging Sparky by the skin strips until she's on its wing perch.

Slowly m-uuu-m walks them to the stranger who bends forward, chattering to Sparky with a deep, soft rumbling. Its head is too near to hers. She looks into its brown eyes. It looks back into hers, brings a wing toe to Sparky's face. She pecks at it, a speck of red welling up. The stranger doesn't flinch, just keeps chattering, low and steady, as it touches her chest, legs and feet, turning the ring around her ankle that she's so used to she'd forgotten. Next the stranger unfolds her wings, rippling feathers. A jittery trembling inside Sparky urges her to flee. She tries to flap but her wings are held too strongly. The stranger lets go, stepping away. Sparky flaps again, her wings beating now as she jumps up only to be jolted down;

m-uuu-m has trapped her. She calls out raspily, foot-jerking, trying to pull herself free as m-uuu-m stretches out its featherless wing to the stranger. Sparky finds herself lifted up, forced to perch on this new human's wing toes. She looks to m-uuu-m.

Raindrops trickle down its face. It meets her eyes, quickly glances away, staring at the ground. Rain drips off its unbeak.

The ground rushes up to Sparky as the stranger crouches. She's pushed into dimness inside the box. Swivelling her head, she finds no way out.

The box rises, bob-floats through the air, a swinging feel to the motion. There's distant familiarity to this. Through small neat holes in the box's sides she watches her space retreating, then her territory, the perch where she flew with her mate, the huge structure her humans roost in; it all falls away behind her as, up ahead, a moving growler comes into view.

Sparky huddles at the rear of the box, toes curled, talons pricking the furry ground, legs straining to keep her standing steady as the box swings gently towards the moving growler.

The swinging stops. Her leg muscles relax. A bang, and another bang, shudder through her. She's been swallowed again, inside this box, by the growling mover. She head-shakes, pecking around her ankles, tapping the box's sides, opening her wings to feel feathers bending, the space closed in around her. She calls out to m-uuu-m, for its protection.

But the growling noise smoothers her calls. The box jolts forwards, she's stumbled off her feet as outside movement shakes her from wingtip to wingtip. The growling motion seeps into her. She's been here before. She doesn't know where she's going next.

HHH

Who gets a kid a barn owl? Christ knows how they didn't kill you, Sparky. Little sod didn't even come to say 'bye to you. The mum was pretty upset and so she should be, should've known he'd get sick of you.

But all good now. Have you home ASAP, kiddo. Onwards and upward.

Now

16th June 2022 (cont.)

HHH

On the drive home I pick over the director's new Sparky story, a hunter ripping apart a fresh kill. She was, is, from a major tourist attraction down south, he said, one with a large animal collection. Her aviary was damaged in a storm last winter and they had nowhere to house her so sent her all the way up here because they know him. The story's holes gape at me, a mouth with teeth punched out. Why would such an established, successful attraction need to send one barn owl to be accommodated off site? Surely they had somewhere they could house her temporarily. If not, why send her such a long way? They must have contacts closer to home that could've helped. If I believe him, the centre director was an animal keeper there but even so… And where was Sparky for the four months after her aviary was damaged but before she arrived here? Certainly this major tourist attraction isn't the previous owner the director described, the person who surrendered Sparky because they mistook her imprinted friendliness for aggression, so at least one, probably both, of these tales is a lie.

If Sparky's story was a novel I'd berate the writer for concocting such a implausible plot, one that readers would tear apart in disgruntled one-star reviews. Clearly Sparky isn't going where I've been told because, clearly, she didn't come from there. So where is she going? Why is the centre director lying about it unless something dodgy's happening, maybe even something illegal? Whatever, I can only deduce it's wrong for Sparky or he'd not have lied. I resolve to investigate, see if I can challenge the lie, save Sparky from whatever shady fate is lined up for her.

This is the dramatic climax, rising like a mountain, out of my spiralling concerns that this centre isn't the safe sanctuary for animals in need that I'd assumed it was. It's more like Joe Exotic's caged collection than Noah's rescuing ark.

When I get home I contact the falconer; now I'm desperate enough to ask, beg, a favour. I tell him the latest Sparky tale. Birds of prey are his livelihood, his life; he knows that world and agrees that what I've been told is cockerel-and-bullfinch, which makes me feel less like a paranoid conspiracist but even more anxious for Sparky. He suggests I contact the IBR where Sparky's leg ring is registered, to see if they have any information about her that might help. He also says, with overwhelming generosity, that if I can get the centre to hand Sparky to me he'll help me with caring for her. That's the good news. The bad, awful, news is that I'll have to expose the lie before I'd have any grounds for asking to adopt Sparky myself. To do that I have to gamble on letting this play out, potentially staking Sparky's life.

Before

September–November 2019

OOO

When the growling and moving finally stopped, Sparky felt the box rising up, bob-floating along. She stayed hunched into herself at the rear where threats could only come at her face to face. But no threats came.

The strange new human took her into a large, cool, dim structure. She couldn't see much through the neat tiny holes in the box but she heard plenty; chirps, shrieks, caws. They passed into these sounds which settled around her, finding their place in her auditory map of the surroundings, as the box was lowered. When it opened, she was looking up at the stranger crouching in front of her. Behind it, she saw a space like hers but much larger. The stranger chattered briefly then put a pair of mice on the ground close to her, nudging them towards her: an offering. It stood, only its muted leg plumage and dark toeless feet visible. Sparky listened to and watched it walking away.

HHH

There you go, kiddo, lunch. I'll let you settle in. Check you tomorrow.

OOO

Now she's on her own. The chirps, shrieks and caws quieten. She risks a quick lunge forward into the dim light outside the box, snatching a mouse, retreating inside to eat. Her immediate need to secure a meal, to survive, met, she edges forward again, grabbing the other mouse and stashing it in the box. She can satisfy her hunter's curiosity and venture out now she has a hide-e-hole with stashed food to dart to if she's attacked.

Standing at the box's in/out, ears scanning further afield for anything approaching, Sparky regards the space around her, eyes gathering details, mind mapping. There's a long, tall perch in the middle, a large water pool over there, a thick branch perch hanging from above over here. She shuffles forwards, drawn out by the amount of space, reckoning the many wing-beats she'll need to cross it, more than in any of her before spaces. She leaps up, finding enough air to circle the space. She swoops this way, that way, lands on the tall perch, takes off, gliding around again, landing on the hanging branch perch which sways as if breeze blown.

Her balance steadying, Sparky cranes her neck. Overhead is a patch of sky, lines scored across it. She sprints up, finding the lines are set into the top of the space so she can see, but not fly, out. She spirals downward, noticing now a box high up at the rear of the space. It has a Sparky-sized hole in the front of it, a short perch beneath the hole. She lands there, poking her head inside: empty. She hops into the box, stretches out her wings. They just touch the dark sides. This is a better roost than the box on the ground. She retrieves her stashed meal and returns to this high-up roosting box, settling into its sheltering darkness, securely surveying this new space through the hole.

She has a safe roost, perches to fly to, water for bathing, food. It's not her space with her mate but it's enough like her space and the differences are improvements; she could be contented here. Maybe the strange human will be enough like m-uuu-m, like d-aann-y-elll was, that she can pair, be contented, with it.

It's night. A call, collected by her heart-shaped face, funnelled into her precisely attuned ears, wakes Sparky.

Keee-w-ickk.

Ears tracking the call, eyes piercing the darkness, she flies to the tall perch, hunting the caller.

Opposite, separated from her space by a gap, there's another set of criss-crossed lines. The keee-w-ickk call came from behind those lines. Sparky's eyes catch a glimmer of movement in the darkness.

The glimmering movement flashes sharply.

Keee-w-ickk.

Out of the darkness of its space, the caller flies to its criss-crossed lines, grabs hold and hangs there, looking out: looking at her. Inquisitive, Sparky swoops to her criss-crosseds, reflecting the keee-w-ickk caller's pose.

She gives her soft raspy screech. It returns with another keee-w-ickk. Hanging onto the lines with their hooked talons, wings outstretched, they stare at each other with forward facing eyes set in flat, round faces: each other's likeness. Except for their plumage; the keee-w-ickk caller's is darkly speckled where Sparky's glows whitely.

They're both fliers. The keee-w-ickk flier is more like Sparky than any flier she's seen before. They're the same, not in every feather, but they share a shadow. She feels its similarities in herself, recognises her differences in it, the innate awareness she lives by, survives by, confirming they're both of a kind.

Keee-w-ickk pushes off, disappearing into the darkness of its space. Sparky stays another moment, then she flies off too, turning in the air, lapping her space before scrambling into the box to roost.

Ss-p-aaarrr-kkee.

At the sound of her call, Sparky pokes her head out through the hole and into the brighter morning light. The stranger's in her space, holding up its featherless wing to her, prey wriggling there. She's not hungry and doesn't know if it's safe to go to this human so she doesn't.

It climbs closer. She darts inside the box only for the whole front of it to open, the stranger reaching in for her, standing her on its wing toes as they climb down, leave her space and go into the gap.

Sparky glances at where the keee-w-ickk flier appeared last night. It's on its perch now, calls out, stopping them. The new human chatters briefly, Sparky's call mixed with other sounds.

HHH

Sparky, meet Della the tawny. Della, this is Sparky, newest recruit to Matthew's Bird of Prey Days, the soon-to-be, must-see attraction at country shows across the UK. Be nice to her, eh? I'll introduce you to Reggie I. Peregrine and Keith Harris-Hawk later, Sparky. Just gotta get your weight then we can see about training you up, eh?

OOO

Life unfurls for Sparky. She has a new routine, a new space, new territory and a new mate: matt-ee.

It comes to her every day, taking her to balance on a short bobbing perch, then back into her space where it does the raining and clawing that clears her space of droppings, feathers and pellets. Afterwards it goes into keee-w-ickk's space, emerging with keee-w-ickk flier so Sparky gets to see the balancing on the bobbing perch, which is on a flat surface, standing on legs, in the gap between her space and keee-w-ickk's. She also gets to watch the raining and clawing happening in keee-w-ickk's space.

Then matt-ee passes again with other fliers, a dark brown and a blue-grey, perched on its featherless wing. These are less like Sparky and keee-w-ickk, bigger with more pointed faces, eyes on either side of their heads. Their beaks and feet are heftier, for killing bigger prey; Sparky knows they're her foe. They stare into her space, jumping up, trying to attack her. At first she flees to the box but when she realises they can't get her Sparky stays on her perch, returning their menacing stares.

After all this matt-ee comes to her and they go outside to her new territory where there's a tall perch in the middle of a grassy patch and they fly, hunt and feed together, like she did with m-uuu-m and d-aann-y-elll except there's more sky for her to fly through and she flies higher, further, than she used to before she feels the pull on her legs that warns her she's flown as high and far as the tethering line lets her. This is how she and matt-ee learn each other's ways, recognising each other by sight and call, until they're comfortable together, bonded: completing each other. Sparky finds reassuring confidence in matt-ee; this new mate understands her instinctively: naturally. It's more her kin than m-uuu-m and d-aann-y-elll were. Sparky and matt-ee establish themselves as a pair quickly.

This is her new life. She is contented.

Now

17th June 2022

HHH

Heart drumming, stomach squirming and hands trembling as anxiety rushes through me, I ring the IBR. It's a small organisation and the lady who answers my call is the person the falconer said I'd probably speak to. He also said he wasn't sure how much she'd be prepared to tell me. I give her Sparky's leg ring number and ask if she knows anything about this barn owl. Not unreasonably she asks why I'm enquiring. I'm suddenly a contestant on a nightmare quiz show, with only seconds to give the correct response and Sparky's safety depends on my answer. I tell her everything, pouring out the various conflicting stories I've been told about Sparky, where she came from, is supposedly going, explaining I fear something underhand is happening. Why else would I be lied to? I ask her, hoping the question prompts her to agree with me. I fight for coherent; sink into gibberish. Thankfully, she takes what I say seriously; sadly she's heard too many stories of wrongdoing involving birds and she's on the birds' side, always. She tells me what she can.

Sparky's five years old, hatched 5th August, 2017, female, as the falconer said, and legitimately in captivity, bred from captive-born parents. The IBR have the breeder's details, they lodged the leg ring number with the IBR, and the contact details of who they sold Sparky to but data protection means the IBR can't tell me that; they can tell me she wasn't bought initially by the tourist attraction she's supposedly returning to although she could have been sold to them later. I'm as certain as I need to be that she wasn't. After that, Sparky vanishes. Until now: my call is the only report of her for five years. Sparky's first owner didn't keep up her registration.

The IBR can tell me that Sparky originally had the legally required Article 10 paperwork but it's expired. Like a car's log book, each new keeper has to apply for the A10 in their name and that hasn't happened. If I adopt Sparky, they can help me to get her A10 reinstated so I'll be her legal guardian.

If, I think, if only…

Before

November 2019–March 2020

OOO

Today matt-ee and Sparky left their home territory in the moving growler. Her mate was with her so Sparky was calmly curious at this new happening. The growling and moving lasted only a short while. When it stopped matt-ee took Sparky from the box she'd been in, letting her step to its featherless wing before they walked a little way from the moving growler to where they stand now.

Ahead of Sparky lies a vast field: her natural hunting ground. The trees bordering it are so distant they appear no taller than dandelions. The sky overhead sweeps away endlessly. Sparky holding onto her mate, matt-ee walks them deep into the field, where it plants the tall perch it carries in its other featherless wing. Then it retreats from the perch. Sparky leaps from matt-ee's hide-covered wing toes so they can start flying and hunting together, in their new territory, but is jolted out of flight.

Chattering, matt-ee pecks around her ankles, its wing toes attaching a tiny black object with a long bendy tail to her leg. Sparky kicks up that leg, feeling this new weight. Uncertain, she pecks at it.

HHH

Soz, kiddo, but you need a tracker on if you're gonna fly free. Don't reckon you'll nick off but gotta remember the golden rule of working with birds: they can fly better than you. Now, it's a bit blustery today so watch out.

OOO

Matt-ee raises its featherless wing, lifting Sparky skyward. Now they're ready to fly.

Wind ripples her plumage, blowing into her face: a flying wind. Forgetting the new weight around her ankle, she opens her wings. Gusts eddy beneath them. With the slightest hop, she's airborne, flying with the lightness of free-floating that's faintly familiar, recalling d-aann-y-elll. There's no dragging heaviness, her flight's buoyant, gravity disowning her. Sparky glides and swoops with easy wing-beats, sweeping herself higher, looking down from far up, the sky surrounding her, nothing pulling her groundwards. She's free to fly, flying free. She exalts in the feeling.

Matt-ee is far below her, shortened by her tree-tall view of it. A current swirls up underneath her, pushing her even further from her mate. Sparky lets this wind sweep her along, wings silently stroking invisible flying air, eyes and ears hunting the ground. The further from her mate she goes, the further she will return from, reaffirming their bond.

But as suddenly as it swelled, the current ebbs; Sparky plunges, wing-beating faster, hauling herself up, levelling off her flight. New wind pushes her aside, tilting her so this wing points groundwards, that wing at clouds. Now she fights, inborn instinct urging her to defend her place in the sky. She angles wings and tail, flexes muscle, finds herself turned again by wind stronger than her. Looking out and down, land and sky endlessly flee from her in all directions, she an aerial speck speeding through it, her mate a grounded speck static in it, awaiting her return. She heads towards matt-ee.

The wind snatches at her again, blowing her off her flying course. She flaps fiercely, facing where she wants to go, body not following, swirling air funnelling her its way. Every wing-beat is harder than the previous; heavier, sludgier, weaker. Her chest is crushed; she breathes in gasps, surrendering to the gust, letting it down her with a jolt, feet hitting the earth as though it's giant prey.

In her tumbling fall Sparky loses her way back to matt-ee. She treads around on the spot, scanning the field which rolls onward then rises up, limiting her view. Unable to see her mate she listens for it.

A harsh cawing from overhead explodes in her ears. Sparky raises her gaze. Black fliers, many of them, circle above. They call harsh threats to her.

Body stiffened, reflexes sharpened, Sparky readies to flee, tuning in her hearing, collecting up and filtering out sounds, searching for the call that'll tell her where to go.

Ss-p-aaarrr-kkee.

The black fliers still circle, their primary feathers raggedly scraping the soft blue, their caws scratching at her ears.

Ss-p-aaarrr-kkee.

Her other half's calling her.

Ss-p-aaarrr-kkee.

She locates it: over there. Her breathing slowed now, she pushes into a flurried flight, rising up but staying beneath the circling, cawing black fliers, beating laboriously towards her mate, ears guiding her.

Matt-ee comes into view, in the middle of the field, holding out its featherless wing, repeating her call as she nears it.

Feet in front, talons primed to grip, Sparky brings her body from flying to standing, wings fluttering rapid, stuttering beats that hover her back to her other half. Her mate chatters as she eats the prey it's got for her.

Above the black fliers disperse.

HHH

Wind caught you out there, eh, kiddo? It's all good though; the best way for you to learn how to use wind is fly in it. And we now know you need to work on stamina. Don't worry, we'll soon have you flying fit, Sparky. At least you've proved you're bright, for a barn owl, coming to the call like that from out of sight. Reckon we'll make that our show-stopper, eh? We'll be an awesome bird display team, the five of us; you'll be the headline act.

OOO

Most of Sparky and matt-ee's flying is out over the vast field now. That means going in the growling mover but it also means soaring free, as far and wide as she can. Sparky swoops and glides, landing on and launching from the tall perch or matt-ee's featherless wing, circling the sky on swift silent wings. Some flying days the sky's white-blue, the light sharp and clear, the air frozen. Others it's grey, the light dull, the air damp. But whatever the day she flies further, higher, her chest cool and her wings lightweight, energy humming through her. However far she flies, she always returns to matt-ee, their bond invisibly tethering them together.

Sparky's circling high in sky paler than her breast feathers, far from matt-ee but knowing where it is, her return route mentally mapped, when a few white downy flakes appear, floating around her. More emerge from the white-weighted air, settling on her back, wings and head, weightless iciness soaking through her, vanishing softly among her feathers: snow. She's seen it, seasons ago, tumbling from the sky, blowing into her before space. She even walked on it when it covered her before flying ground. But she's never flown through it. Now she's surrounded by tiny fluffy clumps, they flock the air, blurring her sight. Feeling the snow's freezing touch, she looks to matt-ee; it's clouded in swirling whiteness, its outline hazy: fading.

Ss-p-aaarrr-kkee. Ss-p-aaarrr-kkee.

The call is louder that usual, repeating before it's finished: alarmed. Matt-ee wants her back now. Wings sodden, she floats downward, the weight of ice-white wetness sinking her as her ears search urgently through dense, sleet-bleached air.

Ss-p-aaarrr-kkee. Ss-p-aaarrr-kkee.

She tracks the call; matt-ee comes into view, its featherless wing raised for her. She dives towards it clumsily, soggy feathers stumbling her flight. Matt-ee chatters to her, tugging at her ankles while running through the whitening world.

HHH

Soz, kiddo, this wasn't forecast. Soon be at the car, get you home and dried off ASAP.

OOO

Cold clutching at her, Sparky tries to shudder the chilling wetness from her plumage, her blood freezing. The growling mover's stopped now. The box joggles along at a frenzied pace that unbalances her. She shakes out wet plumage again, fluffing herself up to dry herself out but the iciness still presses in on her.

The box lands. Matt-ee coaxes her out.

Ss-p-aaarrr-kkee.

She hop-steps to the featherless wing, sees instantly she's not in her space. Matt-ee stands her on a low perch, tethering her gently. Washing over her from behind, Sparky feels warmth. Turning, she sees the flickering brightness of fire and shuffles round to face it, tucking up a leg, eyes closing, absorbing soothing warmth.

HHH

Soz for the soaking, Sparky. You better kip in front of the log burner tonight. Just try to crap on the puppy pads, not the carpet, eh, kiddo.

OOO

Dry and warm now, Sparky awakes to the sight of dark red meat on the ground beside her. She hops down, eats, hops back to the perch, settling in to study her new surroundings.

The space is smaller than hers, filled with different shapes and colours; so much detail she head-turns frantically, eyes devouring every sight. She sees matt-ee, perching on a long wide low ledge, leaning against the upright rear section of it. There's a rounded softness to this perch; matt-ee looks to be resting comfortably on it. This is matt-ee's space, where it roosts while she's in her space. Tonight they're roosting together. It chatters to her as she maps all the space, alert but calm. There's no danger here; her mate's with her.

Flickering movement and stuttering sound draw her focus to a large flat oblong object standing on legs in the corner. She watches and listens a moment. Human chatter mingles with other noises; clicks, chirps, chimes, hissing, tapping: such a cacophony of sound it clogs her ears. Coloured shadows flit across the rectangular object, changing in a rapid flutter, falling off the edges of it for others to emerge startlingly. She leaps off the perch, flapping up to be hauled down. Matt-ee goes to the object, touches it; the sound and movement vanish.

HHH

Let's shut that rubbish off, eh, Sparky? Bloody scaremongering about some sodding virus. It's not the cough that carries you off, so me nan used to say. How was that bit of duck? It'll put fat on your bones, for sure. Here, have some more.

OOO

Matt-ee drops more chunks of darkly red meat beside Sparky then returns to its perch, stretching out on it, holding something small and flat to its face, staring at it and poking it. A stream of fainter noises trickles to her ears and Sparky traces them to the object matt-ee holds. But it's nothing to bother her so she eats the succulent flesh and goes on with her mapping, taking in this new environment with hunter's curiosity until she's familiar enough with it all to let herself sleep.

They roost together all night, as mated pairs do.

Now

20th June 2022

HHH

The limited info I learn by ringing the IBR is enough to prove, at least to me, that Sparky isn't from the tourist attraction as the centre director claimed. If she was she'd definitely have an Article 10 in place and her registration details would've been updated. Major attractions with known animal collections don't operate beneath the law, they can't risk the bad publicity. But if I confront the director I don't know how he'll react; I might lose the chance to rescue Sparky. It's torture but I have to carry on as normal. At least Sparky doesn't know what's unfolding. I head in for what may well be my last flying session with her; she's supposed to be leaving tomorrow.

She flies brilliantly for me; it's sweetly bitter. We're a team at last, but is it too late?

OOO

T-raay-cee hasn't come for a few days but that's familiar; Sparky knows it'll come to her again soon because it's her mate. She waits on the high ledge, as always, is already in flight, dropping to the perch as t-raay-cee enters, keen ears detecting its arrival before it's in view. But when it's inside their space she senses it's quivering, alert to a danger that's silently invisible to her. So when it calls her, she hesitates, searching for the threat it's identified, so they can protect each other. But she doesn't find sound or sight of the danger, needs to keep scanning until she's sure they're safe. T-raay-cee doesn't want to wait, though, tries to get her to perch on it. Nerves twitching muscles, Sparky springs into flight, darting around her space, t-raay-cee calling to her, chattering softly but still emitting that warning tremor. After a brief chase Sparky's on t-raay-cee's featherless wing and they're in the narrow gap.

Sparky hunts for danger in their territory but after a moment she's reassured; everything's familiar: safe. Whatever danger t-raay-cee senses it's not out here. She focuses on her mate, stood as far from her as it ever has.

Ss-p-aaarrr-kkee.

She flies, the air hers while she travels through it freely, landing with precision on the featherless wing, eating the food offering, claiming the air again as she swoops back to the perch.

They hunt for many flights, in rhythm with each other, flowing in life's eddy, alive together: whole. Sparky doesn't need the lure of prey or even her call; she just needs her mate, to fly to it and away from it so she can return, nurturing their bond.

They fly until her chest has filled with exhilarating effort. T-raay-cee's eyes fix brightly on hers and its face hole stretches into the upward curing line. Sparky senses their shared elation as they go home. Hopping onto her perch, she takes the mouse t-raay-cee holds out for her. As she eats, it leaves a pair of mice on the perch beside her, proof they're successful hunters together.

HHH

Before I leave I pop back to Sparky, standing outside her aviary, fantasising about stowing her in the boot of my car, claiming she escaped when I was flying her because someone, yet again, ignored my warning sign and opened the outer door. A friend suggested this plan; I wish I was brave enough to act on it. If this was a heart-warming YA animal rescue novel I would. It isn't; I don't. I just stand there, Sparky staring at me as I tell her what a great little barn owl she is, how I've enjoyed my time with her, hope she'll be safe and happy wherever she ends up. Just as I always introduce myself to new arrivals at the centre, I try to say goodbye to those lucky enough to be rehomed or released. But Sparky's farewell has none of that optimism. I drive home wretched with worry.

OOO

She's eaten the mice, is resting, when t-raay-cee reappears. It doesn't usually come to her again like this. Sparky expects it to enter her space but her mate stays outside, looking in at her, chattering softly. Sparky flies to the criss-crossed lines, landing close to t-raay-cee's face. They eye each other unblinkingly; the elation of their hunt together has faded, replaced by the quivering tension of approaching danger. T-raay-cee stops chattering, turns, leaving their territory, Sparky still hanging there, her whiteness and her outstretched wings making a ghost of her. She tracks her mate with eyes and ears until it's gone too far to follow.

Before

March–September 2020

OOO

Sparky and matt-ee stop going in the moving growler to the vast field to hunt together. Something's changed. Not between them, they're still a lifelong pair, their bond unbreakable. But something's changed their life. So they adapt to survive.

Now they fly like before, on the grassy patch between Sparky's and matt-ee's spaces: their home territory. But Sparky flies free here, like in the field, not held down by the line as she was previously. Even so she can't fly as far or high as in the field; there isn't the endless sky, the far-rolling land, to soar and swoop up into and out over. She still flies as much as she can, though, returning from afar to matt-ee.

When they start flying their home territory again, she goes to and from the perch planted in the grassy patch. After several days of this matt-ee doesn't point her at the perch, it just gives her to the air. She flaps up then straight back down to its featherless wing. It chatters to her.

HHH

Soz we're locked down here, kiddo. You know I want to be able to take you, all of you, out to fly properly, but we'll make the best of it, eh? I'll teach Keith a few tricks, have Reggie doing steep stoops, maybe get Della flying circuits and see about you following on, be great for the show. Assuming we're allowed our livelihood, our lives, back in the foreseeable, Sparky.

OOO

Matt-ee offers her the air again. As she takes off her mate starts circling their territory. Sparky follows, flying above, ears and eyes tracking it, waiting for her call.

Ss-p-aaarrr-kkee.

She drops down to it, eating the prey it has for her then leaping confidently back into flight; she knows what her mate wants them to do. She flies, matt-ee walks, both patrolling their territory, by foot and wing. Around they go. It's not distance from her mate, but lengthening moments apart that reaffirms their bond now, Sparky flying until whenever matt-ee calls her back.

Patrol-flying, hunting and feeding on their home territory together becomes their new life. Matt-ee flushes prey out through the air beneath Sparky. She races to where it lands, hovering above it then pouncing, talons first, to snatch it up. When she's eaten matt-ee stands her on the featherless wing, holds her into the breeze; she launches into flight and they circle again until matt-ee flushes out more prey somewhere else in their territory. The chick lands under a tree. Sparky fixes on the fluffy yellow body, pinpointing where it lies hiding motionless in long grass, and strikes. She returns to matt-ee for the next attempt…

Unless it's raining or gusty, they hunt like this every day, Sparky catching prey that matt-ee finds, flushes out, flies to her. It's easy hunting, she hones her skills quickly, snatching mice, chicks, or bits of them, chunks of meat even, from wherever they go to ground. Then the hunting gets harder, prey landing on top of the large structure her space is inside, on top of matt-ee's space, on the moving growler that's now silenced and motionless. She learns to fly up after prey as well as down onto it. She even snatches it from the breeze. It's a full enough life, hunting with her mate although their home territory is close around them, hemming them in. Sparky longs for the vast field, where they quartered open ground: where they flew wildly free.

October 2020

OOO

Matt-ee's in her space, today they're flying the few wing beats from perch to each other and back. Up this close to her mate, Sparky notices its face is paler, the skin sallow. Its eyes are dark-shadowed, sunk deeper into its skull, it's body thinner, skeleton pressing through flesh. Its steps are slow, plodding. Its plumage is bedraggled, needs preening. When she perches on its featherless wing she feels a trembling spreading into her feet. This isn't like when d-aann-y-elll changed. That was growing. This is something else, something she knows intuitively, as all animals do; it's damage, injury, illness: dying.

Matt-ee's chatter is croaky, the sounds muffled, her call fainter, duller than her ears are accustomed to; she has to retune to it. Distress fills her; although her mate is still here it might soon be lost to her. She can only wait for it to die or recover.

HHH

What a complete mess, Sparky. Christ knows what's gonna happen with this bloody virus carry on but whatever, it's seriously bad for us, kiddo. No work on the horizon. Cupboards emptying. Skint. The end's in sight 'cos there's no end in sight. What the hell're we gonna do, eh, Sparky?

OOO

A night passes and a day then another night. Matt-ee doesn't come. Sparky flies from her tall perch to the criss-crossed lines fronting her space, to the swaying perch, back to the lines. She hangs there, watching: waiting. Maybe her mate's died. Hunger grows inside her but she can't do anything about it. She needs matt-ee to come, taking her out so they can hunt together. But if it's died…

Across from her keee-w-ickk circles its space, flying to land on the lines with hooked toes. Sparky and keee-w-ickk stare at each in knowing and wondering, live reflections of each other. Keee-w-ickk gives its call. Sparky gives hers. But their calls aren't to each other; they're to matt-ee, who hasn't come to either of them so they can fly, hunt and feed. She and keee-w-ickk are more like each other than Sparky and matt-ee but they aren't a pair, so she doesn't call to keee-w-ickk and it doesn't call to her. They both call to matt-ee. The night silence deepens, darkens.

Sparky's on her swaying perch. The day is old. Matt-ee appears at last, staggering weakly, quivering like a feather in a breeze. As it enters her space, Sparky flies straight to her mate who's injured but still alive, has returned to her with the last of its strength. It doesn't, can't, raise a featherless wing for her. So she drops onto its head ledge. It chatters gently to her as it stumbles about her space.

HHH

Soz, kiddo, I lost it there for a bit. Just didn't know what else to do 'cept get blind drunk. Gotta face it, though, it's a dead cert now: we're sunk. Business shot down thanks to this bullshit. I've had to take a job delivering smiley-faced parcels to every poor sod on house arrest.

OOO

As it chatters it flies chunks of meat across her space, Sparky on them in a wing-beat; matt-ee slips out of her space, heading to keee-w-ickk. Hungry, food clutched in her foot, she focuses on eating: surviving. If only matt-ee will survive too. Without her mate she'll be incomplete again.

Matt-ee comes earlier the next day, looking more alive now, walking more steadily: recovering. It does the raining and clawing in Sparky's space, chattering to her, the sound more resonant. She flies to its head ledge, talons pricking the furry plumage, and stays there while it clears away pellets, feathers and droppings. It doesn't normally let her perch there so long but this is a way for them to be together: bonding behaviour. The raining and clawing done, her mate lifts her onto its bare wing toes. She feels their fleshy softness, tries to balance without stabbing, as it raises her until they're face to face. Its is twisted into a killing face. Then the face opens, relaxes, and raindrops fill the pale eyes. Matt-ee points Sparky towards her perch but she turns her head, keeping watch on her mate as it blinks and rubs its eyes. The featherless wing judders under her but she tightens her grip, unwilling to leave it. Matt-ee walks to the perch, pressing Sparky's legs against it, urging her to step to it, giving her call again and again, buried in amongst chatter that bubbles wetly. Sparky holds on to her mate.

Matt-ee shakes its head, the face hole stretching into the upward curving line. It's eyes dry up, brighten. It walks them now to the in/out so they can hunt over their home territory.

HHH

It was gonna be the best life for you, Sparky, and Della, Keith, Reggie. And me. We were gonna be the greatest bird display team in the country. Fantastic free flying for you, showing off how awesome you all are, top-whack money, cordon bleu rations, five-star home, easy living and happy days. Wish I could make it happen. Life's a… yeah, well…

C'mon, one last flying session, eh, Sparky?

Now

21st June 2022

HHH

I contact the animal centre. By now Sparky should've been collected, taken to wherever she's going, but there's a delay, the director tells me, she'll be gone by lunchtime. If I don't hear anything I'm to assume she's on her way. More lies. What the hell's happening? But I can't do anything except wait for it to happen.

22nd June 2022

HHH

There's been no more communication from the animal centre. So this morning I'm to assume Sparky's gone. The director wants me to believe him, so I give him what he wants, ringing the place he said she was returning to. But because it's a big tourist attraction the only phone number is a ticket sales line. I wait in a telephone queue, nerves stretched tight, at snapping point when the call is answered by a polite, script-reading woman who tells me her name is Victoria. I scribble it down in case I need to know later who I spoke to. She asks how she can help. I suspect she can't but proceed to explain, as casually as my thudding heart lets me, that I'm ringing from the animal centre to check Sparky arrived O.K. with them, is settling alright. Victoria is baffled; she doesn't have a scripted reply to my enquiry. I can't be put through to one of their animal care team, the call centre doesn't have that capability. Why would it, they just flog tickets? She'll get someone to ring me back.

I fidget around the house, edgy, phone within reach, puzzling over the ridiculous story that's supposedly Sparky's. It perplexes me because it's so implausible; one phone call might be enough to explode it. Having learnt her Article 10 paperwork isn't in order, making selling her illegal, I suspect an under-the-perch deal. Suspect; can't prove. But I can't think of any other reason for that lie.

Before

November 2020 (cont.)

OOO

This morning matt-ee appears, walking quickly, passing Sparky's space. It returns, on its featherless wing the blue-grey flier which points its heavy-hooked beak towards Sparky, the eye nearest her staring menacingly 'til they're out of sight.

Matt-ee returns, alone, passing Sparky's space, not looking at her. When it reappears the dark brown flier perches on its featherless wing. Seeing Sparky, the flier screeches, splintering the air between it and Sparky. She warns it off with outstretched wings and harsh hissing until matt-ee's taken it from view.

Matt-ee enters keee-w-ickk's space now. Sparky watches as keee-w-ickk flies to the featherless wing and matt-ee brings them from keee-w-ickk's space. Sparky goes to hang on the criss-crossed lines as matt-ee and keee-w-ickk disappear.

She's still gripping the lines when matt-ee comes to her; she flaps up to its head ledge. It chatters to her, lifting Sparky's skin strips so she flap-jumps onto its wing toes. A raindrop falls from an eye, sliding down the pale round face, as matt-ee takes her through the in/out. She head-bobs, searching out what's happening now, curious but calm. This is her mate, she's safe with it. Maybe they're going to fly together over their home territory.

Matt-ee puts her in a box. She hears the growling, feels the movement. This is what happens when they go to the vast field to fly. Anticipation flutters in her.

The moving and growling finally ends. Her box bobs along. Normally matt-ee takes her out of the box as soon as the growling mover stops, and they walk together to the field. She peers through the neat tiny holes in the box's sides for a glimpse of the field; sees a large grey structure looming ahead, tall and wide, with an in/out that leads to darkness. Matt-ee keeps walking. Sparky's nerves tingle and muscles stiffen, every sense intensely focused, her whole body anxious about this change to their routine, the danger it might become. They pass into darkness. Her eyes adjust quickly but the tiny holes only let her see speckled snatches of her surroundings.

Her box lands, the front opening. Matt-ee crouches, peering in, then reaching in. Sparky hops to its featherless wing. Whatever happens she's safe with matt-ee. They're a pair, protecting each other. She scans the area for threats, rapidly gathering and stashing sights and sounds: a space, smaller and darker than hers, a single perch in the centre, shallow water pool on the ground; a strange human, large egg-shaped body, white chest plumage that looks eggshell stiff and ready to crack, a smooth shiny egg for a head: egg human.

It comes towards her. Sparky leaps from matt-ee's wing perch, flapping furiously, getting nowhere. Egg human bends close, ogling her. She struggles again. Matt-ee hushes her call. Egg human chatters then, to matt-ee, as it prods

Sparky's breast, unfurls her wings. She pecks and kicks but can't manage to injure it. It retreats; matt-ee turns away, shielding her from it, facing her at the perch, pushing her towards it.

But she doesn't fly to the perch. Twisting sharply, short quick wing-beats bring her round in a tight circle, back to matt-ee. It doesn't hold up its featherless wing for her though. Instead, it flies a mouse towards the rear of the space. The mouse passes Sparky in mid-air. She turns again, a stumbling, clumsy flight, instinct driving her to chase the prey matt-ee's flushed out for her. When she's caught the mouse, beaking it up, she jumps into flight, rotating as she takes off, to go to matt-ee, her other half.

But it's already outside the space, criss-crossed lines between them. She crashes into them, feeling them cuttingly as her feet grip, hold on. Matt-ee holds on too, from its side, wing toes curled around the lines, staring down at her, chattering so quietly only she hears.

HHH

I don't want this either, Sparky, honestly, kiddo. But this fat bugger'll give me £700 for all four of you; knows he'll sell you all on for double that when things pick up, bloody pandemic parasite. But no one else's buying now and I gotta sell. He'll look after you, though; scrawny owls don't fetch top whack. I'll do my damnedest to buy you back, kiddo, promise. Don't worry, you'll get a good home whatever, a bonny bright barny like you. Jesus, Sparky, if there was any other way… soz, kiddo.

OOO

Sparky gazes up at matt-ee. It stops chattering, turns to egg human who gives matt-ee a small flat brown object. Matt-ee lifts a flap, slides out purple leaves, nods and slides them in again. Egg offers up its wing toes but matt-ee keeps its tucked inside its plumage. So egg head-shakes and turns, walking towards the glow of daylight. Matt-ee throws her a final glance, a head-bob, a wing-flap, then walks away.

Sparky hangs on the lines until matt-ee's gone where even her hearing can't follow. Then she flies to the tall perch, waiting for her mate's return.

Now

22nd June 2022 (cont.)

HHH

While I'm waiting, het up, for Victoria from the tourist attraction's call centre to ring back about Sparky, my mobile buzzes: a text, from the animal centre director. 'Sparky has been signed over to us, so will remain with us.' What the…? I reach for the landline, to ring John, then the falconer. But before I can dial my mobile buzzes again: the centre director again. 'Why don't you think about taking Sparky on yourself?' What the hell is going on? My heart throbs, I'm breathless, adrenaline flooding me. And does it matter what's going on? I can get Sparky out, get her safe.

I don't need to ring John now. He'll say, 'win it then worry about it'. I ring the falconer instead. He's already said he'll help but that was when this was a hypothetical; now it's reality.

'Tell him yes, you'll take her,' he says, 'I'll help with whatever you need.'

So, green-lighted but bracing for impact, I ring the animal centre director, fingers fumbling as I dial, heart throbbing as the call connects.

When he answers I keep it as casual as I can, playing it like I'm mildly surprised Sparky's been signed over to them. He doggedly bites down on his lies. I make out I believe him. Surely he knows I know this is a sham, that we're acting our parts? But I'm too close to saving Sparky to risk losing her now by calling him out. 'Yes, of course, I'd love to adopt her.'

He talks me through their rehoming procedure, a much less rigorous vetting process than I've experienced when adopting cats; all I have to do is email him a photo of an aviary suitable for Sparky. Once I would have put this down to the fact that he knows me, has seen I'm a responsible animal carer from my volunteering. Now I realise this is another black mark against the centre's duty to care for the animals there. At least I know Sparky's coming to a safe home.

The timing is terrible though. We're on holiday next week so Sparky'll have to stay at the centre 'til I return. I itch to drive up right now, bundle her into a cat carrier belted to the back seat before speeding off so he doesn't have chance to change his mind. But that's not practical. At least it gives me time to sort out appropriate accommodation for her. And we're staying at a holiday cottage called 'Two Owls Lodge'—surely a good omen.

After I get off the phone, I do ring John, tell him, ring the falconer, tell him too: Sparky's free. Her sentence overturned anyway.

I'm basking in relief that it's over when Victoria, from the tourist attraction call centre, rings back regarding my enquiry about Sparky. She tells me they've contacted my animal centre. Panic pounds in my ears and scorches my cheeks; it never occurred to me that they'd investigate my call to them about Sparky by ringing up the animal centre. I'd imagined their head raptor keeper being radioed while going about his business in some aviary, a crackly conversation in which, head-scratching, he says he knows nothing about a barn owl returning to them from an animal centre up north, then a quick return of my call exposing the lie about Sparky. I'm so sideswiped by this I'm hardly listening as Victoria is confirming the barn owl in question is safe; I don't need to be concerned about her. Mumblingly, I thank her for letting me know and hang up; asking awkward questions is pointless now. I realise what's happened:

Bamboozled by my enquiry, the tourist attraction rang up the animal centre, spoke to the director, said they had someone on the phone, asking about a barn owl that was supposedly returning to their raptor collection from his centre, a barn owl they knew nothing about. God knows what he told them to cover the fact that I'd caught him out in a lie, but, knowing I'd busted him, he texted me, inventing the nonsense about Sparky being signed over to them, following it up by offering her to me. She's an bribe, a pay-off: take the owl, that's what you want, and stop making trouble. I don't care. I'll play his game, win, get Sparky safe. Then I'll make whatever trouble I need to, for the good of the animals still at his centre.*

* I learnt later that his response on the phone to the tourist attraction was, 'Yes, I'm aware of that individual [meaning me]. Just tell her the owl is safe and not to be concerned about it.'

Before

November 2020–March 2021

OOO

Matt-ee has only been gone a short while when Sparky hears footsteps. Flying to hang on the criss-crossed lines, she tracks the nearing sounds keenly only to realise the thud-thudd is too heavy; they aren't her mate's footsteps. She retreats to the perch.

Egg human appears. Sparky hisses and opens her wings in warning. Egg ignores her hostile display, entering her space, its rounded body encroaching, and points a small flat black shiny object at her. There's a sharp flash of bright whiteness. Lightning startled, Sparky leaps off the perch, sheltering in the darkness at the rear of her space. Egg strides over to her with a single step, grabs her skin strips and yanks her onto its featherless wing, pointing the flat black thing at her again and chattering but not giving her call. There's another blinding flash, then it shoves her towards the perch and leaves.

Sparky stays on the perch, panic trembling her inside-out, fear crushing her chest, breathing in gasps, listening to egg leaving: listening for it returning.

HHH

Let's get your photo for Facebook. You're a good looking barn owl, not too speckled for a female, Disney eyes. Should sell fast once this covid kerfuffle dies down, and you were a bargain so I'll make a decent profit… come here… there, that'll do.

OOO

Long nights and short days pass. The smaller space that matt-ee left her in is now Sparky's space. The egg shaped human comes, flying prey to her, mostly fluffy chicks, never mice. When she tears into the chicks' bellies a gooey yellow liquid bubbles out, running and oozing. It sticks to her feathers, feet and beak as she eats. If there's more food than she needs she scratches and scrapes at the ground, digging a hollow that she stashes spare meals in, saving for lean days; matt-ee's not here now to hunt with her. Matt-ee's gone.

Her feathers fall out. She isn't flying so she doesn't need them, her body dropping them so new, fresh, crisp feathers can grow, ready for when she flies again, when, if, matt-ee returns. Fluffy white down covers the ground, a light snowfall. Then stiff white-dappled leaves fall from wings and tail, giving her dingy space a faint brightness. She bathes in the small water pool then preens on the perch, dislodging old broken feathers, grooming pristine replacements.

This is her existence: waiting for her lost mate to return.

Egg human appears as usual to fly food to her. But today, before it sends prey in through the lines, it stares around her space, head-shakes and chatters. Sparky braces to spring into flight; if it enters her space she'll try to swoop around it and through the in/out. But it doesn't enter. It launches a pair of chicks towards her. They land on the ground beneath her perch. Sparky doesn't drop down to them until she's heard egg's footsteps thud far away.

HHH

God, I'll have to get Abbie to muck this place out. She should be glad to have an excuse to get out of the house right now instead of being stuck inside glued to Instagram.

OOO

Someone's coming, not egg human, Sparky knows because the footsteps don't thud-thudd. She flies to the lines, craning to see. It might be matt-ee.

It isn't. It's a new human, tall and thin, with a young face: a juvenile.

The new human doesn't look at her, give her call or hold up a featherless wing for Sparky to perch on. It just enters and does the raining and clawing.

In this small space Sparky can only stand on the perch, eyes and ears guardedly following it. She detects a muffled thumping, shooshing noise coming from its ears: doooff-doooff-doooff. She hasn't known a human make noise with its ears. Curious, Sparky flies across to land on this strange human's head ledge. The doooff human squawks. Sparky pecks around its head, where the doooff sound is louder. The stranger reaches out a featherless wing. Brushed off, Sparky flaps up, hovers, drops down, wing-beating for balance. Doooff chatters now, a harsh rapid stream, the sound coming from its face hole, and shoves Sparky off again. She flies to the tall perch. Doooff human carries on raining and clawing, glancing at Sparky often.

HHH

Oi, get off! You're making this a harder job than it already is, sitting there, flapping and pecking. Bloody barn owl. You're too flamin' friendly. I hate it when one of yous is friendly. There's no point us being friends; you'll not be stopping here.

OOO

The nights get shorter and the days longer. The only humans that come and go are egg and doooff. Egg brings food but stays outside, flying yellow chicks in to

Sparky. Doooff enters but doesn't offer her food, just does the clawing and raining. Neither of them call her to their featherless wings. Neither wants to be her new mate. And matt-ee hasn't returned. It was looking injured, like it was dying, before it brought her here and it's been gone so long she knows it isn't coming back, is probably dead. But Sparky's only half herself without a human to share life with. She keeps flying to doooff when it enters but it always flaps her away or, if she lands on a head ledge, shoves her off. Sparky wouldn't fly to egg even if it entered her space; she doesn't want that human for her mate.

Sparky lives an empty half-life; flying the few wing beats from perch to lines, perch to ground, perch to water pool, eating, bathing, preening and roosting. Many days go, many nights come. Sparky exists, surviving until a new mate arrives to make her life fulfilled: whole.

A pair of humans is approaching, Sparky hears their chattering but doesn't fly to the lines to watch; it'll be egg and doooff, sometimes they appear together.

But it's not doooff with egg, it's a new human that glances into her space and, seeing her, stops, facing her, chattering with egg. Sparky studies this new human closely for any behaviour that might mean it's wanting to be her new mate. It raises a featherless wing, poking wing toes into Sparky's space. She flies to the lines. It chatters more, looking at egg, then her. Suddenly it gives her call. She hasn't heard that sound for so long she'd forgotten it until hearing it again now. She clambers across the lines, closer to the new human that gave her call, that wants her to come to it. If it comes into her space she'll fly to it; if it doesn't flap her away it could become her new mate.

HHH

Sparky, eh? She's cracking. What's her story?

Only three and a half years old, in great shape. An imprint, been properly trained. Great little bird. Bargain at £250.

Nah, I've only got one spare aviary and I need another peregrine for pigeon clearance, that's the only work these days. Maybe if the country shows get going again this summer and there's flying display work I'll come back for her. Sorry, Sparky.

OOO

The new human turns away, following egg.

It passes her space again soon, going where it came from, a familiar blue-grey flier perched on its featherless wing. Both human and flier look in at her. The flier screeches; the human bobs its head. They walk on.

That human didn't want to be her new mate. But there might be other humans who come that do want to share their lives with her, flying and hunting together.

Sparky starts watching for new humans: potential mates.

Now

21st June–2nd July 2022

OOO

T-raay-cee doesn't come. Sparky waits, watches, but it doesn't appear for them to fly, hunt and feed together. Instead other humans come. They fly prey in to her. They rain water into the pool. They stay outside her space. They aren't her mate so they don't come to her and she doesn't go to them. If too many nights and days pass and t-raay-cee doesn't come it'll stop being her mate. Then the waiting for a new human to share life with will have to start again. But t-raay-cee could appear today, raising its featherless wing and calling ss-p-aaarrr-kkee. Or the next day. Or the next. Or the… Her hunter's focus keeps Sparky in the now of waiting for t-raay-cee to return.

HHH

Across the valley from 'Two Owls Lodge', hiding in the pine forest, wild owls call to me gloomily as I spend another sleepless night pacing the patio. Thoughts of Sparky stuck at the animal centre, not knowing I'm coming for her as soon as I can, haunt me. Is she missing me, wondering where I am, thinking I've abandoned her? I've never been good at waiting, especially when I can't do anything more to secure the outcome than float text messages to the falconer and animal centre director, arranging with the director to collect Sparky on a day when the falconer is free to help me settle her in to her new home. Finally the date is fixed: Sunday, 3rd July. I claw myself closer and closer to that moment: to Sparky.

On the last night of our holiday the wild owls call out more hopefully.

Before

April 2021

OOO

Egg and doooff stand together outside Sparky's space, staring in and chattering. It's different. behaviour for them, could mean change is happening.

HHH

Finally sold this one.

Oh, who too?

Some barmpot, Allie something-or-other. She'll be here at the weekend, so get the aviary mucked out.

Barmpot?

Yeah, said when she saw it on Facebook she knew it were hers. Rambled on about some budgie she'd had as a kid, taming ducks in the park, a jackdaw she kept in her kitchen 'til it's wing healed. But she didn't haggle.

She'll look after her though?

Huh, yeah. Said she's gonna have it as a house owl so it'll be living in its natural environment, haha.

Whaddya mean?

Barn, house: same thing. Well, close enough.

Will Sparky be O.K. living like that?

Why do you care? Pays your wages this week, it does.

OOO

Egg and doooff go. Nothing else different happens that day.

The next day egg brings a new strange human.

They stop at her space, looking in, chattering. The new human is taller than egg. Sparky claw-climbs her way up the lines, high enough to view egg's shiny pink head-shell from above, high enough to study the new human's face. The unbeak is hooked, more like a flier's beak. Its skin is pale yellow-brown, stretched tightly over its skull. Its eyes are dark. The head plumage is pale at the top, dark where it hangs down, touching this head ledge but not that, as if it moulted and hasn't regrown on that side yet. Its body plumage is brightly red-blue-green-pink-orange in patches, lines and speckles, floating loosely around its scrawny limbs. It stares at Sparky. She stares back. Then it chatters to egg who head-bobs and they come through the in/out.

Sparky flies to the perch, giving her raspy caw call. The new human responds.

Ss-p-aaarrr-kkee.

It's calling her to go to it but its featherless wing stays by its body so Sparky stays on her perch, unsure what this behaviour means.

Ss-p-aaarrr-kkee.

It's been a long while since any human called her to it like it might want to be her mate. But still it doesn't raise its featherless wing. She could fly to a head ledge, see if it flaps her away.

Ss-p-aaarrr-kkee.

She jumps across to the many coloured plumage with a wing-beat.

It doesn't shove her off. It turns to egg, clap-clapping its wing limbs together, like her before human, d-aann-y-elll, sometimes did, and chatters singingly.

HHH

Hello, Sparky, aren't you a gorgeous girl? And bright too, you know your name, came when I called you. You want to come home with Allie, don't you? We're going to be best friends, Sparky. Allie and Sparky; Sparky and Allie: for ever.

OOO

Twisting her neck, Sparky studies the new human, admiring its bright plumage. Humans are like fliers; different colours for face, plumage, eyes, wings, even legs and feet. Her inspection reaches its feet now. Human feet are a rounded shape where Sparky's have toes. But not this human's feet. It has toes, more than Sparky, at the front. The toes wriggle. Sparky floats down to them.

Its feet toes are stubbier than hers, without her long talons; they're more like humans' wing toes but stunted. Sparky hops around to inspect the heel: no toes there where she has toes pointing backwards. The feet stand on a flat surface a bit bigger than them with skin strips wrapped over the feet, near the toes and around the ankles, joining the flats to the feet. Sparky stretches across, pecking a skin strip, feels familiar toughness, like the skin strips around her ankles. This human is more like her than other humans she's seen.

A squealing noise; the foot slides away. Sparky glances up. The new human is watching her. Egg bends to Sparky, yanking her onto its featherless wing; unbalanced, she jump-flaps.

As egg stands, Sparky teetering on its wing perch, new human steps closer, its face hole wide, curving upwards. It sing-chatters again, gives Sparky's call again. She tries to fly to its head ledge, away from egg, but egg holds her down. Egg's almost never held on to her but now there's a human behaving like it might want to be her mate, egg won't let her go. Sparky head-shakes, rubbing her beak over the thick hide covering egg's wing toes, pecking with sharp jabs but egg doesn't release her; it takes her out of her space.

Sparky faces new human. It follows, eyes fixed on hers, as they head towards daylight.

When they get outside brightness blinks Sparky's eyes. Between blinks she glimpses the sky, whitely smeared and glowing bluely, still there for her to fly up into so she can fly down to her mate again. If she finds a new mate.

She's still marvelling at the sky, its potential, when egg stoops, bringing her rapidly close to the ground. Sparky flap-jumps, fighting away from the hard grey surface rushing to collide with her. Egg pushes her into a box just as the ground's almost on her.

Inside the box Sparky see the front has criss-crossed lines and hops to them, peering out.

The new human peers back at her, singing its chatter. Then it stands; all Sparky can see is its scrawny many-coloured legs beside egg's fat black legs. She can hear them chattering though.

HHH

That's alright for her, isn't it? It was Sylvester's. He was a naughty boy, tried to eat my poor little Jackie so I had to…

Yeah, it's fine.

And she'll be O.K. on the bus? I don't have a car, they won't let me sit my driving test because…

Huh, erm, yeah, people take dogs on buses so why not? You've got my money, have you?

OOO

The box rises up, starts bob-floating along. Sparky keeps watch through the criss-crossed lines, spots doooff human standing a short distance away, staring at her. Sparky calls to it with a croaky screech. Doooff raises its featherless wing, fluttering its wing toes at her before turning its back to her.

Now

3rd July 2022

OOO

Humans approach her space. Sparky recognises t-raay-cee's chattering scattered amongst the rest. It's returned to her: for her. Sparky darts to the ledge so when her human enters they can start their flying, hunting and feeding.

The humans appear in the territory outside Sparky's space. It is t-raay-cee. But shrivelled human is with it and another that Sparky recognises from when it's watched her fly in the narrow gap. This other human walks close to t-raay-cee, like they're a pair, leaving shrivelled human walking alone behind them, a solitary stalker. T-raay-cee's human mate carries a box like those Sparky's been in before when she's gone to a different territory. She knows today something that she's needed to happen for a while is happening: her mate's taking them to their new home territory.

T-raay-cee's inside now, holding up a featherless wing: calling her. Trusting it, Sparky goes to it; they're a pair, completing each other. When t-raay-cee lifts her to the box, Sparky willingly steps inside.

The box bob-floats along. Sparky sees t-raay-cee walking ahead of her, shrivelled human beside it. They walk the length of the narrow gap and through the in/out at the end.

HHH

Finally, almost a fortnight since seeing her, I'm collecting Sparky, John with me, back up in case the centre director reneges on our deal: on Sparky. He follows us, like he's stalking prey, as I lead John to Sparky's aviary. She's on the ledge, waiting for me. I call her. She comes straight away but why wouldn't she? As far as she knows we're about to fly as usual. Once we deviate from our routine she'll know something's up; then I'm in the unknown with her. Cats are the only animals I've transported before. Handily Sparky fits in a cat carrier, the plastic type with a metal grill at the front. Helpfully, she steps into it.

We go to the car, John carrying her, the centre director chatting to me friendly and casual; like I don't know he's a liar and he doesn't know I know he's a liar. He advises me I need a smaller carrier for her. I thank him, say I'll get one. He asks if I have food for her. I say, yes, I've been to a local reptile shop and stocked up on frozen chicks and mice. Just smile, nod, play along, and get her in the car.

OOO

Sparky feels it, as a coolness, before she sees it: the sky. They're out under it. Fresh air creeps invisibly into her box. Sparky looks beyond t-raay-cee; the vista, smoothly blue and white, rises up over the far away horizon, arcing overhead, mantling everything but enclosing nothing: pure freedom. She hasn't seen such a view in far too long. She absorbs it while she can. Up ahead a moving growler comes into sight.

HHH

John lifts her into the car, sits in the driver's seat. I go back inside to do paperwork; at least she's in our car now. If anything goes wrong John's under instructions to drive off. I'll leave on foot, run if I have to; he can pick me up down the road. It doesn't come to that. The adoption form is one side of A4 asking for only basic details, with places for me and the director to sign, confirming I've adopted Sparky. I've already emailed him the aviary photo he asked for and, because no money is changing hands for Sparky, this single flimsy piece of paper is all I need to prove Sparky's legally in my care. He tells me he'll get a copy sent to me. Yeah, righto. I photograph it. I don't care what he thinks of this; I know I need this proof she's come to me legitimately, however he came by her. Finally I tell him I won't be in tomorrow, my usual volunteering day, as I've got things to do after my hols and want to make sure Sparky settles O.K. He doesn't, can't, challenge this. Clearly I'm not coming back but we've reached this drama's final act, no point in breaking the fourth wall now. I leave, heart throbbing, sweating anxiety and trembling with relief.

In the car Sparky's fairly calm. She must've travelled like this before, all she does is flap a bit, arriving unscathed at her new home.

OOO

Soon the growler's rumble shudders through Sparky and they're moving; her, t-raay-cee and t-raay-cee's human mate. T-raay-cee turns, peering in at her, and chatters.

HHH

Thank God. Bloody hell. You're safe now, Sparky.

OOO

The growling mover stops. Sparky's box bob-floats along again briefly. They must be at their new home territory. She tunes ears, focuses eyes, eager to map the space t-raay-cee's claimed as theirs.

HHH

It's over. I'm drained but also exhilarated; Sparky's escaped. Now I need to get her into her new aviary. The falconer, quickly becoming a friend, is on hand to help. He checks her over, confirming she's in decent condition, given what we know, can guess, about her previous life: lives. Whatever her past's been, I'm determined her future will be her best life.

OOO

The box lands and t-raay-cee opens the in/out. Sparky steps onto its featherless wing, head swivelling, ears and eyes inspecting the large new space surrounding her. Wings fluttering in readiness, she hunts for danger in this new large space, especially any fliers that might attack. She sees only humans; t-raay-cee and its human mate plus another with dark face plumage. She's seen this face plumage human before, a while ago, in the fliers' space, t-raay-cee brought it, she perched on its bare wing toes and it held her steady. There's no danger here. Sparky folds her wings away, starts mapping her new space.

There's enough air for her to circle the space with many wing-beats. A long branch perch sways in the centre and short slanting perches are set high up the sides. A large water pool is on the ground and half way up that side is a big deep hollow, somewhere sheltered to roost. This is a suitable space, with everything she and her mate need for a contented life together. She leaps into the space's air now, circling, landing on the long swaying perch.

T-raay-cee faces her, offering a chick and calling to her. Sparky flies down, snatches the prey, takes it to the big deep hollow where she scrambles to the rear, scratching in the fine grainy ground, stashing her meal for after she's explored, is ready to eat and rest.

She hops back to the hollow's front edge. T-raay-cee's pale eyes stare at her. Sparky stares back with her dark ones. They share a knowing: you're safe.

Before

April 2021 (cont.)

OOO

The new human's fluttery bright plumage brushes against the box on its bob-floating flight, Sparky slipping around inside it. From nearby a familiar growling races towards then away from her and, through gaps in the box's sides, Sparky glimpses many moving growlers passing, faster than flight.

After a while of the box bob-floating it lands and she relaxes legs stiff from balancing. She's at ground level, the growling movers swooping past. Sparky huddles against the box's rear, eyes and ears alert for danger.

The new human's face appears at the in/out, staring eyes on her, chattering to her with its sing-song. In amongst its chattering Sparky hears her own call several times, followed by a new sound pattern, a-ll-eee: the new human's call.

HHH

It's going to be great, Sparky, the two of us. Sparky and Allie. Allie and Sparky. We'll be best friends, two girls together. Allie and Sparky. Sparky and Allie. Here comes the bus, the wheels on it go round and round; the wings on the owl go…

OOO

A-ll-eee's face disappears as a long growling mover appears, stopping beside them. It's growling is a roar.

The box jolts upwards. And again. And again. Then down but quickly up and bob-floating on as the mover starts to growl fiercely, move slowly and the box swings up and out, as if turning in flight. Sparky slides from here to there, bumping against the sides. She struggles up, feet clenching the furry ground, wings flapping for balance, feathers bending. But at last the box is still although the growler is on the move, moving Sparky, and the a-ll-eee human beside her. A stream of singing chatter washes over Sparky.

HHH

Sparky and Allie sitting on a bus, a jolly ride home without any fuss.

You'll love your new home, Sparky, lots of rooms for you to fly around and explore. Plenty of windows so you'll be able to spy on the outside world. Allie and Sparky living in a house, eating tea together: pizza and a mouse.

You'll soon settle in, I'll give you the tour tomorrow, Sparky, but tonight we'll just chill out in the lounge. It's going to be great.

Thank you, Universe, for bringing Sparky and Allie together.

Allie and Sparky happily ever after, lots of good time and plenty of laughter.

Nearly home, Sparky.

OOO

The moving goes on and on, jerkily stopping and starting over and over; Sparky slithers around inside the box, feathers crumpling as she flaps to right herself. Underneath the constant growling she hears the new a-ll-eee human beside her, chattering its high pitched singing with squeaking mousey tones that Sparky's ears instinctively tune to. The a-ll-eee and ss-p-aaarrr-kkee calls are repeated often. The glimpses Sparky snatches of this a-ll-eee human are of it peering down at her.

Finally the box rises, is shaken around, swung about. Sparky falls off her feet, clawing and flapping herself upright as the coolness of fresh air washes over her. They're outside; the growling fades. The box bobs along, carried by the a-ll-eee human. If it's taking her to a new territory it must want them to become a pair. Sparky can't do anything until they are where they're going and she can leave the box. Eyes half-closed, feet locked into a gripping hold on the box's furry ground, she rests.

Stillness rouses her. She shuffles to the front of the box, looks out between the lines. They're in a new space, familiar, though Sparky's never been here before, because she's able to match it to a space she mapped a few seasons ago; after she flew in snow, got wet and chilled, she was taken into a similar space where she warmed up and dried out: matt-ee's roosting space. This space is alike enough and different enough for her to know it, without knowing it, as a-ll-eee's roosting space.

A-ll-eee appears, opening the box's in/out and chattering.

HHH

Welcome home, Sparky. What do you think? This is the living room, we'll spend most of our time here. Come out and I'll show you around.

OOO

Sparky leans forward, stretching so her head's outside the box but her body's still safely inside. With neck turning all ways, she starts mapping this new space that recalls matt-ee's roost to her. There's an array of objects, small and bigger, scattered here and there, some perching on narrow ledges up the sides; a pair of human perches, like that matt-ee rested on, a flat surface on legs beside each perch. There isn't a perch for her, that she can see. She hops out of the box, searching for somewhere high, where she can survey the space for hide-e-holes and threats. She spots a large black rectangular object in a corner. She could perch on top of it. With a jump, Sparky's airborne but as soon as she lands, turning to view the space from this vantage, the a-ll-eee human rushes towards her, flapping its featherless wings and loudly singing its squeaky chatter.

HHH

No, no, no, Sparky. Naughty, Sparky. You mustn't sit on the TV. It's the landlord's, you mustn't break it. Come on, off you get.

OOO

The a-ll-eee human is close enough to grab her: hurt her. Panic charges through Sparky; now it's behaving like it's attacking her, doesn't want to be her mate, wants to chase her from its roosting space. She's got an instant to escape. With a head-turn, Sparky sees a wide opening to the outside where, close to, humans are walking, growling movers passing. Further away there are trees. Above it all is the brightly grey sky. She's caught the sight of all this even as she's leaping into flight, gliding towards her escape, wings tingling with energy. She reaches the wide opening, is about to pass through it…

Bang.

Something solid strikes her, or she strikes it, whacking her head-on. A thudding throbs in her ears. She drops out of the air, crash-landing, stunned.

Quivering energy passes through her, enough for her to scramble to her feet, talons scratching for grip. She's on a sturdy ledge. Shaking herself back together, Sparky looks out, up, at where she should be flying. She collided with something but there's nothing to collide with. She reaches forward, pecks, feels hardness. She pecks across this way, back that way. She sidesteps along the ledge, still pecking, still finding a solid surface where there should be untouchable air. She jumps into a short vertical flight, pecking up this way, down that. But everywhere she pecks she finds an invisible solid surface. She can't see it or go through it, she can only see through it, like the ice in her water pool during winter. She recalls seeing through an expanse of ice like this a long time ago. Her before mate, d-aann-y-elll was behind it, neither of them could get through to reach each other.

Sparky turns sharply now, hunting for the a-ll-eee human who was coming to attack her. It's standing motionless, across the space. Its eyes and face hole are wide, its wing toes holding its head. It gives her call, but quietly.

Sparky doesn't fly to it. It doesn't want her to, isn't holding up its featherless wing for her to perch on and isn't calling her in the bright, strong tone that humans use when they call her to them. She stays on the ledge, watching it nervously. It takes a step towards her. She opens her wings, tilting them, displaying her diamond-dappled tan, black and grey, making herself threatening, shaking her lowered head and hiss-cawing, warning this human off. A-ll-eee stops in mid-step. It sing-chatters softly.

HHH

Sparky, oh Sparky, are you hurt? The window, you didn't know. I'm sorry. Please, let me… no, O.K., sorry, sorry. Please, I won't hurt you.

Little Miss Sparky crash-landed did she, shaking her head to and fro; along came poor Allie, to help her best friend, making sure she's soon on the mend.

I know what'll help. Just a jiff, Sparky.

OOO

A-ll-eee leaves through the in/out, closing it, trapping Sparky. Alone in this new space, she scans it, eyes and ears hurriedly mapping so she can navigate in flight, find safe hide-e-holes and vantages.

There are some ledges high up the sides; she flies to them but sees they're too narrow for landing on. Across the space from the expanse of ice is something that looks perch-like: a tall skinny trunk but instead of a straight branch there's a dome. She flies to it, landing with a wobble. The domed top of this odd perch is a taut thin surface with a hole in the middle. Talons pricking the surface as she curls her toes, Sparky peers down inside; there's an egg. She bends, legs tensed, wings outstretched for balance, and pecks but her beak can't crack it; it's not an egg, too hard and slippery smooth. If it's not an egg, this isn't another flier's nest. She can perch here safely enough. It's not the most stable perch but it's tall, gives her a view of the whole space, including the in/out so she can see danger approaching, and it's in a corner so nothing can attack from behind. If she's staying in this space she'll perch on this dome. She's balancing there when a-ll-eee returns.

HHH

Where are you, Sparky? Come out, come out, wherever you… oh, there you are, on the lamp, look see what I've got you.

OOO

Sparky stiffens, claws clenching at the taut surface. But a-ll-eee doesn't pounce towards her. Chattering, it goes to the ledge beneath the ice, puts something down, retreats. Sparky sees yellowy fluffy chicks, the sight of food awakening her hunger. But a-ll-eee's close to the meal. She considers the risk of flying to the prey this new human has brought her, now behaving again like it wants to be her mate. Cautious, Sparky waits. A-ll-eee picks up a chick, wriggling it, holding it towards Sparky and calling her. Still she waits. A-ll-eee shuffles away from the prey until it's retreated enough for Sparky to risk flying off her safe dome perch for the chance to hunt.

She strikes the prey. A chick in her beak, toes gripping the other, she flies back to the dome perch but it wobbles as she tries to hold the chicks securely while eating. She needs a more stable place to feed: the ledge beneath the ice. Sparky wing-beats back to it, landing side-facing a-ll-eee, wings hiding her catch from this unsettling human. When she's eaten both chicks she faces a-ll-eee again. It's still standing away from her. It clap-claps its featherless wings together and its face hole stretches into an upturned line. It sing-chatters.

HHH

You're alright, Sparky, not hurt, thank goodness. Hope your tea was nice. I wanted us to eat together on our first night but never mind. We'll do that tomorrow.

Little Sparky owl, sat on a windowsill, eating her chicks for tea.

OOO

Night rises. Sparky stays on the ledge beneath the ice, watching through its solid invisible expanse, her motion-tuned eyes finding and tracking each flitting flicker: humans walking, growlers moving, trees swaying, fliers swooping. As the view becomes familiar she swaps to staring into the sky, reliving the freedom of flying high and far through clear air before returning to her mate, them sharing the exhilaration of hunting together.

A-ll-eee darts between this and that perch like it can't decide which to settle on. It leaves and returns. The upright black oblong that a-ll-eee chased Sparky off flickers and stutters. Sparky recognises it now from matt-ee's space. She doesn't try to land on it again.

When it's night dark a-ll-eee comes towards Sparky on her ledge with the sky view: the sky ledge. Mistrustful, Sparky flies to the tall dome perch. When she looks back at the expanse of ice it's gone, the night black sky vanished by a pale speckled yellow surface. Now a-ll-eee heads for Sparky again so she circles the space awkwardly, wings dodging obstacles her night vision alerts her to. Suddenly the darkness brightens dimly. A-ll-eee returns to its perch. Sparky flies to the pale speckled yellow surface where the ice was, holding up her feet, fumbling to grab a landing but the pale yellow surface sways away from her; she returns to the dome perch. The space's dull light comes from within the dome. As she lands Sparky glances into the hollow, where the egg-like thing is. Brightness blazes up at her so strongly it whites her vision entirely. She closes her eyes, shaking blinding brilliance from her head, facing away from it, eyes feeling pierced by the light. When she's had enough soothing eyes-closed darkness, she opens them a crack, careful not to look into the brightness, settling there, a leg tucked up.

The night deepens. A-ll-eee stays in the space with Sparky, like matt-ee did long ago. Matt-ee was her mate, they roosted together, were a pair. A-ll-eee is behaving like it and Sparky are a pair now, even though they haven't bonded yet.

Sparky's ears collect the rustling of muffled movement. She glances up; a-ll-eee's going to the pale, speckled yellow surface, peeling it away; the ice, and the sky beyond it, reappear. Sparky flaps to the sky ledge, passing a-ll-eee in mid-air as it goes to her dome perch. A moment later the space's light vanishes and a-ll-eee is singing, Sparky's call mingled with the tuneful chatter; she turns to the sound.

A-ll-eee is by the in/out. It flaps a featherless wing then leaves.

HHH

It's bedtime, Sparky. Nighty-night, see you in the morning.

Now we lay us down to sleep, we prey the Lord our souls to keep: Allie and Sparky Madison.

OOO

Alone, cloaked in night, Sparky explores this, her new space, flying, walking, perching, pecking and clawing. The ground is furry, the sides harder than wood. She finds a ledge that's wide enough for her to stand on, midway up the side opposite the in/out. It's littered with small flat objects that lean backwards on a single leg but Sparky can hop around them. It's another perching place for her: the littered ledge. She tries the human perches too; the wide flat ledges of them are too soft for balancing steadily, her feet sinking into them, but the rear uprights are firm enough for her to stand on. She steps from a human perch to the flat surface on legs beside it, feeling woodiness as she walks across it, feet splaying. This isn't like her other spaces but she's here: it's her new space now; she'll have to adapt.

When she knows every nook she returns to the littered ledge, tucks a leg up underneath her, closes her eyes: rests and reflects. The a-ll-eee human brought her to this space, but it chased her, then brought her food, gave her call, roosted with her for some of the night. It's not like her before mates but it's with her, they're together. They might bond, become a pair, completing each other, sharing life; if she accepts this strange mate she won't be alone, only half of herself.

Now

July 2022

HHH

Sparky's in her new home now but I was so focused on her escape, which came about so dramatically, that I couldn't think beyond getting her safe. Now she's escaped the animal centre, has a proper aviary of her own, I have to decide what's next. It's not everyday a barn owl comes into your care. I'm nose-to-beak with 10–15 years of responsibility. Her wellbeing for all that time is absolutely and utterly on me.

For now I can cope. I've got a chest freezer for storing her food in, much to the horror of a friend who shuddered to learn I keep dead mice in with our food, a lot of which is other dead animals anyway. There's a lawned area big enough for her initial flight training and access to a field if we dare to spread our wings. Any equipment I need, like jesses, perches, tracking gear, is available online. And, crucially I've got the friendly falconer who's willing to work hand-in-gauntlet with me. I've learnt enough to manage Sparky's daily needs but I'll need his expertise when problems crop up. I can't race her to my cat vet if she breaks her wing. If I don't control her weight correctly she could starve to death in a sudden cold spell. At some point her beak and talons will need trimming, more challenging than clipping cat claws. And she can fly, escape far more easily, be far more unreachable than even my acrobatic ninja tabby who once ended up on the porch roof. A knot tied too loosely and I'd be sentencing Sparky to fight for her life in the wild.

Rescue over, reality weighing on me, I'm doubt-riddled, the feeling like maggots crawling over my skin. Have I done the right thing, or the thing I wanted to do? Have I done the right thing for Sparky? Or, having saved her from one potentially awful fate have I condemned her to another with me? I'm a novice, albeit with an expert on speed dial. But it's not enough to keep her alive; she has to live her best life. For that I need to regularly fly her free. Am I going to be able to do that?

These worries peck away at me until one morning I drive to a local owl centre, a small but well-run tourist attraction. I pay the entry fee and wander slowly around the aviaries, stopping at each, inspecting how well they're maintained, scrutinising the birds for signs of illness or injury. Not that I know what I'm looking for but they all appear healthy; alert and active, feathers smooth, eyes bright, feet tidy. And the aviaries are spacious, appropriately appointed with plants, perches, baths, as clean as I keep Sparky's.

They clearly know what they're doing. This place has been up and running for years, has experienced bird keepers on staff and, unlike the animal centre that I, now, no longer volunteer at, it has to be licensed and veterinary inspected, because it has non-native birds on public display. Sparky would be safe here. They'd know how to look after her properly and she could be part of their flying displays. She'd be a hit with visitors, especially children, and she'd benefit from their professional training. But, after what she's been through, I have to be beyond certain about her future welfare.

I return to the ticket office and ask if they take volunteers. The head keeper comes to talk to me. He seems knowledgeable, genuinely committed to his animals. But so did the centre's director; it took me too long to see the animals there weren't being rescued so much as collected in what I now see as a pseudo-zoo; they were, in my opinion, props for his head keeper fantasy. I can't be scorched twice: despite her feline familiarity, Sparky doesn't have nine lives.

The owl chap takes my details but tells me they currently have vet students on placement there so no volunteer vacancies over the summer. Once the students finish he'll be able to take me on; he'll be in touch in September. The fact that they get student vets on placement is reassuring. I know from my teaching life that placements are thoroughly scrutinised. Any mismanagement, any problems with animal welfare, any dodgy goings on, would soon be exposed. Sparky'd be O.K. here. I think…

Driving home I wrestle logic and emotion. She'd be better off with professional care. But I'm attached to her now; we've been through it together. And she's had so much upheaval in the short time I've known her, possibly worse before. Now I've taken her on is it fair to put her through more change, rehoming her again? Is it fair not to, if this owl centre can give Sparky her best life? I decide not to decide anything yet. I'll look after her over the summer, see how we go, at least the weather'll be warm so I'm unlikely to accidentally starve her to death. Come autumn I can volunteer at the owl centre, suss it out thoroughly and, once I'm convinced it's the right thing for Sparky, see if they'll take her. There's a better chance they will if they know me through volunteering. And, if I'm volunteering there, I'd still have her in my life.

OOO

Sparky's new space becomes her space. Of all the spaces she's had it's most like the space matt-ee found her, where life was comfortable. It will be here too; plenty of air for her to fly through, perches to flit between, a safe roosting hollow and a wide, clean water pool. She can see the sky overhead too; it's still there for her to fly up into so she can return to her mate from high and far.

But for now they fly in her space, her and t-raay-cee, because they need to establish themselves as a pair here. Their bond's the same but their territory isn't. Sparky knows she's safe with t-raay-cee, it'll protect her, fly with her, bring food for her, share life with her. She doesn't know the territory beyond her space, if strangers will trespass, attack them, whether the sounds she detects outside could bring danger into her space. So she's cautious. If she needs to wait, watch, listen, before she flies to t-raay-cee when it calls her, she does. T-raay-cee reassures her with routine, hunting in a small, safer way together inside their space.

As days and nights pass familiarity develops and Sparky grows easier, relaxing into this life with t-raay-cee. Becoming more confident, Sparky's inquisitive urges bubble up; she stops shying from, starts investigating, anything new appearing in her space. When t-raay-cee's human mate and the human with dark face plumage enter there's no rising panic pulsing her chest, stiffening her muscles and tingling her nerves. Her life is settling. When she and t-raay-cee start flying, hunting and feeding together outside, her mate releasing her, Sparky soaring overhead, returning when it calls to her, then their life will be all it should.

Before

April 2021 (cont.)

OOO

Dawn comes. A-ll-eee enters Sparky's new space, its head plumage ruffled, needing preening. It starts chattering as soon as it spots Sparky on the sky ledge. In amongst the chattering is Sparky's call but, though a-ll-eee repeats her call often it doesn't holds up its featherless wing for Sparky to fly to so she stays on the ledge.

HHH

Morning, Sparky. Did you sleep well and have sweet dreams? I was dreaming about you all night, Sparky, the fun we're going to have. I'll just have breakfast, Sparky, then show you round your new home.

OOO

A-ll-eee leaves, returns carrying a tiny water pool and a short shiny stick with an end like half an eggshell. Except for that night with matt-ee, Sparky hasn't seen what humans do in their own space. Hunter's curiosity makes her stare now, fascinated, learning.

A-ll-eee perches, holding the tiny water pool under its face, dipping the shiny stick into it then putting the eggshell end into its face hole. After its done that a few times Sparky's interest peaks, overruling caution. She flies across to the rear upright of the human perch, far enough from a-ll-eee that it can't grab her but close enough to peer into the tiny water pool. She sees it's full of creamy liquid, clumps floating in it. Some of the liquid and clumps are scooped up by the eggshell ended stick, disappearing into a-ll-eee's face hole. This is a human eating.

A-ll-eee turns towards Sparky, chattering, offering her the eggshell ended stick, filled with liquid and clumps.

HHH

Sorry, Sparky, how rude of me. Do you want some honey nut clusters?

OOO

Sparky tilts her head, inspecting the offering. It doesn't look like food but this human is eating it, offering it to her. She sidesteps along 'til she's close enough, stretches forwards and pecks. The liquid has a sticky runniness a bit like the blood of prey. She taps about blindly, finds a clump, crushes it. It crumbles easily in her beak, like mice heads, but it isn't meat and bone. Sparky drops it and flies to the sky ledge, resuming her watch through the ice.

A-ll-eee finishes eating, stands, chattering, steps through the in/out but doesn't close it again. Alert to the possibility, Sparky stares.

Ss-p-aaarrr-kkee.

She flies to the littered ledge from where she can see straight through the in/out. A-ll-eee's there, calling her to fly to it but not holding up its featherless wing. Sparky's confused. What does this human want?

HHH

You just come out when you're ready to explore, Sparky. I'll be upstairs. I need to get ready for the charity shop, today's my day.

OOO

A-ll-eee walks from sight, reappearing a moment later, walking back in the same direction but climbing upwards until it's out of view again.

Her hunting instinct urges Sparky to explore; her survival sense warns her to be careful. She wavers between opportunity and jeopardy, listening for danger, hearing only the distant sound of raining and the a-ll-eee human's singing.

She flies through the in/out. The space beyond is narrow and high so she flies upwards into it, above many rising ledges that a-ll-eee climbed. She heads for a patch of sky, dropping down there onto another sky ledge, facing another expanse of ice, confirming the invisible hardness that she can see through, but not fly through, with beak taps. Then she turns, studying the space around her. There are more in/outs, all of which are open. Thinly white air drifts towards her from the nearest, bringing the noise of rainfall and feel of dampness, like fog.

Keen to map this new territory, learn it so she's safe in it, Sparky flies through the dampness into a space that's brightly white with swirling fog, the rainfall thunderous to her amplifying ears. She tries to land on the curved white edge of a water pool, empty of water and standing on a thick leg. But the edge is hard and slippery; her talons can't grip it, her feet slide away from each other. She spots a safer perch, protruding like a ledge, beside the water pool. When she lands there her toes clutch the blue fluffy fur hanging over the perch, letting her stand upright without slipping. She settles there, absorbing the details of this new space.

The raining is from a shiny branch sticking out of the side across from her. A-ll-eee is under the raining branch, its head plumage wetly flattened to its skull. Sparky sees pale yellowy-brownish skin covering its whole body; it's moulted all its plumage suddenly and is now bathing under this raining branch, not in a water pool.

A-ll-ee faces Sparky, eyes opening.

HHH

Oh! You startled me, Sparky. Good thing we're girls together. It wouldn't be right showering with a boy watching. Sorry, Sparky, but I need that towel, please.

OOO

The raining stops. A-ll-eee stretches its featherless wing towards the perch Sparky's on, grabbing the furry covering and tugging it away. Sparky has to spring up, flapping into foggy air. She heads back through the in/out, to the sky ledge.

A moment later a-ll-eee appears from the bathing space, goes through another in/out. More confident now she's started exploring, mapping, Sparky follows.

It's a big enough space for her to circle so she does, scanning for a landing spot. Against that side stands a very tall, very large box, like a gigantic nest box but without an entrance hole. She flaps to the huge nest box, scrabbling onto it, head plumage lightly brushing the solid surface above. From here she can survey the space, which is mainly filled with a human perch much longer and wider than those in the space below. A-ll-eee settles on it now, rubbing its skin with the large piece of fur it pulled from under Sparky's toes. After the rubbing, a-ll-eee steps to the huge nest box, reaching out a featherless wing. Sparky leans forward to watch as the front of the nest box opens like an in/out, a-ll-eee's featherless wing disappearing inside. Sparky readies to flee; another flier could be inside, might emerge and attack.

But no flier emerges. A-ll-eee pulls out a brightly coloured bundle and covers its yellowy skin with what Sparky realises is fresh plumage. Humans don't grow plumage; they find it and cover themselves with it. Sparky stares at a-ll-eee in the new plumage. It sing-chatters and spins around before leaving the space.

HHH

This is my favourite dress, Sparky. I'm wearing it today in honour of you, to celebrate you being here. Do you like it? I feel like a princess in it; Bella, Bella, bell of the ball.

OOO

The new plumage swirling around its legs, a-ll-eee leaves the space. The feeling she should follow because it's brought her to this new territory and is, now and then, behaving like it wants to be her mate, swells inside Sparky. Although it's different from her before mates there's enough to show her this human could become the half of her that she lost when matt-ee vanished. She flies down the rising ledges, returning to the space she started from, her new space, landing on the rear of a human perch, waiting for what a-ll-eee does next.

It stays at the in/out, chattering.

HHH

O.K., Sparky, I have to go, my bus'll be here soon, but I'll be back this afternoon. You guard the house for me. I'll just close this door, keep you safely inside.

Now

July 2022 (cont.)

HHH

I put the owl centre plan aside until autumn; I have a summer with Sparky ahead. I'll do as much as I can to make up for what I know, and imagine, she's been through. Luckily the falconer's as pleased as me that Sparky's safe and keen to train me to care for her; I'll be his oldest apprentice.

But the familiarity of Sparky's old home, the routine we'd established, is lost to us; we need to start again, develop a new routine, settle into Sparky's new home, new life: learn to fly all over again. Except now I don't have the security of a long barn to fly her inside. If I want to let her stretch her wings she'll have to fly outside, over the field where she'd be a white speck in a green and blue ocean, free to fly away if she chose. I put that dread thought aside, rewind to the beginning by flying her inside her aviary prior to walking her around outside on the fist, where she can see the house, hear the road noise, feel sun and wind, visit the lawn where I'll start flying her tied to a creance line as soon as we're ready.

OOO

Today, when they've flown in her space several times, they go out together, Sparky perching on t-raay-cee's featherless wing. Looking up she sees the sky, wide and blue, and jumps towards only to be pulled down. She's tethered to t-raay-cee; it's not ready for them to fly yet.

They walk away from her space. Sparky takes this chance to map her new territory. There are trees and bushes; a large structure she recognises as where humans roost; a pair of growling movers; a grassy patch like those she's flown over before, a tall perch planted in the middle of it, waiting for her.

They walk for a while then return to her space. This routine is new for a time but it ages quickly, becoming their life.

Before

April 2021 (cont.)

OOO

A-ll-eee moves to step through the in/out. Sparky flies to join it, landing on the head ledge because the featherless wing is folded away. As soon as she touches down, a-ll-eee stops, turns, walks Sparky back to the sky ledge, still chattering.

HHH

No, sorry, Sparky, but you can't come. You have to stay here. They only let guide dogs in the charity shop.

OOO

It crouches beside the ledge; Sparky's nudged to jump across to it. But as fast as a-ll-eee stands, walks to the in/out Sparky flies to join it.

They do this a few times. It's not the flying, hunting, feeding she shared with her before mates but going to a-ll-eee's head ledge as it walks away is still flying to a human, which is what Sparky knows and does. If they fly together, they'll bond, become a pair. A-ll-eee turns more sharply, runs from her. But Sparky can fly quicker than a-ll-eee runs; she's always on a-ll-eee's head ledge before it reaches the in/out. A-ll-eee starts giving Sparky's call in a stream of rapid chattering, so she keeps flying to it because that's what the call means.

HHH

Naughty Sparky. I'll miss my bus. Please, stay in here. I'll be back soon, Sparky. I know you don't want to be apart but we have to, Sparky, just for a little while, Wednesdays, Thursdays and Saturdays. No, Sparky, naughty.

OOO

Sparky doesn't know what the new n-orr-t-eee sound means, only the ss-p-aaarrr-kkee sound, so she flies to it now, learning from this new human's behaviour how to be with it.

After more of this a-ll-eee, with Sparky on its head ledge, walks into the high narrow space, along to the far end and into another space there. Sparky scans around it, storing details, mapping it: another sky ledge at another expanse of ice; a water pool like that in the bathing space but deeper, more square shaped, with a curved shiny branch over it; a large, tall box like that a-ll-eee took the new plumage from but white, not brown. Singing, a-ll-eee goes to this large white box, opening its front and reaching inside.

HHH

Young Mother Madison, went to the fridge, to get naughty Sparky a chick.

OOO

Sparky leans forward, peering around, into the white box. A jumble of different-shaped objects perch on ledges. A-ll-eee snatches at something; Sparky's quick eyes see the wing toes pounce on a chick. This is where prey can be caught: the hunting space. A-ll-eee hides the chick amongst its plumage and takes them into Sparky's space, near but not to, the sky ledge. The chick appears now, flying towards the ledge. Sparky chases it, powering down on it with killing force. She foots it up to her beak, wings hiding it from a-ll-eee, still wary of this human, its unpredictable behaviour. With the chick secured, she twists her neck, looking over a wing to see a-ll-eee disappearing, the in/out closing.

Now

July–August 2022

HHH

I sound out the falconer about the owl centre plan. He doesn't know the head keeper but has heard good things about him. It's an option, if they'll take her. But for now she's fine where she is. She has a home, a better one than before, maybe the best she's ever had; she's safe, been lucky, ending up with you, he tells me.

I'll only believe this myself, when, if, I dare to fly her properly, free, out over that terrifyingly wide, wild, field. That's where Sparky deserves to fly, like she was born to, as wild barn owls do on their hunting flights, quartering open grasslands. If I daren't do it she'll have to go to someone who will. I owe her that and I'll make that decision, no matter how deeply losing her would cut, if it's right for her. That trite expression about letting go of those you love is literal, not metaphorical, for me now.

I set about re-establishing a routine for Sparky and me. Routines are reassuring because, with enough consistency, animals, including people, can believe we know what's coming and be ready for it. But routines take time; how long do I have, how long can I wait, how long does she need? I can't both move Sparky forward in her training and keep everything the same for her day after day. Inevitably her routine needs to vary: progress. I try to think only of the next step; the destination lurks over the horizon.

OOO

They've stopped walking in the middle of the grassy patch, beside a tall perch. This is different but familiar. Sparky flaps her wings, readying herself.

She's stood on the perch. T-raay-cee walks away facing Sparky, just a few paces, then raises its featherless wing.

Ss-p-aaarrr-kkee.

Sparky knows she can fly to her mate. It's only a few wing-beats. She's flown further to it before. And she trusts t-raay-cee; it took her from the fliers' space, flew with her in the narrow gap, brought her to this better territory, they go outside together where she sky watches. But she can only trust herself to flight when she's accustomed to her world, their life together. When something's different she's uneasy, tension stiffening her wings and constricting her chest, making her feel she can't fly even though all she has to do is leap into the air, wings beating. So she doesn't fly now, not even the few wing-beats needed to reach t-raay-cee.

After a long moment of waiting, Sparky on the perch and t-raay-cee a few strides away, t-raay-cee comes close, holds up its wing and calls to her, the sound warm.

Ss-p-aaarrr-kkee.

Sparky hops to it and they return to her space, fly in there, as usual, where she's sure of their safety.

HHH

Once I've got her flying as easily to me from the perch in her aviary as she did at the animal centre I take her out, just as I did there, walking around with her tethered to my still pristine falconry glove. But this new step is a backwards one. She'll perch calmly on my glove in the aviary but bates off it when we're outside. I persevere until she's unfazed by the sights and sounds of her surroundings; road traffic, walking people, chirping songbirds, grazing sheep, ploughing tractors. Then, under supervision, I give her the chance to fly to me outside while she's fastened to a creance so she can't escape. Another step backwards. Although she flies to me as soon as I call her in the aviary she won't come at all from the perch on the lawn only to come straight away once we're back in the aviary. It's frustrating. If only I knew what she was thinking: feeling. I carry on, being steady with her, observing closely and recording what happens so I learn from her. She'll tell me, as all animals do, in her own way, what she needs from me; I just don't speak her language yet.

Before

April 2021 (cont.)

OOO

A-ll-eee returns later that day, Sparky spotting it through the ice as it walks past outside before she hears it enter their territory. She flies to the littered ledge where she can face it when a-ll-eee appears, which it does almost instantly, calling her to it.

Ss-p-aaarrr-kkee.

She flies straight to the head ledge. Most humans Sparky's known made her perch on their featherless wing but not a-ll-eee; its behaviour is puzzling, different, but not threatening now. It wants to be with her, wants her to be with it; they can bond in this different way, still become mates.

Singing its chatter, a-ll-eee walks, with Sparky perching on it, back into the high narrow space, climbing the rising ledges. Sparky springs into flight, reaching the top before her human, landing on the sky ledge there. When a-ll-eee catches up it goes into the bathing space. Following, Sparky finds a-ll-eee on a perch different again to those Sparky's seen before. A-ll-eee only perches there briefly. When it stands it touches the perch's top. There's a sudden gushing of water. Startled, Sparky flies out, settling on the sky ledge again.

A-ll-eee emerges.

HHH

Sorry, Sparky, did that frighten you? Tinkle, tinkle, little me, I had to go and have a wee.

OOO

Climbing down again, a-ll-eee goes to the hunting space. Sparky flies ahead, landing on a broad ledge that rests on a bank of boxes half as tall as a-ll-eee, set around most of the space's sides. Her feet slide apart as she walks across, investigating the different objects perching here and there, managing to step-slide over the broad ledge's slippery surface, pecking that, footing this. While she investigates a-ll-eee darts around the space, opening some of the boxes under the broad ledge, then opening the tall white box where prey hides.

After a moment a-ll-eee leaves the hunting space, carrying things; Sparky stays behind to empty herself, coughing up an oval pellet, moist but solid, leaving the bony fragments and matted down of her last meal on the slippery broad ledge.

Ss-p-aaarrr-kkee.

Tracing the sound to her new space, Sparky heads there. A-ll-eee's watching for her; as soon as she swoops in it flies a chick to the sky ledge. Sparky hunts it down. Catch secured, she sees a-ll-eee perching and eating. She eats too.

Meal swallowed, Sparky's attention is drawn across the space when stuttering sound appears. That upright oblong object a-ll-eee chased her off is flickering with movement again. Inquisitive, Sparky lands beside, not on, it. A-ll-eee instantly springs off its perch, flapping featherless wings at her so she returns to the sky ledge, absorbing the vivid view behind the expanse of ice. A-ll-eee reperches, face turned to the flickering and stuttering that mimics the world Sparky's focused on.

It grows dark outside, darkish inside. A-ll-eee rests. The in/out is open. Sparky takes this chance to patrol her new territory. Gliding from space to space, drifting, fluttering, circling and swooping, landing here, there, pecking and footing, Sparky adds features and routes to her mental map, learning this new territory's every detail. There's only her and her human occupying it. There are several distinct spaces in it. Below the rising ledges is the living space, where they do their flying and eating, and the hunting space where they find prey. Above the rising ledges is the bathing space, the space where a-ll-eee found new plumage and another smaller space littered with boxes and different objects of odd shapes and sizes. All the spaces have in/outs and sky ledges beneath expanses of ice. There are lots of perching spots but no perches like she's had elsewhere. Both water pools are empty. It's not like any of her before territories or spaces but it's safe; she can fly here, has a-ll-eee to share it with. If they're going to be a pair then this will be their space, their territory, so she'll adapt to it, survive, maybe even thrive, in it.

Sparky returns to the living space. A-ll-eee is upright.

HHH

There you are, Sparky. Right, beddy-byes time. C'mon, lets climb the wooden hill to dreamland.

OOO

Having climbed the rising ledges Sparky flies to the sky ledge; a-ll-eee enters the bathing space, dropping onto the water-gushing perch. Then a-ll-eee heads to the new plumage space. Sparky follows, wing-beating to the top of the plumage box. From there she watches a-ll-eee bury itself feetwards into the long wide perch, nestling itself on and inside the flat part, its head near the low upright part.

With a single flap, Sparky floats down, finding softness under her feet. As soon as she's landed a-ll-eee faces her, chatters briefly, reaches out a featherless wing, touching an object beside it. The space's light vanishes. Through the darkness Sparky sees her human huddle deeper into itself, eyes closing. It gives a final call.

G-u-dd-n-iii-tt ss-p-aaarrr-kkee.

Then it stays silent and still. There's only the faint sussing of it breathing.

A-ll-eee is roosting. This is a roosting space; that's not a perch, it's a nest.

Sparky's never been with a human when it's in its nest. Uncertain what to do, she steps over to a-ll-eee's head, which is all she can see; the rest of it is hidden inside the nest. Sparky's feather-light body doesn't ripple the soft surface enough to wake the roosting human. When she's beside a-ll-eee's head, she stretches to her full height, craning her neck to get the clearest view. Its eyes and face hole are closed. Her ears trace the soft breathing to the unbeak. The head plumage is ruffled. She listens for a moment before wing-beating to the top of the plumage box. It's asleep. Tucking a leg up, eyes closing, she sleeps too.

Day breaks, the light from outside creeping into the roosting space, growing brightness waking Sparky. A-ll-eee stirs, stretching and sitting up, singing its chatter. Sparky flies down to the nest when her call is sung.

HHH

Morning, Sparky. Did you enjoy our first sleepover, girls together, BFFs?

Sparky Owl, Sparky Owl, what did you do last night? I explored my new home in silent flight. And Sparky Owl, Sparky Owl, what did you make of it? I found it a good home from which I'll not flit.

We've got a whole lifetime together, Sparky, a sleepover every night. It's going to be so, so great.

Now

August 2022

OOO

They're outside on the grassy patch again, Sparky on the tall perch, t-raay-cee a few paces away, calling her, its featherless wing ready for her, the wing toes trapping prey.

But this is still too new, to unfamiliar, for her to risk leaving this perch where danger can't stalk her. She needs to see and hear what's to be seen and heard, mapping this new territory, learning it's safe over many days and nights. Until then she won't fly to t-raay-cee. She'll stay at her lookout, letting the world move around her, ready to face it.

Sparky scans the scene, head swivelling with sharp snaps, darting eyes checking for approaching threats, scanning ears searching for distant dangers nearing. There's so much to see and store; different structures and objects, many colours, things shiny and dull, bigger and smaller. Just as she's reassured herself a movement distracts her; fliers buzzing close or soaring over head, shadows flickering, branches swaying. Her eyes can't help seeing every movement any more than her ears can help hearing every noise; human chatter, the caw-caws, screeches and chirrups of fliers, movers' growlings, bangs and thuds: a whole acoustic world of unidentifiable clacks, snaps, clicks, crunches, whistles, hisses, taps, whooshes, trills, screams and whoops, all demanding her attention, making her turn this way, that way, absorbing them like rain soaking her plumage, overwhelming her, no matter how far afield they are.

She can't fly until these sounds and sights are familiar enough to become the scenery of her world.

HHH

Days become weeks. Sparky still refuses to fly to me outside, tied to the creance line: I'm disappointed. She'd made progress at the animal centre, coming 15m to me; now she won't even jump to my glove. I remind myself she's been through so much change recently, needs consistency. It's a cross against trying to rehome her with the owl centre; a tick for her staying with me. I keep to our routine.

Then she surprises me, on a day when she seems particularly unsure about even leaving her aviary and I'm resigned to her not flying again outside. A friend's unexpected arrival, walking fairly close to where I've set up the perch and am standing calling Sparky, panics her; she takes off, brought to ground by the line. I'm cursing because, now spooked, there's no chance she'll fly to me. But after she's calmed down, the friend's gone inside and I've taken her to the perch, she does, coming when called, several times. Maybe being spooked into the air reminded her of the joy of wafting herself through summer sky. It's encouraging.

OOO

A strange new human springs into view, its feet sharply crunching as it strides over the ground. It's a sudden assault of movement and noise: a threat. Reflexes propel Sparky into scattering flight. This is why she stayed on the perch, watching and listening, not flying to t-raay-cee, so she was ready for danger. She wing-beats urgently, sprinting skyward, racing the panic pulsating in her chest. She's just gaining reassuring height when a sharp jolt drags her down. She tries flying forwards instead of upwards, finds herself in stationary flight. She flaps frantically until, chest throbbing, she has to drop to the ground.

She lands near t-raay-cee who crouches beside her.

Ss-p-aaarrr-kkee.

The call is soft, quiet: soothing.

But the sudden burst of activity has shocked her into stillness; Sparky can't step up to her mate, even though it wants her to.

A gentle tugging coaxes Sparky to lift her feet, step onto t-raay-cee's featherless wing. Her mate walks them to the tall perch. As she hops to it she studies t-raay-cee's face, searching for alarm in the eyes, unbeak and face hole. Nothing she sees in her mate's expression is different to what she's seen in its face before. Everything's usual: safe. She cranes forward, looking behind t-raay-cee. The new human that appeared so suddenly is gone. But the feeling of flying stays, humming through Sparky's body, a vibrating of nerves and muscles quivering with energy: life.

This time when t-raay-cee takes a few steps away from Sparky, raising its featherless wing and calling her, she flies to it.

Before

May–December 2021

OOO

Life with a-ll-eee as her mate settles. Sparky learns its ways: sleeping laid in the nest; moulting then bathing under the raining branch; flying, hunting and feeding in the living space with her; leaving their territory some mornings, returning as the day ages. When it leaves Sparky's trapped in the living space but whenever it's in their territory she's free to fly around all the spaces, perching anywhere. She goes often to the sky ledges, reliving the freedom she used to fly into. It's a different life than she had with before mates but she adapts, becoming contented in it, teaching a-ll-eee her ways.

Like when she showed it she needed somewhere to bathe; she found the pool in the bathing space full of water and jumped in, splashing around, rinsing her feathers until they were clean then climbing out to preen them, get them in flying order. Now she always finds that water pool full for whenever she needs to bathe.

A-ll-eee teaches her things too. She's not to perch on the stuttering, flickering rectangle in the living space. She's not to fly to a-ll-eee when it's closing the living space in/out. She doesn't understand all its behaviour though. Sometimes when she's emptied herself, coughed up a pellet, it'll flap a featherless wing, its song screechier, then it rubs away the dropping or drops the pellet in a tall hole in the corner of the hunting space. Other times pellets collect on the ground in the hunting space, where Sparky mostly coughs them out, and some surfaces in the territory become spattered with white-brown droppings. This inconsistency is unlike before humans she knew. And it's often fidgety, like it's panicked even though there's no danger. Sparky senses something unstable, an imbalance, about it.

The biggest difference is their hunting; a-ll-eee finds and flushes out prey, flying it to the sky ledge in the living space, not calling Sparky to its featherless wing for the catch. If she's not hungry, Sparky takes whatever she doesn't eat to the littered ledge where she stashes food, hiding it behind the objects on the ledge. Only she knows it's there so only she can find it, which she does when she's hungry later.

They never go outside to fly, hunt and feed together.

Still, Sparky grows comfortable with this puzzling mate. No strange humans ever invade their territory, it's just them, together, a pair: whole. Their life is safe and simple, their world small and secure; nothing threatens them.

Now

August–September 2022

HHH

After getting Sparky to finally fly to me outside a hot spell scuppers us, sun scorching the grass yellow. It's too hot for walking so definitely too hot for flying. Sparky stays on the perch, head turning to sounds and sights invisible and inaudible to me. I keep calling her, not expecting any flight; she leaps into the air, flies up and away, presumably startled by something utterly imperceptible to me. The creance line brings her safely to ground. I pick her up but, unlike other occasions, she doesn't follow this with flights to me. She just sits there, panting. I worry she's overheating, return her to her shady aviary. In there I try calling her to me again, for a chick foot. She comes towards me immediately but, halfway, circles back to her perch. I try again with a wing, a piece of leg. Nothing. Then I get the mouse, the main course when she's flying. She launches like a rocket, the cheeky madam. I've been calling her to me for the mouse when we're back in the aviary; she's obviously sussed this, was waiting for her rodent reward to make a flight worthwhile. At least I've learned what a bright spark she is.

OOO

The sun burns into her wings and dazzles her eyes as Sparky stands on the perch. The heat throbbing through her is cumbersome, pressing down on her, solid air pinning her wings to her body. T-raay-cee calls her to it, but Sparky doesn't have the energy to carry this hot weight in flight. She'll save her flying for if she needs it.

T-raay-cee comes closer, coaxing her to it. Sparky steps up to it, showing her mate she wants them to be together, just that today, in this heat, she can't fly to it. She goes to the perch, t-raay-cee goes to its spot further away, calling to her again. But hot air fills Sparky's lungs. She pants it out, searching around for cool shade; there isn't any close enough. She knows her space is shady. Mustering scant energy, she flaps off the perch but doesn't have enough in her to go far, not even to strain against the pull groundward. She drops down. T-raay-cee comes to her, letting her step up to it and carrying her, at last, to her cool, shaded space. It's understood her, what she needs. They're learning each other's ways, becoming a pair that can depend on each other.

Before

January 2022

OOO

Sparky's resting on the sky ledge in their living space. A-ll-eee's resting too, focused on the flickering stuttering oblong.

A pair of humans walks along the grey ground beyond Sparky's territory. She spots lots of humans walking there; they don't spot her. These humans do, though, looking through the ice right at her, heads turning to keep eyes on her as they pass. The human nearest Sparky raises a featherless wing to her as they vanish from view.

D-ii-nnnggg-d-oo-nnnggg.

The sound comes from outside, entering their territory. Sparky head-turns, scanning for threats, sees a-ll-eee is standing, staring at the ice, where the pair of humans passed by.

D-ii-nnnggg-d-oo-nnnggg.

A-ll-eee chatters harshly now, the sing-song vibrating through Sparky, stiffening her muscles.

HHH

What do they want? I told them never to come here. What are they doing coming here, Sparky?

OOO

Wings unfolded, flight ready, Sparky watches a-ll-eee leave the living space, closing the in/out. She hears a fainter d-ii-nnnggg-d-oo-nnnggg, flies to where she can face anything invading her space, ears tuning to the out-of-sight sounds: a bang; harshly screeching sing-chatter; softer coaxing chatter; footsteps.

HHH

What do you want?

We're worried about you, love. The landlord rang, complaining you won't let him inspect.

It's my home. He can't come in. He'll scare Sparky. You can't come in either.

Sparky?

Love, we just want to make sure you're O.K.

Yes, Sparky, she lives here with me now. We look after each other. We don't

need anyone else.
Who's Sparky, love?
My barn owl of course. You saw her, in the window. I caught you staring at her.
It's a real owl?
Of course she's real. If you don't believe me, you can meet her. She won't like you, though. She only likes me. We don't want you here.

OOO

The in/out opens. Body crouched, wings outspread, Sparky prepares to take off. A-ll-eee appears. Sparky starts to refold her wings then sees the pair of strange humans are there, chasing a-ll-eee. A throbbing pulses in Sparky's chest, energy swarms hotly through her whole body. Wings displayed menacingly, she hisses a warning: this is hers and her mate's territory. A-ll-eee steps further into the space; the pair of humans stay by the in/out, scouting the space, considering challenging for it. Sparky studies their grey head plumage and sallow, worn face skin, withered like winter leaves. She hasn't seen humans with these features before but their appearance recalls matt-ee when it was injured, dying. These are old humans, an established pair searching for a new territory. They're resilient: survivors.
To ward off their attack, Sparky hisses her raspy caw screechily, wing-flapping: threatening. The pair shriek-chatter at a-ll-eee, the taller human stepping towards it while the shorter human head-shakes.

HHH

Oh my god. Love, you can't live like this, look at this place.
You can't keep a barn owl here, Allie. This is wrong.
Says who?
If the landlord finds out he'll evict you.
He won't find out. He's not coming in. I won't let him. He can't make me. It's my home, mine and Sparky's.
You're not well. You need help, love.
Have you stopped taking your medication again?

OOO

Sparky springs off her ledge, circling the living space in a wide arc, wingtips brushing the sides as she swoops over a-ll-eee, turning deftly towards the invaders, diving towards the shorter human that blocks their escape. As she races to pounce on, claw at, its grey head plumage, it flaps both featherless wings at her. Sparky feels a touch on her flight feathers, wing-dips sharply, beats rapidly, fighting to stay airborne, flying herself through the in/out, calling with her raspy croak, for a-ll-eee to follow.
Sparky rushes up, into the roosting space, scrabbling onto the top of the

plumage box which is so deep and wide, so close to the sides surrounding it, it's almost a hollow hide-e-hole. Sparky scrambles into hiding, hunches against the solid surfaces behind, beside and above her where the shadows shield her. Her attack failed. The old pair are occupying their territory, their living space. Her mate's alone with them but maybe it can fight them off. Many seasons ago d-aann-y-elll fought off an invading human. She doesn't know if a-ll-eee will fight off, survive, the challenge to their territory. She can only hide and wait.

Harsh chatter screams up to her from the living space, bristling her every nerve.

HHH

You're poorly again, Allie.

I'm calling the doctor.

You're not. Give me that. Just go away, leave us alone. We're fine.

How can you be? People don't live like this.

Then they're idiots; Sparky's amazing. We're best friends.

Maybe we should consider Victoria House, they helped you last time.

I'm not going back there. Never! We don't need that place, or you.

But Allie…

Get out of my home, right now. Leave or I'll scream.

Love, we just want…

Aaaarrrrgh…

OOO

An agonising yowl. An ominous bang. Suffocating silence. Soft footsteps.

A-ll-eee creeps into the roosting space. Sparky peers down at it. It doesn't seem injured. She calls to it. It looks up. Sparky blinks darkly at it.

Ss-p-aaarrr-kkee.

The call is soft, comforting. Sparky shuffles towards the edge.

Ss-p-aaarrr-kkee.

She doesn't fly down. Her mate chatters, its singing gentle; Sparky hears her call often but still doesn't fly down.

HHH

It's alright, Sparky, promise. They've gone. I chased them. I won't let them come again, Sparky, honestly. I'm so sorry they scared you. It's O.K., really. Please come down.

Allie had a little owl, its feathers tan and white. Every time that Allie cried, her owl made things alright.

I know what you need, a treat, Sparky!

OOO

A-ll-eee returns with a mouse that it throws onto the nest.

Ss-p-aaarrr-kkee.

She doesn't get mice often, there don't see to be many in their hunting space. A few wing-beats float Sparky down to the rare prey. She grabs the mouse, swallowing it voraciously as a-ll-eee steps from the space, heading for the rising ledges, singing.

HHH

Sparky owl went up the hill, to hide from Allie's folks. When they had gone, and all was safe, Sparky owl came swooping down.

OOO

Sparky stays on the nest, listening. After a while of only the familiar sounds of her territory drifting up, she flies to be with her mate. Entering the living space, she looks for the grey humans. They're gone. A-ll-eee chased them off. This is still her and a-ll-eee's home territory. They're established here, paired for life now. Nothing will break their bond.

Now

September 2022

HHH

The weather cools. We head into a settled spell. Sparky starts flying to me when I call her. But progress is ragged. She'll do ten decently long flights one session, coming as soon as I call her and raise my arm. Next time she'll only do a few shorter flights. Sometimes she's focused on me, too keen even, snatching food, scratching me. Other times she ignores me, attention focused on her surroundings, and won't fly no matter how I encourage her with food and the signal to come: calling her name plus two tongue clicks, my gloved arm raised, wiggling the food so the movement catches her hunter's motion-tuned eyes. I remind myself this'll take time but I want it to happen quickly, before I have to decide about rehoming her at the owl centre who should be contacting me soon about volunteering, my way of vetting them before deciding Sparky's future: our future. If we do well before then maybe I'll convince myself she could stay here. I prepare for both outcomes with some paperwork.

Firstly I buy a second notebook for my training log, one with a barn owl on the cover, keep up my record of her weight, what she eats, how far she flies each time, now adding weather conditions as she's flying outside, and anything significant that happens during the flying session. I'm looking for patterns, a formula: weight + weather / Y behaviour = X flights. But she's not an automaton with predictable results; she's alive, has her own mind. She decides if, when, she'll fly to me. Only she knows why she does, or doesn't.

Secondly I apply for her new Article 10 certificate, with the help of the IBR lady who's glad to learn I rescued Sparky. I need this document because, ironically it'll be easier to rehomed her once she's officially mine. The owl centre wouldn't want a bird without an A10 as they couldn't use her in flying displays or even have her on show to the paying public. With the A10 in my name I'll formally be her guardian. Actually the form says 'owner' but I don't believe in claiming ownership over animals. They're as alive, as sentient, as me; I've got no rights to them, just responsibilities for them. Plus I sense, or want to believe I sense, a bond between us. She flies to me; she won't fly to others. This isn't me owning her, her being mine; it's a mutual relationship, maybe even a friendship?

OOO

T-raay-cee takes them out to fly, hunt and feed together often now. It's a life Sparky's had before but the memory of it is shadowy. Gradually it brightens, even when something new, different, happens during their flying.

This day the wind ruffles Sparky's feathers from behind as she's on the perch. T-raay-cee moves the perch so her feathers are ruffled from the side instead, which Sparky knows makes flying to her mate easier. But the view of their flying territory is different now; before she can fly she has to familiarising herself with it: remap it.

This day a strange buzzing chirruping interrupts them after they've only done a few flights. Sparky traces it to t-raay-cee, sees her mate pull a small black object from its plumage, put it to its ear and chatter to it then tuck it away again. They do another couple of flights, fewer than usual, before t-raay-cee takes her to her space and leaves.

This day, just as they're flying as high and far as they have, as far as Sparky can without being pulled groundward, there's a drenching downpour. T-raay-cee rushes to Sparky, lifting her onto its featherless wing then dashing under shelter. They have to wait there, rain falling thunderously, for a while. Then they fly again, as if the rain hadn't been.

This day, while standing on t-raay-cee's featherless wing, hopping on that leg, prey held in the other, Sparky over-balances trying to get the food to her beak. She drops it and it escapes into the grass. T-raay-cee crouches down, scrabbling around, brushing aside the soft green leaves. Sparky hops down too, pecking about. Finally they recatch it, t-raay-cee pecking it up in its wing toes, Sparky jumping up to eat so they can go on flying.

There are lots of days like this, when their flying, hunting, feeding routine isn't eggshell smooth, because they're both still learning to live life together. Sparky's facing the wrong way so t-raay-cee can't nudge her into flight, towards the perch. She flies to t-raay-cee too quickly, landing to find it hasn't trapped any prey for her. She loses sight of the perch, has to circle the grassy patch as wide as she can, to find it. The line yanks her out of flight. Strangers appear so they have to wait, watching for threatening behaviour, until the strangers leave.

But however their flying goes they're bonding, becoming a stronger, more devoted pair every day.

Before

February 2022

OOO

Many days and nights pass without the pair of grey humans returning to challenge Sparky and a-ll-eee for their territory; a-ll-eee successfully chased them off. Sparky and a-ll-eee's life goes on as before.

The changes, when they start, are small, happening little by little, autumn leaves falling. Sparky's aware of these changes but unconcerned by them: they don't affect her. A-ll-eee bathes less; doesn't change its plumage as often; rests in daytime, on a perch in the living space not at night in the nest in the roosting space; chatters more and more but less and less to Sparky. It doesn't eat when it wakes. Or it eats then eats again a short while later. It doesn't leave their territory, spending all its days in the living space, perching laid flat, eyes watching nothing. Then it leaves their territory again, for longer and longer; Sparky's alone, the in/out open so she patrols, stopping at all the ices for sight of a-ll-eee reappearing, which it does as day becomes night, then soon after day becomes night, then in the depths of night, stretching out how long they're apart until it's gone from dawn to dawn. But Sparky still has the safety of her home territory, food to eat, a pool for bathing and her mate always does return to her. As long as the changes settle, the new becoming familiar, their shared life will be as it should.

It's night. A-ll-eee didn't catch any prey for Sparky. She's hungry. While a-ll-eee's roosting, in the nest tonight, Sparky restlessly drifts around their territory, scouting for prey, survivor's wildness urging her to keep flying: hunting. She's unsuccessful. Maybe a-ll-eee will catch prey for her during the day.

It's dusk again. A-ll-eee appears with prey for itself. Sparky still hasn't eaten, doesn't know why her mate's stopped offering her food. If it wanted to break their bond it could leave, like her before mates have, but it's staying with her, in their territory, in their shared life. It just isn't behaving like her mate. Confused, hungry, Sparky flies over, hops onto a featherless wing, leans close and pecks at a-ll-eee's meal. Her beak feels fleshiness; she snatches the meat, flying to the sky ledge with it.

A-ll-eee stands quickly, calling out harshly.

N-orr-t-eee ss-p-aaarrr-kkee.

Sparky gulps the fleshy chunk into her stomach with effort. It was large for her to swallow whole but she needed it inside, sating her hunger.

A-ll-eee comes towards her, flapping wildly, chattering loudly.

HHH

Naughty, Sparky, stealing Allie's tea! Best friends don't steal each other's chicken.

OOO

Sparky gives her hissing raspy caw. She hasn't called out for a while because there wasn't reason to. Now instinct, born when she scratched and scraped her way from her shell, first knew hunger and was fed, urges her to call to her human.

A-ll-eee stands as still as dandelion blossoms on a windless day. Sparky hiss-caws urgently. A-ll-eee stares at her. Sparky stares back, croaking her gentle screech again. A-ll-eee disappears, quickly reappears, coming to Sparky, sing-chattering softly, and flies a chick and a chick and a mouse to her. Then it goes on perching, eating and sing-chattering.

HHH

Oh, Sparky, no, Allie forgot. Poor starving Sparky. Here, look, food, lots of it. You were trying to tell Allie, that's why you stole. You're a good girl, you wouldn't steal from your best friend. Did you get your tea last night? Please say you did, Sparky. I can't remember.

Sparky owl in the house, eating chicks and a mouse. She puts down her beak and pecks up some meat. Now she's full up from her meal.

OOO

Sparky eats the mouse, then a chick, then the head of the other chick. That fills her so she darts to the littered ledge, stashing the headless chick in her hide-e-hole there.

Later that night a-ll-eee suddenly leaves the living space. Sparky follows it into the hunting space, where it catches a chick and a mouse from inside the tall white box. Noticing Sparky standing near the water pool, her mate drops the prey on the broad ledge beside her. Sparky pounces on the chick as a-ll-eee chatters, the sound whitening until Sparky can only just hear it.

HHH

Sorry, Sparky, I nearly forgot your tea. I'm all of a dither. It's because of them. They want to split us up. But don't worry, we won't let them. We'll survive together, Sparky: friends forever. As long as you love me it'll be O.K. I couldn't stand it if you turned against me too.

OOO

A-ll-eee reaches a prodding wing toe towards Sparky. It's strange, potentially threatening, behaviour. Sparky screeches a warning, stepping away, wary eyes on her disturbing mate. They both freeze like winter water. Then rain floods a-ll-eee's eyes. The unbeak gives a snff-snff sound. Its face crumples. A deep howl bursts from it, startling Sparky into a hovering flight as A-ll-eee runs from hunting space, thundering up the rising ledges as though chasing prey.

Tonight the changes in her mate begin concerning Sparky; it might not be her mate lifelong. Soon she might be only half of herself again: alone. She searches for somewhere to stash this new catch, spots a crevice at ground level, behind the tall white box and flaps down, stuffing the prey into this new hide-e-hole, hunter's mind knowing the importance of preparing for life's lean days.

From overhead sounds of her mate sing-chattering in high, shrill tones, drift down.

HHH

There once was a barn owl called Sparky that Allie loved with all her might, but when Allie came close her friend Sparky screamed loudly in fright.

Why did you scream at me, Sparky? Don't you want to be friends anymore? If you stop being my friend I'll… I need you, Sparky. Forever friends, remember?

OOO

The changes are larger now, looming over them like a predator's shadow. A-ll-eee's strange behaviour is cold and sharp, a frost on them. It's the change from autumn to winter; gradual and overnight.

A-ll-eee doesn't leave their territory now. It's always night for them, day banished by loose swaying coverings hanging in front of all the ices. Sparky can still reach the living space sky ledge by hopping onto the rear edge of the human perch beside it and scrabbling behind the covering, but she can't get onto any of the others so that's her only sky view.

Their territory becomes littered with debris; feathers, pellets, droppings, half-eaten prey, scraps of this and that, discarded human bits and pieces. Many straight-edged white and brown leaves drop into the high narrow space, a pile of them growing near the in/out that's their territorial boundary. Objects disappear from their spaces, a-ll-eee hiding them in boxes that themselves vanish through another territorial in/out in the hunting space. Strange black markings appear on the sides in some spaces; squiggles, loops, lines and dots. A-ll-eee makes these markings with a thick stick gripped in its wing toes.

A-ll-eee doesn't always have plumage now; Sparky sees its pale skin pulled tight over its bones. Some days her mate doesn't look at Sparky, give her call, let her land on its head ledge or even catch prey for her. It's as if a-ll-eee can't see or hear her. Other days it calls to her constantly, patting its head ledge, offering her more prey than she can eat, coming too close, reaching out grabbing wing toes. Sparky stashes prey for the lean days, lands on her mate's head ledge when it calls her to it, perching there as a-ll-eee patrols their territory, going around and around and around. But Sparky always retreats from the grabbing wing toes, screeching fearfully. Then it chatters harshly, flaps her away or runs from her, howling. There's something frantic, wild, about a-ll-eee, as though it's endlessly fighting to escape danger.

All these changes distress Sparky. Her mate is suffering so Sparky suffers too. Their bond is breaking down, withering, dying. If these changes continue they'll stop being a pair. Sparky tries to protect her mate, staying close to a-ll-eee, calling often to it, perching with it, preening its tangled head plumage. While a-ll-eee sleeps, Sparky patrols their territory, searching for the silent, invisible threat that's brought all these troubling changes.

It's another night. They're in their living space. Sparky's eaten a chick and a mouse and added another chick to her stash; she has enough for several lean days now. A-ll-eee's eaten its own prey, although it's left some uneaten for later. The black rectangular object across the space doesn't flicker and stutter but a-ll-eee focuses on it anyway, not noticing Sparky who's on the dome perch where she can watch for danger approaching.

A-ll-eee stands suddenly, glares at Sparky, jabbing a wing toe towards her, chattering harshly then leaving the living space.

HHH

I thought you were my friend, Sparky. But I realise now you're just like all the others. I warned you what'd happen if you stopped being my friend.

OOO

A-ll-eee goes to the bathing space. Sparky follows, guarding as it bathes; her mate doesn't usually bathe at night. When it's bathed a-ll-eee goes into the roosting space, puts on new plumage and spends a long time preening. Then it patrols their territory, sweeping aside the swaying coverings that hang in front of the ices, revealing sky views. Sparky flaps down to each sky ledge as it's exposed, then follows a-ll-eee as it continues its patrol.

They return to the living space, settling on a human perch, a-ll-eee curled up on the flat bit, Sparky standing behind on the top edge, where she can jump to her mate if it needs her. It doesn't call to her so she doesn't try going to a head ledge.

A-ll-eee picks up a thin stick and a little flat white object, scratching the white surface with the stick, leaving black marks on the white like those it's made in their territory. It puts both objects on the perch. Then her mate stays motionless, as though hiding from a predator.

Sparky calls out, as gentle a croaking as she can. A-ll-eee looks right into Sparky's eyes. They are beak to unbeak. This close together Sparky can't see her mate's features clearly. She steps back. As she does, a-ll-eee chatters briefly.

HHH

I thought you were my friend, Sparky.

OOO

Its eyes are raining. Often, after a human's eyes rained, Sparky didn't see that human again. She gives her hissing raspy call. A-ll-eee replies.

Ss-p-aaarrr-kkee.

But faintly, sounds stumbling, as if the call hurt. Then her mate faces away from Sparky. She stays with it though, on the perch; a-ll-eee's her other half and she's its, their life is together. She won't abandon her mate.

Sparky's on the sky ledge in the living space, eyes hunting the blackness beyond the ice. A-ll-eee went to the roosting space a while ago. Sparky went too, watching as her mate swallowed many tiny white morsels of human prey before burying itself in the nest. Then Sparky started her night patrol. Now she's watching outside for approaching threats. Only the trees opposite move, windblown. The only sounds are faint, distant.

A shrill cry breaks the night's stillness, coming from behind and above Sparky. She turns sharply, head then body, wings opening. The cry repeats, a loud, long shrieking that pierces Sparky's head, echoing around her.

Then silence. Sparky darts to the dome perch, waits listening and watching, for the screaming danger to attack. It doesn't. The moment's silence stretches out. Still there's no attack. Sparky launches into flight, circling the living space, swooping into the hunting space, powering up the rising ledges and all around their territory. Her night vision sees everything according to her map. Her high-frequency hearing detects no strange sounds. She returns to the living space. The shrill threatening cry doesn't repeat.

The day dawns greyly. Sparky listens for the usual sounds of a-ll-eee rousing; hears nothing. In morning's eerie tranquillity last night's high pitched cry reverberates in her mind's ears.

Sparky flies out to the narrow space, landing on the lowest rising ledge, ears searching above, finding only emptiness. She hops up several rising ledges, stops, listens again. Still nothing. She flaps-jumps into flight, wing-beating to the sky ledge at the top.

From here she can see into the roosting space, to the mound in the nest made by a-ll-eee burying itself there to sleep. Needing to know her mate isn't hurt Sparky glides into the space, landing on the nest, talons gathering up loose nesting material as she steadies herself, eyes and ears alert.

A-ll-eee's head pokes from the nest, head plumage spread out, eyes closed, face hole open, a dark patch of something trickled from it. Sparky steps across to a-ll-eee's head. There she bends to examine the darkly trickled patch, pecking it, feeling a gloopey wetness like blood. She hops around the edge of the damp patch and pecks another spot; it's stiff, crispy like dried leaves.

Sparky straightens up, focusing on a-ll-eee. It hasn't moved, isn't awake. She calls to it. A-ll-eee just lies there, eyes closed, unmoving. Sparky calls again. When her mate doesn't respond she climbs onto the mound that is the rest of a-ll-eee, buried in the nest, walks to where she can reach its head. She pecks and calls, pecks again. It still doesn't wake.

Sparky steps off her lifeless mate. She knows what this silent stillness means. She's a hunter; death is her life, she eats it: she kills. She feels death's emptiness in her beak, her ears and eyes recognise its frozen hush. She understands death's nothingness. Her mate is dead.

She's lost mates before; she's never found her mate lifeless before. Sparky's wild impulse impels her to escape from stalking danger. But this is also her other half, who makes her whole; her human rearing urges her to stay close, be with it.

Sparky flies to the tall plumage box, a safe vantage overlooking her mate. After long enough passes without danger approaching she flies down, landing by a-ll-eee's head even though she knows it won't, can't, call her to it.

The roosting space darkens, day ending around Sparky and a-ll-eee. When it's fully dark Sparky flies to her living space, eats a chick from her stash and perches on the sky ledge, watching the living world outside.

Days pass. A-ll-eee lies dead, in the nest. Sparky has to make a new life for herself; she's a solitary hunter now, her only aim surviving until she finds a new mate.

She vigilantly patrols her territory, perching on the sky ledges, watching through the ices for approaching danger. She lands here, there, viewing her spaces from every vantage. She bathes in the bathing space, in the pool that was full of clear water before her mate died but is now half-full of murky water. There's no one to flush out prey for her so she eats from her stashes.

Tonight she eats the last of her stashed prey. Tomorrow there might be more prey, there're might not, she doesn't know. She carries on living because she can't not.

The following dusk Sparky feels the beginnings of hunger. She flies into the hunting space, perches near the tall white box where prey hides. She can't get in to it so she waits for prey to emerge. It doesn't.

By night her hunger has grown, an emptiness consuming her. In the dark stillness her predator's eyes spot prey moving outside her territory. She focuses all her energy on the scurrying mouse but the ice prevents her ghostly killing flight; the meal scurries away.

Another day, the hunger has swollen insider her and there's a sludgy feeling. Sparky can only fly a few wing-beats before needing to rest. She rests more than flies, eyes closed, a leg tucked up, the other supporting her until it aches and she swaps. She opens her eyes now and then, noticing the day getting brighter then darker.

It's fully dark now. She's on the sky ledge in the living space, spots a familiar pair of grey humans walking along outside her territory. They stare at her; she stares back at them. Faintly she hears them chattering. They keep walking: disappear.

D-ii-nnnggg-d-oo-nnnggg.

She turns sharply, facing the sound, watching for the grey humans entering: invading.

D-ii-nnnggg-d-oo-nnnggg.

They don't enter. Some short sharp tap-tappings sound, hardness against hardness, then the d-ii-nnnggg-d-oo-nnnggg noise again and more tap-tapping. Sparky stands hunter-still, watching and listening.

A-ll-eee. A-ll-eee. A-ll-eee.

Her mate's call, given by another human who wants a-ll-eee to come to it, doesn't know it can't. Willing herself into flight, Sparky drifts out to the narrow space, landing on the ground at the in/out that's her territorial boundary. She can hear humans chattering beyond it, calls her rasping hissy caw as loudly as she ever has. The chattering stops. She calls again. The chattering restarts then footsteps move rapidly away. Sparky gives a final cawing rasp, leaps into the air, flapping desperately to the sky ledge in the living space, landing as the pair of grey humans walk past the ice. Her flashing white halts them. She calls again, beak stretched wide, wings opened wider, making herself as large as she is. They stand as if frozen, then face each other, both chattering, flapping their featherless wings, turning sharply, vanishing from view.

Sparky waits to hear the tap-tapping or the d-ii-nnnggg-d-oo-nnnggg; hears a loud thump-banging. This new sound might bring danger so she stays on her ledge, conserving the last of her energy to escape or attack.

The thump-banging shatters into a sharp splintering, the sound of a tree cleaved in half. The pair of humans appears. Sparky recognises their grey head plumage and withered face skin. They see her: stop. The short grey human covers its face with its wing toes. The taller human steps into her space. It's going to challenge for Sparky's territory again and a-ll-eee isn't here to chase them off. Sparky leaps from the ledge, wing-beating towards them. Both humans step into the darkness behind them, the in/out closing before Sparky reaches it. She drops to the ground, exhausted, only the urge to survive keeping her body alert, wings open, eyes and ears searching. Footsteps climb the rising ledges, then walk overhead. Sparky tracks the sound as it goes to the roosting space.

A scream pierces the silence, the sound of agony: death. It ripples fear through Sparky. She stumbles to the littered ledge, nearly missing her landing, clumsily scrambling up, facing the in/out, chest throbbing. Now she has nothing left. All she can do is rest and wait for whatever's happening to happen.

Footsteps pad around above then descend the rising ledges. Furious chattering and high wailing flood Sparky's ears.

After a while blue flickering brightness illuminates the living space; beyond the ice growling movers appear, stopping outside her territory, and humans, a flock of them, emerge from the movers. The taller grey human appears, flapping a featherless wing at the flock and Sparky hears them all crossing into her territory: invading.

Noises clog her ears; a cacophony of chattering, a trampling of footsteps, thumps and bangs, beeps and buzzes, clicking, scratching, soft high stutterings, animal sounds. The noises last a long while but no humans enter her space. Finally footsteps descend the rising ledges and leave her territory. Perching on the sky ledge, Sparky sees a pair of humans carrying a long flat object between them; on it is a mound, like the mound a-ll-eee made when buried in its nest. The rest of the flock walk beside or behind this mound-carrying pair, the grey humans coming last, holding onto each other with their featherless wings. They stand, watching the rest of the human flock leave, then the grey pair disappear from sight to reappear in sound, chattering outside Sparky's living space.

HHH

Oh, Michael, why didn't she let us help her? We should have made her see the doctor, got her in Victoria House.

We never could make Allie do anything, love. We did what we could, don't blame yourself. This would've happened no matter what.

You can't know that. If only we'd...

OOO

They're outside, could come in now, attack her. Sparky calls out, mustering her harshest shriek.

The chattering stops, restarts.

HHH

What about that? We can't leave it in there. It must be hungry, it's been six days since...

I think we need to go home now, love.

No! It was important to Allie. I can't go until I know it's alright. It's the only thing we can do now.

Fine, Peter might be able to help.

Peter?

He's good with birds.

With parrots!

I'm sure he'll know what to do, though. You go home. Peter'll bring me back when we're done. I won't be long and there's no use you staying.

OOO

Her call frightens away the shorter grey human. Sparky sees it walking past outside. But tall grey is still in her territory. She'll have to chase it off if it attacks her. Or she'll have to escape, surrendering her territory. She huddles into herself.

Growling outside wakes her to the sight and sound of another human invading her territory. Chest fluttering, she shakes herself, readying for a final flight as humans chatter behind the in/out.

HHH

I'm so sorry about Allie, I can't believe it.

Neither can we. Thanks for coming. I didn't know who else to call and Judy wanted to make sure the owl's O.K. It was something Allie loved so…

Of course. I've had a quick look on line. Brought some beef, Barbara'll go mad when she finds it missing, it was tomorrow's tea but I'll take her to the Dog & Gun instead. Do you know if it's got a name?

I think it's Sparky.

Sparky.

OOO

Ss-p-aaarrr-kkee.

Her call, from behind the in/out. She stands tall, stretching her neck, wings unfolded. The in/out opens. Tall grey human appears but steps aside, letting the new human enter her living space. She studies this stranger slowly walking towards her, learning its movements, body and face, especially its face, so she'll know it. It's taller than tall grey and thinner, with darker head plumage. Squares surround its eyes, making its eyes appear large. She's not seen a human with squares around its eyes before, is so focused on this new feature that she lets it get quite close. It chatters, a soft, low humming that gets louder as it gets closer until she realises it's close enough to attack.

Sparky opens her wings, lowering her head, hissing at it. The square-eyed human stops walking, raises a featherless wing, the toes at the end of it covered with a thick dark skin like her before mates had when she flew to them. Clutched in its grip are red chunks of flesh. Sparky folds her wings away at the sight of food, bobbing her head, balancing the risk of harm with the reward of food if she flies to it. It keeps chattering, her call in amongst the low humming.

HHH

It's alright, Sparky. Don't be scared. Look I've got food for you. Are you hungry? Shall I put it here for you, Sparky? What's this? Oh…

OOO

It's offering her food and calling her to it but Sparky doesn't know this square-eyed stranger. She daren't fly to it no matter how hungry she is. She shuffles along the littered ledge, trying to get further away from it. Square eyes stops beside the human perch that Sparky and a-ll-eee occupied together that final night.

Reaching down, square eyes picks up the small white flat object that a-ll-eee scratched with the short stick. Dropping the meat, square eyes retreats to the in/out where it offers the white flat object to tall grey.

Sparky makes herself wait a moment, wary of being attacked while she eats but the humans stay at the in/out, tall grey staring at the white object while square eyes stands, body turned away from her, lowered eyes glancing at her.

She hop-flaps to the food, stands with wings spread to hide her meal and gobbles down chunk after chunk until she's full. There's some left. She checks on the humans. Their heads are bent together, tall grey's head ledges are shaking and square eyes has a featherless wing around it; they aren't watching her. She takes the chunks to the littered ledge, stashing them. Behind her the in/out closes with a tiny click. She's alone in her space again. But she's not hungry now. She can rest comfortably.

Sparky goes to the dome perch, settles there, a leg tucked up, eyes closing.

Now

September 2022 (cont.)

OOO

T-raay-cee's walking them a different route back to her space after today's flying, hunting, feeding. Nerves and muscles in Sparky's wings, legs and chest quiver in a readying flurry of anticipation.

They stop a few strides from the grassy patch, facing a structure with criss-crossed lines at the front. Sparky peers through them for other fliers but the space is unoccupied. T-raay-cee takes them inside.

It's a wider, lower space but with as much air for flying through as in her space. It's not her space, though. So when the ankle tugging stops and she knows she's untethered from her mate, can fly off into this space, Sparky doesn't. She takes a moment to explore it with eyes and ears.

There's a pair of ledges for her to perch on high up the rear side. There's a pair of perches on the ground; a shiny and black curved perch and rock perch. There's also a water pool on the ground. And from the front she can see out over where she and her mate fly together on the grassy patch, can watch all that happens in her territory. This is a suitable living space.

T-raay-cee chatters to her now. Sparky hears her call but in the soft, low tone of the surrounding chatter; she isn't being called to fly. She's offered a chick. Sparky beaks it, scanning this new space for somewhere to eat her meal. The ledges look to be high, safe places.

T-raay-cee crouches down to the shiny and black curved perch, holding Sparky out to it. But it's too low to the ground for her to be comfortable eating there. T-raay-cee lowers Sparky so much that she has to step onto this low perch or be grounded. As soon as t-raay-cee steps away, Sparky jump-flies, almost vertically, to the nearest ledge. Landed, she transfers the chick to a foot while she examines this perching place up close. There's plenty of space for her to stand upright, her feathers not brushing against the sides behind or overhead. She settles on this ledge.

T-raay-cee is outside now. It bobs its head at her and the face hole makes the upward curving line. Sparky keeps her dark bright eyes on it. This is her new space, their new space. T-raay-cee's found it for them, like it's found spaces previously, each more suitable than the before space. This is their home. Sparky tears into her meal.

HHH

Sparky gets a new aviary, one better suited to her needs because it's sited beside the lawn, what's now her flying ground, where she can watch life's comings and goings, including people, which, as an imprint, is better for keeping her stimulated. I still don't know if it will be her forever home but as long as she's in my care I want to give her the best. And give myself the best chance of knowing if it's right for us to stay together. The new aviary makes me feel less guilty that I'm still reluctant, afraid, to fly her free.

Before

February 2022 (cont.)

OOO

The square-eyed human appears the next morning, chattering to her with its low, steady humming, as it enters her space. She hears her call amongst its chatter.

Ss-p-aaarrr-kkee.

It offered her food, is calling her to it. Maybe square eyes wants to be her new mate; it's behaving like it does. She'll only know if she flies to it and isn't flapped away. So she launches herself over, fluttering down onto its head ledge. Square eyes doesn't push her off; it keeps chattering, face turned to her, so close the squares around its eyes are within beak-reach. Sparky leans forward, pecks lightly, tapping a familiar hard invisible surface, like tiny ices. She leans away, focusing her vision, absorbing this uncommon detail. Square eyes chatters softly rumbling sounds then walks her to the sky ledge, crouching until she's lower than it. She jumps across.

HHH

Morning, Sparky. Oh, hello there. Guess you know your name. Pierre used to sit on my shoulder like that. Mind the specs though, Sparky. Come on, lets get you off there. Was the chap on YouTube right? Oh, yes, that worked. You'll have to excuse me, Sparky, I'm new to owls. You're amazing though. Here, I've got breakfast for you, proper owl food today. Lets see if you'll come to me. Sorry about the improvised glove, it's really for gardening but I think it'll be O.K. Sparky.

OOO

Square eyes retreats a few paces, raises its featherless wing, wing toes trapping a mouse.

Ss-p-aaarrr-kkee.

She knows this routine, if not this human; memory of her before mates, flying to them, hunting with them, like this, buzzes through her. At her call she takes off, flies, strikes the mouse, takes it to her ledge, swallows quickly, eyes on this new human that's trying to bond with her. As the tail slips down another mouse appears.

Ss-p-aaarrr-kkee.

She flies as the call is still sounding, taking her catch to her ledge again. This new human's familiar behaviour makes it easy for her to understand it, to begin bonding with it, flying, hunting and feeding as though they're a pair.

After their flying and feeding Sparky follows as square eyes patrols her territory, watching it for more bonding behaviour. It goes into the hunting space, gets an upside perch but with twigs, not talons, at the end, and a tall round water pool that it fills from the shiny branch over the square pool. The water has foamy whiteness, like snow, floating on it. This too is familiar.

HHH

Right, that's breakfast. We'll have a tidy up now, Sparky, make this place decent for you. You'll have to stay here until we find you a proper home but don't worry, I'll be in every day to look after you.

OOO

Square eyes takes the twig-ended perch and foam-filled water pool to the living space where it drags the twig-end over the ground before rubbing the perches with a soggy blue leaf that it pulled from the foamy pool. Where it rubs the browny-white streaks of droppings disappear. This is like what her humans did in her before spaces.

Next it climbs the rising ledges, Sparky following, reaching the top before it, landing on the sky ledge there. The roosting space's in/out is closed but the bathing space is still open; square eyes heads inside. It drains the murky water from the pool, rubbing until the white shines. Then they descend the rising ledges, Sparky leading.

Square eyes goes into the hunting space again. Sparky perches on the broad ledge as it collects her old pellets, casting them into a tall hole in the corner. Then it opens the white box where prey hides. Sparky leans forward to peer inside. Square eyes chatters to her as it picks things off the ledges; some it drops into the tall hole, others it lifts to its unbeak, inhaling sharply before replacing them on the ledges. Sparky spots a nest of yellow chicks. Hissing raspily, she leaps in onto them, talons gripping. But square eyes tugs on the skin strips around her ankles, making her step off the nest and onto its featherless wing.

Sparky tries to jump free but it holds onto her, walking them to the living space. There, when she tries to jump off again, she finds herself in flight and flaps to the littered ledge. When she turns around the in/out is closed, square eyes gone. But it soon reappears, chattering and carrying a water pool more like those she's had before. Sparky's gaze flits between the human and the water pool. She hasn't bathed in fresh water for a long while but she doesn't trust square eyes enough to bathe with it there. It chatters; she waits for it to leave.

HHH

That's better for you, isn't it, Sparky, you can have a bath. Thank goodness for an online crash course in owl husbandry. It's not as difficult as the forums made out.

But maybe you're making it easy, eh? If you are, thank you. I think we'll manage, won't we? At least 'til we find you a good home. I'd keep you myself if I could but I had enough trouble talking Barbara into parrots. Anyway, I'll leave you in peace now, see you tomorrow.

OOO

Square eyes slips out.

Alone, Sparky flutters to the edge of the pool, bending over the shimmering water then jumping in to bathe.

Square eyes doesn't reappear any more that day but if it's going to be her new mate it'll return.

Now

September 2022 (cont.)

OOO

From her new space Sparky sees all the happenings in her territory, learning the rhythms of her world: which fliers appear at dawn, which at dusk; what direction the wind usually bends the trees; where the sun rises and sets; the humans that appear, the moving growlers that bring them; a vast spectrum of sounds. Learning all this the new fades to old, her world more familiar and comfortable each day.

When t-raay-cee appears they fly together. If it appears but doesn't enter her space Sparky drops onto the rock perch near the front, stretching her wings, making herself a striking flash of white against her space's shady interior. She wing-beats, becoming unmissable movement so t-raay-cee will come to her and they'll fly together. And, because they're a pair, it always does come to her, they always fly together, unless its raining or windy. As soon as t-raay-cee approaches Sparky lands on the criss-crossed lines, feet grabbing hold of their thinness, wings opened, facing her mate, climbing up or along to be with it as soon as it's inside. Then she jumps onto a head ledge, the featherless wing or the short perch t-raay-cee brings for Sparky to balance on before they fly. If they've already flown that day her mate doesn't come in to her. Still, whenever it's nearby Sparky flies to the front of her space, getting closer to it, reaffirming their bond which is strong now.

HHH

We relax into a decent routine. Sparky flies reliably to me from the perch on the lawn, securely tethered to the creance that I gradually unwind to its maximum length. She seems contented, even 'happy'? No, that's presumptuous of me. But settled, certainly. If I thought this was good enough for her… Animals live in the now and, for now, her life's as good as it's been, certainly since I've known her, possibly ever. I can't rewrite her past. But I do have to write her future, find the best ending for her story.

Before

February–March 2022

OOO

Sparky spends most of her time alone in her living space, the in/out only opening when square eyes comes, which it does for a short while every day, calling her to it and offering food. They fly around her territory, their territory now, patrolling together. The only difference is that the roosting space's in/out stays shut.

Frustrated that she can't enter this part of her territory, each time they fly together Sparky lands on the ground by the roosting space in/out, looking at it and calling. But square eyes doesn't open it for them to patrol, it just tugs her gently onto its featherless wing.

Every day she tries to make square eyes open the roosting space in/out so she can survey that part of her territory. Finally, this day she manages to jump free when square eyes is holding her on its featherless wing. She circles above it, landing back at the closed in/out which she pecks, hiss-cawing loudly, dodging away from square eyes when it bends to her.

HHH

What's wrong, Sparky? Oh… Do you need to see she's gone? Is that it? Here, look, it's empty. I'm sorry but Allie isn't… she's not… she…

OOO

Square eyes opens the in/out. Sparky leaps with a wing-beat into the roosting space. The nest is there but empty. Dead a-ll-eee is gone. Sparky swoops around the space; everything else is unchanged. Reassured this part of her territory is secure, she goes to square eyes' head ledge so they can continue patrolling. It walks them down the rising ledges, chattering to her.

HHH

I'm sorry, I didn't realise what you were trying to tell me, Sparky. But you've seen now. You know, don't you, missus? It's sad but you'll be able to grieve and move on. Don't worry, I'll look after you for as long as you need me, and I'll find somewhere suitable for you. You'll just have to be patient, there's no Battersea Barn Owls Home!

OOO

After that day the roosting space's in/out stays open; Sparky and square eyes patrol the whole territory together, perching here and there, always returning to the living space where they fly, hunt and feed then spend quiet moments together, being a pair, living their shared life. When it leaves, closing the in/out, Sparky flies to the sky ledge where she watches through the ice as square eyes walks away, always turning, flapping a featherless wing at her, its face hole moving, the faintest traces of its rumbling chatter drifting through to her, before it vanishes from view. Sparky calls back until her new mate's gone. Then she draws up a leg, closes her eyes, resting until it returns the next morning. Her life with square eyes is a bit like her life with a-ll-eee and a bit like her life with her before mates; there's enough familiarity for her to relax. She has what she needs most; a human mate to complete her. And the sky is still out there for flying up into whenever her new mate's ready.

HHH

Morning, Sparky. Sorry about this, missus, but I need to put you in here today. Don't worry, you're not going anywhere yet, I'm still working on that, but the house clearance chaps are coming so you'll be best off out the way.

OOO

When square eyes arrives this morning Sparky knows immediately that today is different: it's carrying a box. Before, when humans have put her in such a box, she's gone to a new territory, been confronted with unsettling change. She flaps to the littered ledge, watching warily. She's only known square eyes a short time, their bond is flimsy. When it calls her, offering her a mouse, she has to decide whether to trust herself to it.

Ss-p-aaarrr-kkee.

Square eyes wriggles the mouse its trapped for her to catch.

Ss-p-aaarrr-kkee.

She'll only strengthen their bond, they'll only be a successful pair, if she trusts it and it protects her. She flies on slowly sweeping wings, dropping to its wing toes, feeling their thick grey hide covering under her feet. She lifts the mouse to her beak as square eyes puts her in the box. Sparky retreats into the small dark space as the criss-crossed lines close and the box rises up, bobbing along the narrow space, into the hunting space and then onward. A cool breeze ruffles her feathers. They're outside. She hops to the front of the box, mouse uneaten in her beak, cranes her neck, looks out and up. A smooth pale grey wilderness fills her skyward vision. Maybe today they're going to fly into it together.

The box lands with a soft jolt. Square eyes peers in at her, chattering. Sparky calls to it but her soft screech is smothered by the suddenly appearing noise of another human's chatter. Square eyes stands; Sparky can only see its legs now. She shuffles around in the box, hunting for glimpses of the other human. Piecing together a view through gaps in the box's sides, she recognises tall grey human, matching its chattering to its appearance.

HHH

I know it's not ideal, Sparky, but at least out here you won't be disturbed by all the upheaval of…

They're here, Peter, have you got the owl out?

Oh, hello, Michael, yes, she's in there.

Will that be O.K.?

Yes, you'll be fine, won't you, Sparky?

OOO

Sparky hears her call, then the footsteps and chattering fade as square eyes walks away, taking tall grey with it. She eats the mouse and settles in the box, waiting for whatever is happening.

But nothing happens. She stays in the box as the day draws on. Nearby there's a chorus of banging, clattering noises and human chatter. Square eyes appears now and then, peering in at her. When it comes the noises get brighter; when it goes they dim again; she locates them as coming from her territory, but can't visualise their meaning. Nothing else happens.

As the sky darkens square eyes returns. Her box rises up, bobs along and Sparky feels the cool fresh outside breeze replaced by inside musty air.

The box lands, square eyes opens it, steps away. Sparky edges to the front, leaning forward, looking. They're in their living space but it's different: bigger, emptier. She leaps to square eyes' head ledge, where she's high enough to survey the space and close enough to her mate for its protection. With rapid head-turns she sees what's not there; the human perches, the objects on the littered ledge, the legged flat surfaces, the stuttering, flickering oblong object, the dome perch: it's all gone. There's just her water pool, the sky ledge, the now unlittered ledge and a new pair of tall perches facing each other.

A tap-tapping on the in/out; a human calls from behind it. Square eyes lifts Sparky onto its featherless wing, replying to the human as the in/out opens. Tall grey appears. Sparky hisses at it.

HHH

We're ready to leave now, are you O.K. to lock up, Peter?

Yes, of course. Is Judy alright?

Tired, sad. But at least this horrible job's done. Any reply yet from that animal rescue centre?

No, I'll chase them tomorrow.

Please, I know the landlord said we had until the end of March but the sooner this is all dealt with the better, for Judy's sake.

Absolutely, I know it's been terrible for you both.

It would've been worse without you. Goodness knows what we'd have done about the owl.

Glad to help, just sorry I can't do more.

You'll miss it, her, Sparky, I mean.

I will but there's no way I can keep her. Anyway, she deserves to go to somewhere she'll get the specialist care she needs.

OOO

Square eyes and tall grey chatter briefly then tall grey leaves. Square eyes walks Sparky towards a new tall perch. As she steps to it, square eyes retreats across the space. There it calls her back to it, offering food. They fly, hunt and feed together as usual until it flushes out a mouse that scurries through the air to land on the sky ledge. Sparky chases it: strikes. When she turns, mouse in foot, towards her mate, it's gone. But it'll be back soon. They're an established pair now. It's showed her that by making their space bigger, more like the spaces her before mates found for her. Maybe soon it'll take her outside where they'll have the whole wild sky for their flying together.

Now

September 2022 (cont.)

OOO

T-raay-cee and Sparky are on the grassy patch, facing the perch. Sparky doesn't wait for her mate to walk her to the perch today; she jumps, flying herself there, knowing now that's what t-raay-cee wants her to do: fly away from it so she can return to it. Landed there she leaps up again, heading skyward. She doesn't need to hear her call or see the featherless wing raising. She just needs to fly with her mate, sweeping herself up high and far. The further she goes, returns from, the more t-raay-cee will know they're an established pair: bonded.

A sharp jolt grounds her. Looking around, Sparky traces the line running from the skin strips around her ankles to the short branch planted in the middle of the grass. It's that tethering line grounding her again. It was there when she flew with d-aann-y-elll and for some of her flights with matt-ee then matt-ee freed them from it and she flew as far and high as she wanted; matt-ee trusted her to return to it: understood their bond. None of her other mates has understood their bond like that, not d-aann-y-elll and m-uuu-m who never flew her without the tethering line and not a-ll-eee or square eyes who never even flew outside with her. And now not t-raay-cee. Maybe it'll understand soon: their bond's all they need to keep them together.

T-raay-cee crouches down, holding out its featherless wing. Sparky steps up to it and they return to the perch. As t-raay-cee walks away, Sparky listens for her call, watches for the featherless wing raising, wriggling prey appearing for her to catch. She'll have to make do with this, for now. At least they're flying out under the sky, its freedom overhead.

But before she's had chance to spring into flight again Sparky's jerked off the perch. Wing-flapping out of the fall, she lands on the grass, sees t-raay-cee on the ground too, pulling at the line which is coiled around its feet. T-raay-cee's been grounded by the line; it's tethering them both down, keeping them from flying free together. If t-raay-cee can untether them it'll see their bond is enough, that they're a lifelong pair now. Sparky needs to wait for this to happen. She's a hunter, waiting for that striking moment is her nature. It'll come if she waits.

HHH

I start to wonder, worry, that Sparky's getting frustrated flying tied to the creance. She takes to jumping off the perch, not waiting for me to call her, heading up and away, circling and swooping only to be hauled out of flight by the line, tumbling like a shot-down spitfire. But if I take that next step with her it could be our last.

The golden wisdom of raptor keeping flashes up in large neon lettering: birds of prey can fly much better than you can.

Then one session I don't help this situation, getting my feet tangled up in the line, tripping and yanking Sparky off the perch where she's been patiently waiting for me to call her. Even the line is warning me it's a hindrance. Talking to the falconer he tells me Sparky should be flying free next week. I silently cower. He's the expert, he knows that's the right thing for Sparky, and me, if we're to stay together. I only know I'm terrified of what happens if I do it; more terrified of what'll have to happen if I daren't do it.

Before

March 2022

OOO

The only thing that's changed for Sparky and square eyes is their territory: it's emptier, bigger, now. There are fewer perching places but more flying space, even if it isn't out under the wide sky. Sparky remaps her bigger emptier territory; it's a suitable home for her and her new mate. They can live here for many seasons. They continue patrolling hunting and feeding together as before.

Today her mate came soon after dawn, has stayed with her for much longer. They've patrolled the territory, square eyes chattering constantly to her, Sparky following, leading or sometimes perching on its head ledge. They've hunted but there hasn't been as much prey as on other days; Sparky's still hungry. Maybe they'll find more later. Maybe that's why it's staying so long, waiting for better hunting.

Now they're in the living space. It keeps half raising its featherless wing, looking at something near the tip of it. Sparky drops down to inspect; it's a shiny disc. She pecks it. Her mate chatters.

HHH

Yes, Sparky, it's time, I'm afraid. You just wait here a moment.

OOO

It leaves the space, returns quickly. It's flushed out a mouse! Sparky swoops over, pouncing on their catch. As she's crushing the skull in her beak she feels a tugging on her ankles. They're stepping out into the narrow space, square eyes putting her into the box she's been in before. She hasn't had chance to swallow her meal when the box floats up, beginning its familiar bobbing journey. Square eyes' chatter drifts down to her.

HHH

Don't worry, we're not going to be in the car too long, missus, and you'll love your new home. The chap that runs it has worked in zoos all his life; you'll have expert care. They're a charity but Michael's made a generous donation, in Allie's memory. You'll have a lovely big aviary, Sparky, lots of room for flying, other owls for company. You'll soon make friends. You can show the wild owls how good life in captivity is. It's sad for them, Sparky. They're too badly injured to be released. All they had was their freedom and they've lost that. You're better off than them because you're used to living indoors, don't miss flying free like they must.

OOO

Growling fills her ears and she feels the rolling movement she remembers from before journeys like this. Her mate is taking them to a new territory. It must have found somewhere more suitable than even the bigger, emptier spaces of their old territory. Sparky rests, readying herself for when they land there. Maybe they'll fly outside at this new territory.

The moving growler stops. From inside the box she sees sky, its infinite freedom, overhead. Her mate's found them a territory where they have the whole sky for their flying and hunting together. Keenly, she hops to the front to sky watch as the box floats from the moving growler.

The box stops floating along, sways statically in mid-air as chattering surrounds her, square eyes and another human whose croaky reply Sparky doesn't recognise. They bob-float again, passing into and through the dimness of a long narrow space that stretches ahead, before turning off it. The box lands. Sparky peers out at a large space with dull white sides. But the box restricts her view so she only glimpses what looks like a pair of perches across the space from each other and a dark tall structure rising to a point ahead of her.

There's more chattering, call and reply, then square eyes appears, opens the box, its low rumbling chatter reassuring. It steps away; she leans out, head-turning, ears and eyes surveying the space. There is a pair of perches, long and wide, there and there, high off the ground: safe vantage points. Nest boxes, set even higher up the sides, there and there, offer sheltered roosts. The tall dark pointed structure opposite needs exploring but that's for later, when she's alone, mapping her new space.

Ss-p-aaarrr-kkee.

Facing her call, she spots square eyes, a mouse trapped in its wing toes. This space has prey for them. She leaps to her mate's featherless wing, striking down on the catch. As she's lifting it to her beak, square eyes walks to a perch. Sparky steps across to it, grips the mouse in her talons and pecks into it, tearing off the head. Jerking it down her throat, she notices the other human: the stranger.

It's grey, like the pair that challenged for her before territory, but it also has the appearance of something lifeless, shrivelled into skin stretched over bone, flesh withered; she's instantly wary of this withered grey stranger that's chattering to square eyes with the croaking sound she heard moments ago. It comes towards her. Pokes at her. She pecks its wing toe. The strange shrivelled human retreats. She turns her back, hiding her catch, but stays facing it, wary eyes watching it, alert ears collecting its cackling chatter, searching out threats.

HHH

A nice looking bird.

Beautiful. Friendly too. She took to me straight away, loves standing on my shoulder.

That's a bad habit for a bird of prey. Professionals won't like it.

I don't think anyone'll object when she's this sweet. She follows me around the house too, coming when I call her. She must be pretty bright.

Hmph, the myth of the wise old owl. Their brains are actually tiny; one of the less intelligent bird species.

Oh, I don't think…

Now corvids, you know, magpies, jackdaws, ravens, they're really clever. We used to put on shows with them, they'll perform all sorts of tricks if they have a good trainer.

You did that here?

No, no, at one of the zoos. I was head of birds there.

She's in good hands, then?

The best. That little barn owl'll be no trouble here. You mentioned a donation.

Yes, absolutely. Can I just have a minute with her, say goodbye?

They're not like dogs, you know, don't bond with their owners, won't miss you.

Still, I'd like to.

Suit yourself.

OOO

Apprehensive of this strange shrivelled, lifeless human, Sparky watches from her perch. Maybe square eyes will chase it away. Then they'll have claimed this space as theirs.

It does; the shrivelled stranger leaves. Square eyes comes close, chattering in its gentle rumbling hum.

HHH

Right, Sparky, I've got to go now. You take care. You're a special little owl; it's easy to understand why Allie loved you. She was lucky to have you in her life. A pity you weren't enough of a reason for her to not… but if you weren't, nothing was. It's been a privilege spending time with you. Sorry I couldn't keep you but this is the best thing for you. Now explore your new home, make friends with your new roommates and be a good girl, missus. Have a wonderful life.

OOO

Square eyes leaves now. Just as it always does. It'll be back tomorrow. Just as it always is. Sparky settles down to eat, roost and wait for her mate's return.

Now

September 2022 (cont.)

OOO

There are several new strange humans on the far side of the grassy patch today. Sparky eyes and ears them as she and t-raay-cee head towards the perch. The strangers chatter amongst themselves, like a flock of featherless fliers perching in a row. Sparky doesn't know what the strangers want here but everything else is the same; Sparky and her mate are doing what they always do: going out to fly and hunt together. So having these strangers nearby isn't any more threatening than when the small brown flier with a red breast perches on the bush, as it does occasionally when she flies with her mate. Sparky doesn't feel the tightening of her wings and squeezing of her chest that she's felt before when strangers have appeared; she trusts t-raay-cee to protect her now.

Each day they come to the grassy patch Sparky needs more wing-beats to reach the perch. Today t-raay-cee stands as far from the perch as it's ever stood. The more, the further, she flies from and to her mate the stronger their bond grows. So she does as much flying as she can. Sparky reaches the perch.

Ss-p-aaarrr-kkee.

She sets off, landing with control onto the featherless wing, eating the prey trapped there for her. T-raay-cee holds Sparky up into the sky, as high as it can, facing her at the perch.

Sparky sets off again, confidently alighting, turning to her mate, listening and watching for the call.

Ss-p-aaarrr-kkee.

This flight, before landing, she hovers above its featherless wing a moment, feeling the power building inside her, energy thrumming through her from all their hunting together. She eats, then she's airborne, soaring silently through wind, gliding effortlessly on her strengthening wings. She touches down, turns, watches and listens.

Ss-p-aaarrr-kkee.

She flies, again and again and again, buoyed by the contentment of flying out under the sky with her mate.

The line pulls tightly on her ankles, hauling her to ground before she reaches the perch. Sparky forgot they're tethered. T-raay-cee rushes over, pecking at the line, untangling it. If only her human would rid them of the line they'd be a pair like she and matt-ee were: free.

T-raay-cee lifts her up. Sparky flies on until t-raay-cee stops calling.

They walk towards the flock of strange humans who ogle her. T-raay-cee chatters to them. Sparky studies them; different head and body plumages, different sizes but each with forward-facing eyes in round faces, like hers, wings hanging at their sides, like hers but unfeathered, legs that walk them about, like hers. They don't arouse her curiosity for long. The only human that matters to Sparky is her mate.

T-raay-cee returns them to her space and they spend a moment there together, Sparky perching on a head ledge before catching a chick her mate flies to her, their hunt successful.

HHH

I'm persuaded to let a friend's teenage son and his mates meet Sparky, see her fly. People are fascinated by owls. Thankfully it goes smoothly enough. Sparky doesn't show any signs of stage fright even when I take her to the gaggle of teenagers for a close-up encounter. While I tell them everything I know about barn owls, which isn't enough yet, she seems as bored by them as they are interested in her. Well, except for the girl who shies behind her boyfriend like I've got a pterodactyl on my hand. One lad even tells me proudly he had a barn owl when he was younger. Then he reveals he kept it in the shed on his gran's allotment and one day someone let it out; he never saw it again, doesn't seem sorry even now though he's old enough to realise what a cruel end his owl faced. I'm plunged into appalling visions of what Sparky endured before I met her, imagining the bleak chapters that her life story might include.

Afterwards, I resolved to make the point, always, that birds of prey aren't pets; don't just go and get one. Do as I say, not as I did. My uncertainty over Sparky's future is an omnipresent shadow as summer becomes autumn.

Before

March 2022 (cont.)

OOO

Since they became a pair square eyes has returned, morning after morning, so Sparky knows it'll be back tomorrow. Maybe they'll go outside to explore their new territory and do their flying and hunting. While she waits she begins mapping her new space.

As well as the perch she's on and its partner opposite, there's a thick crooked branch growing out of the ground, up against the rear side, that she could perch on. The tall dark pointed structure over there has a partner across the space. She's never had anything like them in her spaces so they need investigating. On the ground in the middle of the space is a large rectangular water pool. As well as the pair of nest boxes facing each other high up the sides, there's a sky ledge, even higher. She flies to it, head plumage brushing the top, and pecks at the ice, confirming its invisible solidness.

From the sky ledge she drifts to a nest box, foot-grabbing onto the edge of the hole and pushing her face through, eyes soaking up the black light inside.

A flier, like keee-w-ickk, eyes closed, is huddled there, a darker shadow in the darkness. It's resting, doesn't see or hear her.

Silently, Sparky floats back to her perch.

She's never been in a space with a flier before; at matt-ee's she only saw keee-w-ickk outside her space.

She doesn't know what'll happen between her and this new keee-w-ickk flier here together. She fidgets on the perch, watching the hole, knowing a keee-w-ickk's there. Daylight fades. When it's night, when the keee-w-ickk wakes, comes out of the nest box… Square eyes mustn't have known there was already a flier in this space; her mate wouldn't have brought them to an occupied territory.

Behind the ice, the sliver of sky is turning blue-black when a harsh scraping alerts Sparky to a human entering.

It's a small thin human with fair head plumage reaching its head ledges and small square eyes, a bit like her mate's. It's features are fresh, it's recently fledged, there's a gentleness about it. It notices Sparky, slowly walks towards her, chattering softly, stops a reassuring distance away, and tilts its head, watching Sparky with a soothing stillness, calming them both. Sparky tilts her head to match; they study each other briefly. It chatters to Sparky comfortingly, the sound stroking her sensitive ears. Sparky listens for her call. Doesn't hear it. The human stops chattering, goes to the middle of the space and drops fluffy chicks, lots of them, in a heap on the ground. Then, facing Sparky, this fair, gentle human points at the chicks, chattering softly again, before leaving.

Sparky stares at the glut of prey, far more than she can eat. Being offered so much is new: different. A quivering in her chest spreads through her muscles, right to her wingtips. She hesitates, on guard against danger. Moment after moment nothing happens. So she swoops down, feet snatching a chick from the edge of the pile. Gripping it, she wing-beats a retreat to the perch, clutching her catch. Just as she's landing movement, flickering at the edge of her vision, makes her head-turn.

From a hole in the ground behind her a keee-w-ickk flier scrambles into the space. Sparky's never seen a flier climbing out of the ground before. She's startled motionless, watching as it stands on the edge of the hole, shakes its plumage, head swivelling. It spots Sparky, large brown eyes holding her dark ones, beak-clacks sharply at her, hops to the food pile, grabbing a chick in its beak, another with a foot then hops clumsily to the hole, dragging its catch.

Before the keee-w-ickk flier reaches the hole more fliers emerges from it, all keee-w-ickks, going to the mound of prey as the other disappears underground. This keee-w-ickk flies to the pile with a short, low swoop, landing clumsily on top. That keee-w-ickk hop-flaps into the air with stuttering wing-beats then stumbles out of flight to hop-flap itself airborne again, many floundering flights getting it to the prey. Another keee-w-ickk walks to the food, dragging a wing behind it like an extra leg.

The keee-w-ickk that flew to the mound sweeps its catch to the perch across from Sparky. The hop-flapping keee-w-ickk stumbles its prey to the crooked branch perch, clambering onto the lowest limb then scrambling higher before tearing its meal apart. Throwing its head back to swallow it notices Sparky. As a leg disappears down its throat in a jerking motion, it beak-clacks at her then tears off the other leg. After each beakful it clacks menacingly at Sparky who drops her gaze from it and onto the flier with the dragging wing. It's got a chick and is wing-limping towards the hole.

There's plenty of food for the keee-w-ickk fliers and Sparky but her instincts urge her to eat quickly; she gobbles in the whole chick. It lodges part-way down her throat. She gulps, blinks and head-jerks but has to writhe it out of her beak, tearing it into swallowable pieces, eyes darting frantically between the other fliers who've finished eating, are hunting again.

If Sparky wants more she'll have to catch it herself; hunter's greed warns her to eat as much as she can while it's there. But that means hunting alone.

The other fliers only glance at her as they eat. Now's her opportunity. Sparky leaps on the chicks, grabbing yellow fluff as soon as her feet touch it, springing back to the perch, a pattering in her chest making her pant. She clenches onto her meal, casting eyes and ears around the space anxiously. If her mate was here…

As night deepens more keee-w-ickks appear from their hide-e-holes. A few circle the space in gliding flight, the others only walk, hop, wing-flap or fly stutteringly. Sparky's eyes and ears dart vigilantly from flier to flier.

A different flier emerges. Its plumage is speckled brown-yellow-white like that of the keee-w-ickks but its body is smaller, thinner, and feathery tufts stick up on top of either side of its head: head-tufts flier. Sparky doesn't see where it appears from, only noticing it in flight. As it reaches the food pile a flying keee-w-ickk swoops down on head-tufts flier, calling furiously, grabbing with its talons. A frenzy follows. Her body rigid, wings flight ready, Sparky keeps eyes on the fighting, tracking the fliers as they wing-strike and foot-claw each other while her ears watch the surrounding space for stalking danger. The violence grows: feathers fling off; screeches shatter the night's silence. Then the keee-w-ickk lets go of head-tufts who hurls itself up to a nest box, scrambling inside, calling out a warning hooo-hooo. The keee-w-ickk follows, banging down on the edge of the hole, sticking its head through. There's a too-long moment of vicious shrieking, beak-clacking and hooo-hoooing until the keee-w-ickk tumbles into flight, flapping to perch across the space from Sparky.

Sparky hasn't lived like this before, trapped with fliers that mob each other, gripping with talons, battering with wings, pecking, footing, striking: attacking. She doesn't know living with fliers like this. She only knows living with humans: her mate. But held deep in her bones and blood, muscles and nerves, is an awareness of the danger she's in from these fliers, unprotected: mateless. Until square eyes returns, escaping her from this new space, the fliers' space, she'll have to survive living among them. For that she needs to study their behaviour, learn their ways, like she did with her human mates, only more urgently. She hunches into herself at the end of the perch, fearful.

All night fliers tear up the space; it's too small for them to share. Some dart to the prey pile, catching whatever they can then vanishing again. Others fly around, chasing each other or diving at fliers trying to hunt. Their harsh, loud, high, long calls, the snap-snapping of beaks and the slap-slapping of wings shudders around and through Sparky. She's never experienced the violence of wild-born fliers before. Now she is it's an aural-visual ordeal, sound and sight mangled together into a terrible reality. She watches from her perch, stiff with the reflex to escape, as keee-w-ickks who can't fly get mobbed, pounced on, pecked and footed, their feathers broken or ripped out. They fight back but can't flee. They're the most injured when the attack ends.

Feathers flash towards her; a keee-w-ickk now flies at Sparky. She's never been attacked by another flier before, never fought off an attacking flier. But all that swooping around her territory with a-ll-eee and square eyes has honed her flight; in spaces she's fast and agile. Leaping off the perch, turning and twisting, swooping and diving, dodging the keee-w-ickk, Sparky powers herself up to the sky ledge. Perching there, crouched to fit the narrowness, she opens her wings, filling the ledge, primaries bending against the sides. Up there, like that, the keee-w-ickk can't get at her with beak or talons. It flies towards her, screaming and flapping, circling the space, passing her closely several times. But she holds her position, keeping wings outstretched, leaning forward to beak-jab when the keee-w-ickk nears her. Unable to get her, it flies to the tall pointed structure, scrambling into darker darkness. Wings achy, legs trembling, Sparky stays on the sky ledge panting, resting. She spends the remaining night primed with a fiercely burning will to survive.

At last dawn rises. The fliers disappear underground or into nest boxes. Hooo-hooo head-tufts can't hide in its box because a keee-w-ickk's claimed it. So hooo-hooo settles in the dark shadow under that tall pointed structure, watching Sparky on her perch across the space from it. She watches back. It didn't fly at her and she didn't fly at it. With a head bob, hooo-hooo closes an eye, tucks a leg up: rests.

Sparky rests too. She's exhausted by the night-long chaos but all the prey has been caught; she'll have to wait for square eyes to come later so they can go flying, hunting and feeding together. It can't have known all these other fliers were here; it wouldn't have found them a space already occupied by wild fliers.

Now

September 2022 (cont.)

OOO

Sparky's flying to the perch, as usual, when she sees it, hiding in the grass: prey. It's pink, fleshy, much larger than a mouse, just lying there, an easy kill. Her wild predator self awakes; eyes watching for the prey twitching, ears scanning for its squeaks. But it's still and silent. She's sure of the strike, swivels feet out in front, toes spread, legs braced…

Whap! She's on it, talons stabbing, feet clenching, crushing the squishy body. As she grips it, the prey lets out a high pitched squeaking. Sparky pecks vigorously, ensuring it can't defend by attacking. But it doesn't writhe, doesn't squeak again. A quick kill but she keeps beak-stabbing to be sure, instincts warning her against risking injury, tightening her killing hold, securing the catch.

Faintly, through the ferocity of her attack, she hears her call.

Ss-p-aaarrr-kkee.

T-raay-cee holds out its featherless wing, offering her a yellow fluffy scrap of prey. But she has this whole, large, pink fleshy kill beneath her feet, food to eat and to stash. Survivor's gluttony overwhelms her. She jabs again at her catch, trying to tear into skin so thick she can't rip through it. She's never had anything like it between her beak, in her taloned toes, before. She doesn't know what it is but it's hers; hunter-her won't surrender it, not even for her mate that's calling and offering food. She spreads her wings out, hiding her bounty from t-raay-cee who's crouched beside her, still offering the scrappy yellow morsel for her.

After a longish moment of pecking, stamping and jabbing, Sparky stops, exhausted: thwarted. She can't pierce this prey's tough hide, there's no tearing into the flesh, no succulent meatiness she can rip into beakfuls. Whatever this is, it isn't prey for her.

She looks up. T-raay-cee's still there, still offering its food, still calling her to it, the relentlessness of its call burrowing into her ears, drawing her to it.

Ss-p-aaarrr-kkee. Ss-p-aaarrr-kkee. Cu-mmo-nn ss-p-aaarrr-kkee. P-lee-zz. ss-p-aaarrr-kkee.

Her mate's also head shaking at her while its face hole stretches into the upward curving line and it makes gurgling clucking noises she's heard from humans before. It starts tugging on the skin strips, trying to step her onto its featherless wing.

This is her other half. She needs to make sure nothing severs their bond. The frenzy of her kill fading, Sparky accepts t-raay-cee's prey as her mate walks them to their flying spot on the grassy patch.

Before she sets off for the next flight Sparky studies the ground, curious about the prey she killed but couldn't eat. It's vanished. But there's still hunting and flying with t-raay-cee to be done. Sparky sets off for the perch, gliding on a gentle breeze.

HHH

I've read enough times that captive-bred imprint owls are doomed if they escape; they haven't learnt hunting skills from their parents so face death by starvation. It's one of the reasons, justifications, I'm clutching at for not flying Sparky free. But one day she shows me she's not as dependant on me as I need to believe. She has her first kill, taking to the task instinctively, impressing me with her determination. O.K., she needs to work on prey identification, but she kills the pink plastic dog toy a friend left on the lawn with gusto. I have a struggle persuading her to relinquish her catch and come to me, not helped by the fact that my calls to her are punctuated with eye-watering chuckles.

But it's reassuring to know she does have some hunting aptitude, should a survival situation arise. When I tell the falconer, after we've finished laughing, he says that all captive birds of prey hunt given the opportunity; it's their nature. How successful they'll be is less certain, but that's true of wild-born birds too. It's down to individual skill, experience and luck. Taming an animal doesn't erase its wild wherewithal. I know from my cats, the spider corpses they leave around the house for me and how they attack feathered or mouse-shaped toys, they're only tame because they don't need to be wild.

I'm underestimating Sparky, holding her back. I have to let her go, or let her go.

Before

March 2022 (cont.)

OOO

Sparky doesn't know what's happened to square eyes, only that it hasn't come to her today. It didn't come the day before either and it always came every day. She remembers how her other mates stopped coming to her like this, their bond broken, their shared life ended suddenly.

The harsh scraping noise disturbs her. A new human enters the space carrying a pair of deep water pools which it puts down before crouching to drain the rectangular water pool, rubbing inside it with a small tufted stick and refilling it from the deep water pools. New human heads towards the in/out, readying to leave.

It's not her mate. But if she wants to escape this space, the wild fliers in it, Sparky needs a new mate. She wing-beats to this stranger, silently swooping through the air between them. It sees her coming and stoops; Sparky misses its head ledge, landing on the curly brown-grey head plumage. The human shrieks, flapping featherless wings around Sparky. She springs off, circuits the space, turning tightly to return to the stranger but it's already outside, touching its head then studying its wing toes. Sparky flies into the criss-crossed lines at the in/out, hanging there, watching it. It head-shakes at her, chatters harshly, walks away along the narrow gap.

All that day humans pass outside the fliers' space: the shrieking human that wouldn't let Sparky perch on it; the fair gentle human; a juvenile human; a human with a rounded body like egg human; the shrivelled lifeless human that chatters croakily. None of them enters the fliers' space, calls Sparky or holds up a featherless wing for her. Only the fair gentle human looks in at her, its square eyes meeting hers. But it's not her square eyes, not her mate. Her square eyes doesn't come.

Daylight's fading when fair gentle human comes, piling chicks, many of them, on the ground again. It chatters softly, with calmness, to Sparky, raising a featherless wing towards the mound of food. Sparky flies for the wing perch, even though fair human hasn't call her to it. If she can go to it anyway, she might find it wants to be her new mate. But in the brief moment of her flight to it, fair human drops its featherless wing so there's nowhere for Sparky to land. She wing-beats herself into a hover, rising until she's level with its head ledge, landing beside the long fair head plumage. It doesn't shriek or flap her off. It stands still a moment, chatters soothingly, then walks to the perch, nudging Sparky to hop up before going to the in/out. Sparky fly-follows, landing on a head ledge before it leaves. Fair human returns to the perch; Sparky hops up again. As it moves away

Sparky fly-follows again. She did this with a-ll-eee, a before mate; if she does it with fair human maybe it'll start bonding with her.

When she lands on the head ledge again it again returns her to the perch, behaving like a-ll-eee did. Encouraged, Sparky readies for the next flight to it. But while she's on the perch fair human flies a chick to Sparky. She flutters down to accept the offering, carrying it up to the perch. It flew food to her, also like a-ll-eee did so maybe… When she looks again for fair gentle human it's outside the space watching her. It could be her new mate.

A short while after Sparky's eaten the chick fair human flushed out for her and another she caught from the pile, it's night dark in the space. Fliers appear from the ground hole and nest boxes, the shadows of the crooked branch and hollows under the tall pointed structures. They fly-hop-walk-drag themselves to the prey, catch and eat what they can, attack or are attacked, flee if they can, fight if they can't. They scream, shriek, hoo and screech, beak-clack, wing-strike, peck and foot-claw. Feathers are broken or plucked. Red wounds opened. They're a mob of fliers all together: an unkindness of each other.

Sparky is of them. And not of them. She watches. She evades. She learns.

She survives.

Days and nights pass; a routine solidifies around Sparky in this new space with these wild fliers.

Early morning a human comes, usually any of the several she sees often here, to drain and refill the water pool. Sparky flies to whichever human comes because, even though they're not her mate, not even behaving like they might want to be her mate, her life's always been shared with humans: she's not whole without a human other half. But they dart away from her or flap featherless wings so she can't perch on them, except gentle human who lets Sparky stay on its head ledge. Sometimes Sparky manages to land on another human, on its head because it dipped down so she missed the head ledge. But her feet slip off a cold, hard, shiny half-shell with tiny holes in it that her talons hook through but can grip onto. Then she has to fly away again. The human shrieks at her and when it's outside the fliers' space, Sparky sees it lifting the shiny hard half-shell off its head, revealing curly brown-grey plumage.

Later in the day another human will come, usually fair gentle, but sometimes shrivelled, occasionally new egg, and prey is released on the ground. When it's gentle human Sparky gets a chick flown towards her. When it's shrivelled human she doesn't. Shrivelled human did, for a few days, try raising a featherless wing and offering her a mouse. Sparky didn't go to it; when it left she caught a chick from the pile instead, before the fliers emerged. She doesn't want shrivelled human as a mate, doesn't trust it; it chased square eyes away, trapping her in this unsuitable territory.

The night time routine is the fliers emerging to hunt and fight. Their harsh screeching calls, beak-clacks and wing-strikes tear through the stillness. Their flying and fighting fills the space with fury as they snatch at prey, struggling to survive. Sparky flies when she needs to, often escaping to the sky ledge. She learns how to live, to stay alive, in this space with these fliers. It's all she can do until she finds a mate to take her to a better territory. Square eyes won't return; none of her before mates did.

She has to survive until a potential new mate appears.

Now

September 2022 (cont.)

HHH

'We've decided you're flying Sparky free today,' John announces. The 'we' is him and the falconer, who've been talking about this while I was weighing her.

I know it's been coming, this moment when I have to either let her go free or be resigned to rehoming her. But now she's been in my care for a few months, is settled into life with me, now we've bonded, I feel it's cruel palming her off to someone else, even to that local owl centre who have the skills and facilities she needs. They haven't been back in touch about me volunteering there so, while I could chase it up, I haven't. It feels wrong, a cop out; I rescued her so she's my responsibility, I just haven't accepted that yet. Today's the moment.

Stomach churning, hands shaking, I carry her to the nearby field where there's more flying space. The falconer fits a radio tracker to her ankle so if she does flit off we can find her again: theoretically. He tells me not to worry; her weight is right, she won't even realise she's not tied to the creance line and she'll probably just fly back and forth from the perch to me, as she has been doing quite reliably for the last few weeks. I trust him, he's the expert. I need to learn to trust Sparky, my bond with her, now.

OOO

Sparky's hungrier that usual today so, when t-raay-cee approaches, knowing they're about to go hunting together, she swoops to greet her mate, eager to be outside, flying with it.

As they walk towards the lawn Sparky sees t-raay-cee's human mate and the human with dark face plumage. These are humans she sees often, watching her and t-raay-cee flying, so them being here is safe. She's keen to fly.

But they don't stop on grassy patch to begin flying. Instead they keep walking, all of them. Head swivelling, Sparky gathers up what she sees and hears, adding these new sights and sounds to the auditory-visual map of her territory. This is different but she's with her mate and other familiar humans, not out of her territory, just expanding it, so she's curious, not panicked. Then she sees it: a field, suddenly added to her territory. It's bounded by far away trees and bushes, ideal for gliding out over, the swathe of sky overhead perfect for soaring up into: wilderness above and below the horizon.

She recalls another map, of the field where she flew with matt-ee several seasons ago; this new part of her territory matches that before flying field. When she and matt-ee flew there she wasn't ever grounded by the tethering line.

Face plumage comes close, its wing toes pecking around her ankles. Sparky bends to inspect the long thin tail trailing from her leg now. There's a faint familiarity about this, recalling matt-ee again. That leg is heavier when she lifts it but it's only a little more weight; she forgets it and, as face plumage retreats, launches into flight.

The tall perch is there. She heads for it because that's what they do when they fly, hunt and feed. Only they're in a newly claimed bit of territory, but where there's nothing to threaten her or her mate.

After a few flights, to and from, to and from, Sparky decides to find out if she's free to fly as high and far as she wants.

Ss-p-aaarrr-kkee.

As her mate calls she launches into soaring flight, heading for t-raay-cee, swooping over it, beyond it, landing behind it. Padding feet into cool moist grass, she head-turns, looking to t-raay-cee, standing nearby, and the perch, more distant. She's flown further than she has since she flew with matt-ee. She wasn't dragged from the sky. She's free to fly, flying free. Her mate trusts her fully now, their bonding completed.

Face plumage calls to t-raay-cee who walks away from Sparky, towards the perch. She chases it down, showing her mate she'll return to it, even when it moves away from her, even though she can fly anywhere she wants. As she lands on the head ledge t-raay-cee reaches up to her.

Sparky steps off, into the nothingness of fresh air, wings open wide, wind filling them, and flies to face plumage, landing on its head ledge; somewhere else she can fly to her mate from. But face plumage starts walking toward the perch, crouching when they're beside it so Sparky steps across, eyes and ears focused on t-raay-cee.

Ss-p-aaarrr-kkee.

She can fly anywhere but her mate's here, offering her food, they fly together, so that's where she'll go: always. They're each other's whole-half. They don't need anything else.

She lands on the featherless wing, snatches the fleshy morsel; it spears on her beak, stuck to the hooked point. Reaching up a foot, she tries pulling it off, keeps missing. She grasps at it, toes curling to grip it, always coming away empty-footed. T-raay-cee reaches out to her face now. Sparky pecks its wing toes in reflex, then returns to foot-grabbing at the piece of speared meat as t-raay-cee walks them to the perch, letting her step across. Balanced there, she keeps trying to kick the food off her beak, head-shaking, beak-snapping, gulping and neck-jerking. But she can't get it into her mouth.

Ss-p-aaarrr-kkee.

She looks over at her mate who's offering her another scrap of food. She ignores the stuck piece, is on the featherless wing in a few flaps, pushing the fluffy meat past the fleshy chunk that stays firmly impaled on her beak.

Face plumage calls out, its chatter coming to Sparky from behind. T-raay-cee replies. Sparky glances over, seeing face plumage striding towards them. When it gets there it reaches out its wing toes. She feels a quick tug on her beak, the food is unstuck, pressed into her opened mouth. She swallows it. Face plumage walks away. T-raay-cee points Sparky towards the perch, nudging her into the air.

They fly again, to and from, to and from. Sparky knows she could fly further, higher, but she needs to show t-raay-cee it can trust her not to leave it, that their bond is all they need to keep them together. Small steps will get them where they're going.

HHH

I'm relieved. Sparky's safely back in her aviary. She knew she wasn't tied down, she flew beyond me, as if showing me she understood that was possible, but she didn't fly away, didn't seem to want to. Apart from the kerfuffle of her getting food stuck to her beak it went O.K. She's safely back in her aviary. This time.

Before

March 2022 (cont.)

OOO

Hoo-hoo head-tufts is roosting amongst the crooked branch. A keee-w-ickk that was at the water pool darts underground as the in/out scrapes open. The rest are in their hide-e-holes. Sparky is the only flier not hiding. She doesn't roost deeply all day like the other fliers. Any potential new mate will come during daylight; she rests wakefully, perching ready to greet it when, if, it comes.

Shrivelled human appears, a pair of new humans following it, carrying a nest box that they put near the water pool. Chattering together, shrivelled human faces Sparky suddenly, pointing at her. She tilts her head, sidestepping along the perch away from it, fixing her darkly watchful eyes on this human she doesn't trust, won't bond with even though she needs a new mate to take her from the fliers' space. Shrivelled human head-shakes at her, turns and leads the new humans out.

Alone now, Sparky inspects the box, ears tuning in, eyes focusing down, shuffling along her perch to a better vantage.

A faint scuffling noise, like crisp leaves scattered together by wind, drifts up to her; she pictures feathers being ruffled smooth. Listening intently, the image of a flier forms in her ears. Leaning forward, craning her neck, her body teetering towards overbalancing off the perch, she stares into the box. Her eyes snatch at a white flutter, a flash of mottled tan and grey. A pair of dark eyes appears, framed by the hole. A screech splits the air.

Sparky jerks back.

The eyes become a head, the face white and flat, arching above the eyes, narrowing to a point, a pale curved beak in the centre. The head becomes a body; white chest, thin legs, featherless feet with pale toes; dark talons curl around the hole's edge as the flier scrambles from the box. It stretches wings speckled in a diamond-dappled pattern she knows well. It opens its beak: screeches at her.

It's not a keee-w-ickk or hooo-hooo flier. Sparky's never seen a flier like it before. But she knows this unknown flier like a territory she's mapped but never flown, a knowing born into her and held innately: the knowing of herself.

The new flier leaps into the water pool, preening familiar plumage. When it's bathed it springs back into the box, poking its head out through the hole, fixing its eyes on Sparky again, knowing her as she knows it, screeching at her with its ss-kk-reee ss-kk-reee call: ss-kk-reee flier.

Only her mates call to her, with her ss-p-aaarrr-kkee call; she understands that. She doesn't understand this whitely speckled flier's shrieky calling to her. Wings stiffened, she braces for an evasive dart to the sky ledge. When fliers screech they're readying to attack. But ss-kk-reee flier isn't behaving like that. She doesn't know what it'll do; she hasn't learnt this behaviour.

Ss-kk-reee's head is still protruding from the hole, its beak open from calling.

Sparky flees to the sky ledge. Up here ss-kk-reee flier can't see her from inside its nest box. The screeching stops. Silence presses into her; she fidgets on the ledge, waiting for gentle fair human to come and fly a chick to her.

Fair gentle has been and gone, leaving prey. Sparky's eaten the chick it flew to her and another she caught from the pile. The ss-kk-reee flier's box is close to the prey pile so Sparky hurried, snatching her meal, speeding her catch to the perch. Now she's facing a night trapped in the space with ss-kk-reee flier.

In dusk's shadows the keee-w-ickk that wing-drags scrambles from the ground hole, shuffling to the chick pile. As it gets there ss-kk-reee flier's head pops out of the box; it ss-kk-reees at the keee-w-ickk who beak-clacks, grabs a chick and retreats.

Ss-kk-reee emerges now, dropping with a feather-shake to the mound of prey. It eats a chick, takes another to the box, passing it through the hole. From inside there's scuffling, a muffled hissing. Ss-kk-reee returns to the prey pile, eats again, then feeds another chick to the box. Turning now, it scans its surroundings, springing airborne, soaring as high and wide as the space allows. Primaries grazing the sides, it swoops an arc around the space, heading for Sparky's perch.

Her nights here have taught her about fliers attacking so when ss-kk-reee swoops down onto the perch beside her, Sparky knows to defend this sliver of territory she's claimed for herself in the fliers' space. She wing-beats into her own aerial arc, clattering ss-kk-reee hard with her wings, chest and feet as she powers over it, through it, knocking it off the perch; she's bigger and stronger than it, her body in motion more powerful than its stationary. She dips this wing, circling around, returning to the perch.

But ss-kk-reee flier has resettled itself where she usually perches, challenging for the only scrap of this space that's hers. Unflinching, she dives, hurtling herself at it but, before she crashes down on it, ss-kk-reee leaps into flight, circuiting the space in a swift arc that brings it around behind Sparky.

She's on her perch now as ss-kk-reee chases towards her. She readies to take off, wing-beat at it, knock it out of flight. But it doesn't land on the perch. It keeps heading for Sparky, as if to land on her. She doesn't want this flier, any flier, on her. She wouldn't land on them. She'd only land on her mate. That's the bond she understands, her and her human together, a whole: a pair, holding on to each other. That's the relationship she was raised on, that raised her. She has no relationship with fliers, not with the keee-w-ickks or hoo-hoo head-tufts. Not even with ss-kk-reee who's her reflection on water. In the brief moment of this insight solidifying Sparky's airborne again, racing to the sky ledge.

There she turns sharply, facing into the space, seeing ss-kk-reee nearing, alighting beside her. But this is somewhere up above the chaos of the space. She's safe here. The keee-w-ickks don't fit on the ledge with her standing, wings unfolded, as she does when they try attacking her. No keee-w-ickk has ever got on the ledge with her. But ss-kk-reee flier fits; it's on the ledge beside her now.

From deep inside, Sparky bursts her raspy hissing. Ss-kk-reee doesn't retreat. She hisses again, plunging the note into her own cawing screech. Ss-kk-reee replies with its shrieking call then hops closer, wings opened, feathers bending where they touch the ice on this side, fanning out fully into the space on that side.

Sparky doesn't want this ss-kk-reee flier on her safe ledge, so close. It's a living dying urge inside her, sending a restless heat spiralling through her. She has to rid herself of this cramping twitchy pain that's pulsing her nerves, spasming her muscles, throbbing her blood. She has to fight off ss-kk-reee.

She jumps at ss-kk-reee, grabbing its legs with her feet, talons hooking its ankles, leaning herself back as far as the ledge allows, spreading her wings as wide as the ledge lets her. Holding ss-kk-reee in her taloned grip, Sparky lunges, beak-snapping, at its face and neck, snatching downy white feathering, leaving plucked raw skin. She hisses harshly, lunges, plucks and pecks, beak nipping and jabbing. Ss-kk-reee struggles, kicking against her leg-hold, frantically wing-flapping to free itself. Sparky beats her wings now too, fighting for her grip on ss-kk-reee, her strength, size and fury helping her hold on. She leg-kicks against its kicks as though they're both running in the same air. They flap and kick but only Sparky lunges and pecks. Ss-kk-reee fights to escape. Sparky fights to wound. They tussle in a furious flurry of feathers for a frenzied now. Then stop.

Sparky's chest burns; beak gaping, she gulps air, her body buzzing, volatile. Ss-kk-reee flier's also panting. Sparky flexes her feet, toes tightening their grip on ss-kk-reee's legs. Her wings are as outstretched as they can be on the ledge. She's leaning backwards but still upright. Ss-kk-reee is flat down, pulled prone during their struggle. Its feathers are crumpled here, there. Dark redness blooms on its breast. Sparky fixes her gaze on that dark red: lunges again. Their scuffle restarts as though instantly unfrozen. Her beak contacts flesh. A shrieking call cuts her ears, frantic flapping blurs her vision, chaotic kicking stumbles her balance. Ss-kk-reee twists and thrashes, tumbling off the ledge, pulling Sparky into the fall with it. Plummeting, she releases her leg hold, spiralling into flight, slamming onto her perch, turning to see ss-kk-reee flier scrambling into its nest box.

Sparky perches motionless while the frenzy inside her ebbs, stillness cooling her blood, soothing muscles and nerves. Then she preens dishevelled feathers. A few are broken but no blood stains her white plumage, she feels no pain, only overwhelming fatigue.

Keee-w-ickks emerge, creeping to the pile for prey they were stopped from catching by Sparky's furious fight with ss-kk-reee. The space resumes its nightly routine. The only change is in Sparky; she's learnt she can fight fliers. She can survive for as long as she has to stay in this space with them. But surviving isn't living. For that she needs her own territory, a human mate to share it with.

As dawn fades the darkness she stays on her, now, usual perch in the corner of the fliers' space, where she can watch the narrow gap that humans come and go along, waiting for her new mate to come.

Before

28th March 2022

HHH

I park on the rough gravelled ground outside the animal rescue centre and head into the main building to check where I'm needed today and catch up on anything I've missed while on holiday.

The centre is two long barns. The main one houses those animals on show to visitors, their entry fee helping support the centre. But with no zoo licence the centre is only permitted to have domestic animals on display year round, mostly farm animals and poultry plus some small furries. The second building houses the more exotic animals and, as usual, I'm directed to work in there.

At first I was chuffed to be judged competent enough to be shown what to do in here and left to it. Now the amount of work overwhelms me; there's so much for one person, feeding and watering abandoned reptiles and snakes, poorly hedgehogs and injured wild birds, some exotic mammals, a couple of native wild mammals that can't be released, and copious invertebrates—the tarantulas make me shudder as I nervously top up their water and throw in live crickets for their dinner. But, while I'm here, it's up to me to help every animal in this ramshackle building so I crack on, collecting buckets of water and heading down the corridor towards the owl room, following the routine I've established to ensure I don't miss anyone out, leaving them thirsty, hungry or needing help.

As I reach the doorway I notice a rounded metal object, about the size of half a football, on the floor, conspicuous by its presence. I stride towards it, brain trying to make sense of this unusual item. It's a colander…

Now

29th September 2022

OOO

It's a day like any other for them. T-raay-cee and Sparky head to the field, face plumage walking beside them. Sparky knows what's coming, anticipation of aerial freedom makes her wing-flap vigorously, leaping off t-raay-cee's wing perch, only the short tethering line preventing her leading her mate to their hunting ground.

As they emerge from sheltering trees her feathers flutter, rumpled by the wind's invisible touch. Sparky faces that touch, letting it blow into her eyes, stalling her first plunge into flight until she knows the perch is reachable, that she'll be able to out-fly the wind. Then she takes off.

As she floats down onto the perch t-raay-cee walks around, coming into view in the direction she's facing. Sparky listens, watches and waits.

The featherless wing is raised, food offered.

Ss-p-aaarrr-kkee.

Their flying and hunting begins.

She flies buoyantly, finding her wings, stretching them out, propelling herself forward. Airborne energy swells within her, bringing her to her mate. She gulps the food; t-raay-cee turns, holding Sparky into the breeze again. It wants her to fly. So she does, soaring higher than ever before with t-raay-cee, wings and wind lifting her into solid nothingness, body feather-light. The perch is a sharp straight branch slicing the softly sloping green field. She reaches it too soon. There's all this sky, wild and free: hers. She can fly through as much as she wants, knowing she can return to her mate. This is the moment to show her mate what their bond means: together forever.

She keeps going, over the perch, over face plumage who's nearby, over the trees and bushes bordering the field, all the way out over the next field, which is crumpled brown earth. Feeling heaviness spreading through her wings, crushing her chest, Sparky flutters downward, feet grabbing bare ground as she lands.

She turns, looking from where she flew to where she is, storing the location she left t-raay-cee. Her mate's hidden from her keen eyes by undulating terrain but its position is marked on her internal map of their territory. She focuses on that map image now, waiting for her mate.

It appears, forwards and sideways of her mapped reference, walking to where low bushes mark their territory's limit, eyes fixed on Sparky as hers fix back on it. When t-raay-cee can't come any closer, stopped by a stream and a long straight boundary, her mate raises its featherless wing, calling her to it.

Even if she goes so far from t-raay-cee they can't see each other, they'll find each other again. She can fly freely, fly far, fly away, because t-raay-cee can call her back, she'll hear and return; their bond is unbreakable.

Sparky dives into the air, drawing herself up, hauling herself forward. But she's flown further than she has for a long while. Her wings carry the weight of that flight. She covers half the distance to t-raay-cee before she needs rest.

Landed, she breathes in deep gulps, folding her wings away, the load on them lessening slowly. She'll wait until her wings lighten enough to fly her to her mate who's still quite far away, still watching Sparky watching it, face plumage beside it, them chattering together.

Suddenly, from overhear, there's harsh cawing; it claws at Sparky's ears. She leans back, glancing up. Black fliers circle above her, their primary feathers splaying as they glide through pale grey sky. They're circling wide and high. Sparky looks to t-raay-cee and face plumage. Face plumage is pointing at the black fliers whose grating squawks draw a thread of pain, ear to ear, through Sparky. Circling tighter, lower, now, they ready to mob, like the keee-w-ickks and ss-kk-reee in the fliers' space. Many seasons ago, when matt-ee was her human, black fliers circled her like this and her mate's calls were alarmed; it knew that danger before she did.

Ss-p-aaarrr-kkee. Ss-p-aaarrr-kkee. Ss-p-aaarrr-kkee.

Her call, repeated urgently. T-raay-cee knows the danger too. She needs to return to her mate, must even though her wings aren't yet weightless. She hops forwards into a stuttering flight, dragging herself along close to the ground, far beneath the spiralling black fliers who track her movements, dropping and tightening their whirling vortex. But when she's covered half the remaining distance her wings are feather-and-bone tired. She sinks down.

Her mate's closer but they're still separated by the straight boundary and the stream. Sparky hasn't seen humans crossing boundaries like this so she doesn't know if it can reach her. But she can reach it, when her wings recover. She unfolds them, letting the coolly soothing breeze ripple them. Overhead more black fliers gather, their whorling flight condensing them above Sparky.

Ss-p-aaarrr-kkee. Ss-p-aaarrr-kkee. Ss-p-aaarrr-kkee.

She must go now, must reach her mate. She leaps skyward, wing-beating vigorous, fighting for momentum: lift. Then she's up, gliding, soaring, a cooperative current supporting her return to t-raay-cee. Behind her the black fliers' disperse, their funnelling circle becoming a loosely scattered cloud.

And she's there, hovering onto t-raay-cee's wing, the rising and falling of her chest slowing, surging energy running through and out of her, into her mate, from it back into Sparky. In the moment of their flying so far together they've completed each other.

After a short rest, the rush of energy still vibrating through them, they're ready to fly again. So when t-raay-cee holds Sparky up, releasing her to the breeze she flies not to the perch, which is too close for a pair with their bond, but out over the brown field, this time going deeper into it, swooping onward, gliding with agile ease. Freedom, the spirit of flying, fills her from the feathers inwards; she is flight.

When her wings start feeling solid again she floats down onto a ridge of lumpy earth that crumbles under her claw-grip. Her mate will call her now and she'll return to it so she can fly from it again, return again: endlessly being reunited. They both know now that their life is this: a mated pair flying, hunting and feeding together in their home territory.

Ss-p-aaarrr-kkee.

She soars.

HHH

Today's the third go flying Sparky without the security of the creance. I'm still anxious knowing she's free to choose her own flight path. The fact that she's returned previously isn't enough; now it's me that needs reassuring repetition. But the exhilaration of seeing her flying joyously, unencumbered by the line, is worth the worry. It's a joy I can only experience through imitation but I'm lucky enough, at least, to have flown, passenger in commercial jets, helicopters, a hot air balloon, a light aircraft and, once, a glider. The magic of that flight, just me and the pilot, silently swooping, gracefully gliding, on thermals, chequered fields below, blue sky above, wing-to-wing with the birds, flying free, is what I remind myself of when I untie Sparky, let her go. It's that elation I want for her, it's what she needs, deserves. Mine was only simulated flight: hers is real. My fears can't deny her that.

But I'll only overcome my fear of flying her untethered by doing it. For now I have a wing-man, literally: the ever-helpful and patient falconer. He's with us today so I know Sparky's as safe as any captive bird can be when set free. Eventually I'll have to do this solo though, if Sparky and I are to stay together.

I send her to the perch, from quite close as she seems a little reluctant to leave me. Then I call her. She comes. I'm still astonished she does that; she doesn't have to, she's choosing to. Eons of inherited wildness stack up against her own short lifetime as an owl imprinted on people. Not even imprinted on me, yet she's returning to me, O.K., there's food, but still…

I nudge her into the air, towards the perch, dropping my arm, encouraging her to take flight. Off she goes. Towards the perch. Past the perch. And on, over the low, twisted trees, stunted bushes and wind-battered fence; over the stream, half full and flowing steadily, right into the next field, landing out of sight. My heart thuds. Panicked, I turn to the falconer.

Unruffled, he directs me to move so I can see her. Luckily it's a recently ploughed field so a white owl's an easy spot. We let her settle a moment. Then he tells me to call her. She's so far away. He reminds me her eyesight is excellent but her hearing even better. She's watching me, listening for me. I call. She doesn't move. Even if I could get over the barbed wire fence and wade the stream, she could fly off before I reached her. The falconer tells me it's possible to run a bird down, chasing them with a tail wind so they can't get airborne. Possible for him maybe. But just keep calling her, he says as a murder of crows gathers above her, drawn by the spectacle of a barn owl in the open in daylight. Crows mob barn owls, harrying them into fleeing: killing them. Sparky seems unaware of this, casually glancing at the black shadows tightening their aerial formation above her.

She's more focused on me.

I call again.

This time she sets off, a low laborious flight, gaining height slowly, rising to fly the fence. But it's too far, she's not fit enough, hasn't flown more than 20 metres at a time since I've known her, possibly hasn't ever flown this far. She lands, rests. I'm calm now though; as soon as she heard my call she started returning to me. I believe, finally, that, as long as she's able, she'll always return because she wants to. She lands to rest twice before she makes it. I don't care; she's here. She came. We're together.

The falconer tells me, 'You'll do well to lose her. She's glued to you.'

Bound, I think, warmth filling me, we're bound together, by something insubstantial yet unbreakable.

So when she flies back into that same field, like a wild barn owl quartering its hunting ground, I share the elation she must feel, up there, finally free to fly: finally flying free.

'I'm going to keep her,' I tell the falconer once Sparky's back in her aviary.

'I never thought you'd do anything else,' he says.

Now

Sparky still lives the life she and t-raay-cee established so long ago. With the passing of many seasons she's certain this is her home with her mate: lifelong. They fly, hunt and feed out over their territory most days. She flies as freely now as the wild fliers that circle and soar above them. All this flying free has made Sparky and t-raay-cee's bond the strongest possible: they always return to each other.

There's a reassuring routine to her life but occasionally there's something different, enough to be interesting but not unsettling. Like when, as Sparky stood on the perch in the field, she heard tiny squealing squeaks behind her in the long grass, rousing hunter-her. She pounced onto the sound, pecking and stamping at the ground as her ears tuned in to the prey, locating it precisely. T-raay-cee joined her, hunting with her, searching the tall waving grass with its wing toes while Sparky pecked and stamped. The squeaking vanished; they were unsuccessful but it was a brief, rousing hunt.

Or when she was taken in a moving growler to a different territory, allowed to fly and hunt there with her mate, some new humans who didn't threaten them, standing close, watching. They saw Sparky and t-raay-cee are a devoted pair that would protect each other so they just stood nearby, chattering and pointing small black clicking objects at her and t-raay-cee.

There'll be more moments that bring something different but mostly there's the reassurance of their steady life together. Sparky is contented. She has her space in her territory, with her mate and together they fly and hunt, completing each other. She doesn't know what life would have been if t-raay-cee hadn't come along to share it. She doesn't know how long she would have survived or what she would have endured. She knows only what did happen: this life, paired with t-raay-cee. For as long as this is her life, their life, she'll be her whole self and so will her mate.

They're in the field again, just them, Sparky on the perch, t-raay-cee stood away from her. They watch each other, connected by their invisible, unbreakable bond, knowing what each will do, doing it simultaneously, as only a lifelong pair can.

Ss-p-aa… she flies.

Epilogue

4th April 2025

I upload the file <Sparky story FINAL.doc> to the email.

> *Hi Adam,*
>
> *Here, at last, is the finalised Sparky MS. Thank you for being so patient and for your continued support. It's certainly been the most challenging book I've written but also the most worthwhile…*

The rest of the message typed, I hover my cursor over 'send', giving myself a moment of reflection before committing to publishing the book that means so much to me because of Sparky, what she means; what it means to have her in my life. I wanted to tell Sparky's story as she deserves it to be told, in a way that might open up more empathetic approaches to writing animals' lived experiences. Sadly I don't, can't ever, truly know what life is like for owls, how they experience the world, their feelings when they fly and hunt, their relationship with humans. I'll never know what Sparky lived through before I met her. I can only imagine and, through word craft, try to convey those imaginings. That might not be enough. Perhaps others could do it better. But, even if the book is a failure at least I'm certain Sparky's story is a success because I've been able to write a happy ending for her: that's what she deserves most, her and all animals everywhere.

I click 'send'.

Postscript

'I took that gyr*-saker out of the aviary yesterday,' the falconer announces.

He's the only survivor of a clutch of three, the oldest so the strongest: a fighter. He's been in an aviary alone since his siblings died. Now fully fledged, he's ready to be manned and trained. For their own reasons, his parents stopped rearing the chicks. It's common enough in nature; it's life and death. Perhaps detecting a weakness in the offspring they decided raising the hatchlings was energy wasted. Fortunately for this resilient youngster, the falconer disagreed.

'Is he O.K.?' I ask.

'His feet are damaged, probably by the parents, crushed in the nest.'

'That's a shame. Will he be alright?'

'He'll fly O.K. but he'll always have foot problems. It's an issue with these birds anyway, their feet are prone to sores and infection. Come have a look.'

We wander to where the falcon sits tethered to a perch. I see his legs are bowed and there's an obvious swelling, worse on the left, but present on the pads at the outer edges of both feet, near his little toes. Otherwise he looks grand; bright dark eyes, smooth white and fawn plumage, pale blue beak. He's small though, for a gyr-saker; even I don't need a set of scales to tell his growth's stunted by parental neglect. Lucky the falconer rescued the clutch when he did or all three would've died. It's a tough decision, though, as falcons are better raised by, or with, other falcons instead of being imprinted on people.

'I was planning to train him up,' he says, 'but it wouldn't be fair to work him with his feet like that. No reason why he won't fly fine though,' he adds cheerfully.

'Oh. O.K.' I study the little falcon; he studies me, head titled to the left, body trembling at the sight of two giant wingless creatures looming over him, chattering and gawping at him.

'He's yours if you want him,' the falconer offers suddenly. 'You can train him to fly to you, to a lure. Kept at a flying weight and getting regular exercise would be good for him with those feet. He might be an odd one though, part imprint, part crèche-reared.' When I don't reply he says, 'You don't have to, though. I can move him into the aviary with the birds I'm resting.'

I don't know what to tell him. A falcon? That wasn't in the plot outline for my life. Neither was Sparky but her story's been one I'm so glad to have been able to write.

'Have a think about it,' he suggests.

'Yeah, I will, thanks.'

---

* Pronounced 'jur' (rhymes with 'fur').

Acknowledgments

I need to thank the following people:

Adam and Jan at Cinnamon Press for their patience and encouragement and for keeping a publication slot open for me for so long while I returned, finally, to writing.

Fellow authors Suzanne Stirke (*No Man's Moor* and *Worlds End*), A. J. White (*Tome of Bàirseach* trilogy), Michael Cawood Green (*The Ghosting of Anne Armstrong*) and former English teaching colleague Pam Camm for their invaluable feedback on early drafts of this book.

John for welcoming Sparky into our family and for being endlessly supportive and understanding throughout the challenging task of writing her story.

Ben and Becca for putting up with me all the time and doing me more favours than I can ever repay you for. You're great mates, thanks so much.

Those people who, for various reasons, I won't name, that played a part, knowingly or unknowingly, in bringing Sparky and me together.

Robbie and Poppy who showed me a way of understanding owls that was a helpful confidence booster with Sparky in the early days of getting to know her.

Sparky and the rest of her 'team', Colin, Smokey and Wilf, for teaching me so much about birds of prey and for letting me share in the exhilaration of flying with them.

www.ingramcontent.com/pod-product-compliance
Ingram Content Group UK Ltd.
Pitfield, Milton Keynes, MK11 3LW, UK
UKHW020104310326
469528UK00003B/86

9 781788 641999